LOVE IS WORTH
FIGHTING FOR

I'LL COME TO YOU

JUNE LARK

ISBN:
Ebook: 979-8-9904659-1-6
Paperback: 979-8-9904659-8-5

Published by Amazon KD Publishing

For those who choose love over fear.

1

INVASION

He left. Just like all the other young men in town. After two years of promising he would remain in York, Pennsylvania, Robert Moore enlisted, making me promise to watch over his little sister. It was not right of him to ask that of me. To put that on me. I begged him to wait, to stay unless he was drafted. Still, he chose to leave.

I was hurt, and no matter how often I wrote to him, his brief notes were too few and far between. I should have been thankful I received anything at all. In our last moments together, angry at his desertion—dashing all dreams I had for us—I told Robert of Ethan's proposal. Since childhood, I never saw him so furious ... spitting, shouting at me to be gone, and claiming the righteous Cause. His pension would help his sister, and he would be fighting for the preservation of the Union and the freedom of those enslaved. How dare I keep him from his duty? How dare I ask him to stay when I could give him nothing in return?

"What would I stay here for?" He pushed his hat back from his face to wipe the sweat from his furrowed brow. "Accept Mr. Harris's proposal. Make your folks happy. You will be better for it."

With pressure from Pa and Mother, and a hurt heart, I had surrendered and accepted Ethan's proposal.

Now, as I stood on Main Street, crowds pushed forward, stretching our necks to see the commotion over bowler hats and bonnets. Tension vibrated through the townsfolk. Anna McQuaid locked her arm around mine, keeping us from being separated. Then his eyes connected with mine.

Ethan Harris stood on the street corner, staring at me. He stood a head taller than everyone, his fashionable bowler hat shading his dark eyes. He smirked and tipped his hat, satisfaction painting his features. Was he enjoying this? A shiver ran down my spine, and I turned away from him.

A hum of nervousness rippled throughout York. The streets were muddled with carts, horses, and people. Harold, our livery driver, had to drop off Anna and me two blocks from the post office. Anna gripped my arm as we made our way down the street, pushing through people as we approached York–Wrightsville Railway and the post office. A crowd in front of the post office flowed out into the street. Everyone was demanding their mail and pleading for letters to be sent to family members or soldiers at the front … before it was too late.

"What's happened?" I asked Anna.

"I don't know, Miss Ella." She turned to the gentleman beside us. "What is it?" she asked him.

"Rebels," he said with a stiff, tense face. "They're coming up this way. Everyone is trying to send out letters before they close the railway."

"They're closing the railway?" A wave of trepidation washed over me.

"Miss, this is war. The enemy will destroy everything in its path, and we must be prepared. Get all your mail, send out the necessary letters, and skedaddle. Pennsylvania is about to become the front. My family and I are heading to New York as soon as we're able."

"Should we get our mail too, Anna? This may be my last chance to send word to Robert."

"We'll try." Anna nodded.

We waited for an hour before we reached the counter where Mr. Cravett, the mail clerk, stood, sweating and exasperated.

"Came for the Coburg mail, did you?" he asked.

"Yes, sir, if you please, but only if it's ready. We only came for the package my grandmother sent."

Grandmother Montgomery, my maternal grandmother, lived year-round at her Parisian home now that she was widowed. She complained the war kept her abroad, though we knew she hated Pennsylvania. In her stead, she sent a dress for the honeymoon—something all the girls in Paris were wearing.

Mr. Cravett relaxed his shoulders. "Miss Coburg, you have been the most reasonable voice I've heard all morning. Just a moment while I fetch your package."

He disappeared to the back room and returned with an elaborately decorated box, painted with flowers and tied with gold cord and tassels.

"Thank you very much, Mr. Cravett." I smiled as Anna took the package from the counter. The package was almost half her size.

"My pleasure. A breath of fresh air, I daresay."

Anna and I pushed our way back through the growing crowd.

Anna shook her head, brown- and gray-peppered curls escaping her bonnet. "All these folks gone mad, like it's the end of the world. Now, let's get this dress home before it topples me." I could tell she was nervous as her Irish accent thickened.

Anna McQuaid had been with our family since I was born, and she cared for me as if I were her own. Now she ran our home. I told her my secrets, and she told me hers. I trusted her more than anyone on earth, and she had proven it to me by keeping my secret about Robert.

"Rebels!" someone yelled in the street. Screaming and hollering punctured the hot air in response. A rush of energy exploded through the crowd as everyone pushed to get off the streets.

"Can you see anything?" I yelled over the melee.

"No!" Anna replied.

Looking for Harold and the buggy, we elbowed our way through the people lining the streets as if they were anticipating a parade. In the distance, a band struck up and began to play "Yankee Doodle."

"What's happening?" I stood on my tiptoes, attempting to see over the hundreds of heads, my hoop skirt squishing against the throng.

Anna pinched her lips, considering, then said firmly, "Come."

We found a break in the crowd and turned down the street, only to halt in our steps.

Men in gray marched forward, a Confederate band taking up the middle. An old general sat tall on his mount, leading his troops. He bared his head, waving his hat and flashing a hearty grin on his tanned face. He bowed in his saddle, saluting to the people of York. Everyone stared, astounded.

Will they not loot? Fire? Commit arson?

Instead, the Rebels were treating us to a parade!

"Hurry now! We need to find Harold." Anna led me away. "It looks as though they're heading toward the town square."

We hurried back down the street. We were nearing the square when the general yelled for a halt, and the crowd pushed, gathering around the general and his men. The Confederate general raised a hand to call for silence. A hush fell over the town. I scanned the crowd, looking for someone to raise a firearm against these invaders, to do something to stop them. I searched for Ethan.

The old general bellowed from his perch, "What we all need on both sides is to mingle with each other so that we shall learn to know and appreciate one another. Now here's my brigade. I wish you knew them as I do. They are a hospitable, wholehearted, fascinating lot of gentlemen. Why, just think of it—this part of Pennsylvania is ours today; we can do what we please with it. Yet, we sincerely and heartily invite you to stay! Are we not a fine set of fellows?"

Invite us to stay? I couldn't help but raise my brows in amusement.

To my great surprise, applause broke out. Whether it was out of shock, fear, or not knowing what else to do, we all applauded.

—

"Are we going to leave, Pa?" Elizabeth, my younger sister, asked. She paced on her feet. She was the household's darling. Amenable and prudent, she was everything I was not. All the way to blonde ringlets and plump cheeks, while I had decidedly unruly, light-brown hair and a thin figure. I was often chided for my stubbornness or recklessness.

"No, honey," Pa said, lifting Elizabeth onto his knee. "We have no plans to leave. Life will go on as planned, and your dear sister will have her wedding."

The wedding was mere days away, and my stomach roiled with anxiety. I was trapped inside the parlor, the enemy outside our door, and soon there would be a ring around my finger symbolizing I was no longer my own.

Elizabeth clapped and hollered with glee, jumping from Pa's knee and running off with eight-year-old Cousin Amelia by her side. Pa chuckled, and I knew everything was to continue as before. We were not in immediate danger, and it was as if the whole household breathed a sigh of relief.

Yet, I sat there … itching to escape.

2

SELF-PRESERVATION

1863 JULY 1–3

To my chagrin, and despite the town's Rebel occupation, wedding festivities continued. Our neighbor, Mrs. LeDoux, hosted an afternoon of refreshments in her garden in honor of my approaching nuptials.

A new lawn game was set up for the men with rackets and something called a shuttlecock—a rounded piece of cork with feathers—and a string strung across the yard between two trees. Her son, Daniel, who brought the rackets and shuttlecock home from the university, said the game was popular among the students. Shoulders square and beaming, Daniel explained the rules and demonstrated his exceptional batting skills. Ethan, of course, refused to play, calling it a children's game, his eyes shooting daggers at Daniel over his liquor glass.

I stifled a laugh at Ethan's own childish obstinacy, while

the ladies and I sat around a table, painting with watercolor.

The pleasant afternoon encapsulated us from the war, the soldiers marching in the town square, and the distant boom of artillery in the small town of Gettysburg.

Like thunder in the distance, the explosions reminded us our joy was temporary and fragile. With each cannon blast, my breath caught, and I said a silent prayer for Robert—wherever he was in all of this.

I glanced at Mother, her bow-shaped lips pinched, her green eyes, like my own, large. Knowing how this wore on her nerves. Knowing I was a disappointment. Knowing she was sick. Knowing as soon as one festivity ended, she would retreat to the darkness of her bedchamber, complaining of a headache. She had been a force to be reckoned with before the loss of my younger brother years ago. Now she was a husk of the mother who raised me. I suffered a smile to ease her worries.

I tried not to think of the impending wedding, numbing my senses to protect myself. If I spent too much time thinking about it, I knew I would succumb to fear and grief. So I played my role and pushed dire thoughts down deep, where they could not hurt me, where I could preserve myself and my dignity.

This was how it was supposed to be. It was the natural order of things, was it not? Pa and Mother seemed to think so. Ethan was the most eligible for their eldest daughter. The employer of my father, and the owner of York Ironworks and the large Etherton Estate property. It made sense. Ethan's late father had been Pa's good friend, orchestrating his standing in town, providing him with a home— Woodhue—for his young family.

When I accepted his proposal, I thought I was doing right by everyone. Pa was loyal to Ethan. After tragedy struck with the unexpected deaths of his brother and father, Pa stepped in to run the Ironworks—a business Ethan knew very little about. It was all to go to his elder brother, and now it was thrust upon him. He took him under his wing, teaching him the business and treating him like a son. There was no hesitation when Pa gave Ethan his blessing to ask for my hand.

And I just wanted Mother and Pa to be proud of me.

I also thought I was doing right by me.

I had accepted Robert's call to duty. I convinced myself he was not the right choice for me. He lacked the social standing and wealth with which Ethan was born. But my heart could not accept it. My heart ached with what I was doing, my muscles constricting as if telling me I was going the wrong way.

Engagement feasts were hosted at our home and the Etherton Estate. As each hour ticked by, I felt disassociated with what was going on around me, floating above. It was necessary self-preservation, I convinced myself. Was I weak? Why wasn't I fighting? Should I do something to stop this? No, this was strength. None of this was in my control now.

Something more was happening here.

I saw it in the growing shadows beneath Pa's eyes, the creases in his forehead when he glimpsed at Mother and me, worried. Was that guilt? Was that heartbreak? Was that fear? A secret I was not privy to? It was concealed in the triumphant gleam in Ethan's eyes and the whispers to his employee, Mr. Pocket. They huddled together in dark corridors during social gatherings. They would conference in quiet, and then Ethan would send him off on an errand.

Our guests were oblivious to the darkness as they toasted the soon-to-be-wed and gorged themselves on roast pig and cottage pie.

How could this all be real? How could we celebrate when men were dying in the next county?

Two nights of feasting, two nights of toasts, two nights of forced smiles. I was tired. I was numb. I was an empty shell.

"You can at least pretend to be full of wedded bliss," Ethan accused.

But I knew myself. I knew the fire and strength I possessed. I would protect it, and I would do what I could to protect those I loved.

When the nights were over, I was glad of it. I was one day closer to finishing this. Once I was Ethan's bride, I would no longer have to feign happiness. There was some freedom in that, wasn't there?

Sleep no longer came. The acrid scent of campfires and gunpowder lingered on the evening breeze. Even in the darkness, distant rifle cracks punctuated the silence. Warm and sticky, I suffocated in the quiet solitude. Harsh whispers of anxiety and fear filled my mind, and I could do nothing to silence them.

Walking helped quiet my nerves. Each night, I would tiptoe through the sleeping house, out the front door, and walk Woodhue's twelve acres. No one bothered me then, and the exercise drained the thoughts from my head.

Two days until the wedding, and I desperately needed fresh air. I inhaled deeply, but the smoke stung my lungs. Muffling a cough to not wake the house, I hurried down the front steps until I could bury my toes into the cool grass. I lifted my heavy hair off my back and let the breeze tickle my neck, cooling beads of sweat.

Hoofbeats sounded on the road, and I stilled. It was late, and no one should be on the road, but there were enemies about. I stilled my breath, listening and praying it was not a Rebel soldier. Even on my own property I was vulnerable, standing barefoot on the lawn in nothing but my nightgown.

The horse turned into our drive, and I froze. I momentarily thought to yell for Pa but knew it would wake Mother, and I'd never hear the end of it. What was I thinking, wandering around in the dark in my nightgown?

I readied myself to flee to the house when the approaching rider took off his hat and moonlight cast light on his features.

"What are you doing here, Ethan?" I whisper-shouted, annoyance overshadowing my momentary fear.

His blond hair was disheveled and his face pale. He cracked a smile—a knowing, lazy, drunk smile. A dangerous smile.

"I was just coming to survey what will soon be mine." A slight slur marred his words.

He dismounted the horse, walking toward me. His gaze traversed the front of the house and the lawns and paddock beyond, then came to rest on me, surveying me from head to toe. His brow lifted at the sight of my bare feet. It dawned on me that he wasn't just talking about me, but of Woodhue as well.

"Woodhue was always meant to be mine. Something of my own, separate from my father. It was stolen from me," he continued. "Etherton and the factory were meant for Jeffrey. He would have ruined it all if he had lived."

I took a step back, closer to the house. Drinking made men like Ethan dangerous. At the mention of his brother, Jeffrey, I knew where his mind was. Many versions had been told of their deaths. Anna had shared, in secret, that Jeffrey had ended his life after killing their housemaid, Emilyn Murphy. There was speculation they were lovers, and it had ended badly. Mr. Harris, prostrate in grief, succumbed to failing health, leaving Ethan with what remained of Etherton Estate, the ironworks, and fortune. He had already sold Woodhue to Pa by that point.

"Father would be proud to know what I turned his business into." Ethan was rambling now. "He wouldn't have foreseen this war, but there is much profit in it, more than I could ever imagine." He continued to survey Woodhue around us and then came back to look at me, stepping closer. He was close enough now I could smell the whiskey wafting off him. "You love Woodhue, don't you?"

"My father is proud of what he's built here. It has been my home," I explained, retreating into myself. The less I said, the better.

"Yes, your old man is a proud man, a man who would do anything to protect his family, no matter the cost."

The cost? I narrowed my gaze on him, suspicion rising.

"This war. It makes people desperate. And there is always a cost. A cost to protect. A cost to preserve. Someone has to profit. Someone has to keep this world afloat. It might as well be me." His eyes searched mine, heated, yearning.

I shuddered, a chill washing over me in the muggy night.

"What do you mean?"

Ethan chuckled. "You're a simple one, aren't you, my dear? I should have known you would not understand." He gripped my arm, bringing me closer to him. "We were meant for each other. The moment you were born at Woodhue, the moment your father came to work for mine, our lives were intertwined. This was all preordained. A way to break the curse."

Curse?

"I knew it would come full circle. I knew we were both meant for greater things. This country is meant for greater things, and I am not about to let anything or anyone stand in my way. And if I have to do everything myself, I vow I will. This world has too many simple people; I was really hoping you were not one of them."

He dropped the horse's reins, wrapping his arms around me and hoisting me off my feet. Taken aback, I did not protest while he carried me across the lawn, toward the copse of trees beside the barn and paddock. Then I found myself and started kicking and writhing in his grip, my arms pinned to my sides.

"Let me down," I demanded, finding my voice, willing what strength I had to rise.

"I've wanted you for a long time, and I've wanted Woodhue for even longer. Wouldn't it be apropos to lay together in the soils of Woodhue?" he asked, his voice gruff, stinking of liquor and desire.

"We aren't wed yet. Let me go," I squeaked. Cringing inside at how small my voice sounded.

He laughed deep in his throat. "Whether we share our marital duties now or two days from now, what's the difference?"

"Ethan, please," I begged. I hated myself for begging. "My chastity. I would like to retain something for you on our wedding night."

He laughed again, louder this time. I was afraid someone might hear us, yet also wished for someone's intervention. "Your chastity? You are far from chaste, my dear, and I know it." His eyes flashed dark with rage and jealousy.

"Why would you say that?" I snapped, shocked, trying to draw him into conversation, hoping to stall from what was inevitable.

"You know damn well what I mean," he growled, then laid me on the ground, pinning me beneath him.

It dawned on me then that he knew of Robert. He knew more than I thought and was jealous of whatever affection was between us. But Robert was honorable—more honorable than Ethan ever could be—and never forced himself on me. Anger welled up like blood from an open wound.

"You're drunk, Ethan. Get off me," I implored under his weight. I tried to remain quiet, not wanting to wake the house to find us here in the dark, under the trees, on the ground. Shame and embarrassment rose up with the anger, and I knew I had to do something to stop this.

17

"No, my dear. I know you want me just as much as I want you," he breathed in my ear. "This has to happen. A way to end it."

End what? He was not making sense.

"And if you are as chaste as you claim, it's only a bit of blood, Ella. Nothing to fear."

We both squirmed—he, undoing the holster belt at his waist, and I, moving my legs and pushing him away with my arms, trying to escape.

He set his belt beside us and began to open his pants while he hiked up my nightgown. His hand scaled my leg. He leaned in to kiss my throat and my jaw. His sour breath made me gag. Was this really happening? I turned my face away from him, if only to shield myself from his kisses, and then it was like a message from God. A cloud passed across the moon, revealing a bright streak of moonbeam. A glint of a pistol in his holster caught my eye. I reached out. It was in arm's reach, and I wrapped my fingers around the grip. Before I could think this through, I pushed the revolver between us, pointing the barrel into his sternum.

Ethan jumped back.

I propelled myself to my feet, still aiming the gun at him.

Surprise washed over his face, followed by a confident smirk. "You wouldn't dare. Do you even know how to cock that thing?"

"It's loaded, is it?" I asked, curious but also feeling my own confident smirk creep across my lips. I knew how to cock a rifle. I had seen Pa do it dozens of times. A Colt revolver was no different. I cocked it. "Whatever you think you know of me, Ethan, you have yet to find out. You may be gaining a bride, but know that I will hate you for the rest of your days if you do this. And do not think for one moment that you are safe from ruin."

A flicker of fear crossed his eyes, and I wondered what he thought

I knew. The alcohol seemed to evaporate from his glazed expression, his jaw clenching. Let him think I knew the truth. Something scared him, and now I knew it. Once we were married, I would sleuth it out, and the truth would protect me, my family, my home, Robert, and Katie.

Running his fingers through his hair, his rage and passion evaporated. He looked weary. Whatever alcohol still coursed through him dissolved. He did not touch me as I scrambled to my feet, the revolver still heavy in my hand as I aimed at him.

"In two days, you will be mine, and nothing will stand in our way. Nothing!" His horse had wandered toward us and was only a few steps away. Ethan picked up his discarded holster, turned, and headed to mount. Once on his horse, he looked back at me. His anger flared. He was fuming, but he did not ask for the return of his pistol as he turned his horse around and galloped away into the night.

I stood there in the dark, my breath heavy and rapid in my chest. I wanted to panic, to do something rash and dangerous. I wanted to run. But I did neither. Instead, I stood there, waiting for my breath to calm and the sweat to cool. My hands trembled as I uncocked the gun. I held it close to my side and hurried back inside.

When I was finally safe in the quiet of my bedroom, I saw the ivory grip engraved with *JPH*.

I collapsed on the bed, exhausted. Ethan was calculated. He wouldn't just leave me with his brother's gun. He knew he left it with me. But why? I shuddered. Was this the pistol that took his brother's own life? I recoiled, dropping the revolver on the quilt. I had to hide it.

I spent the night thinking where to put it. There was a loose floorboard beneath my vanity. I grabbed my nail file and pried at the board, but it refused to budge. Dawn lightened the horizon. Birds chirped, welcoming the coming sun. Sweat beaded my forehead and chest.

"Sumter," I murmured. Hiding the pistol in the folds of my nightgown, I tiptoed through the quiet house and back out the door.

The sky was rose gold when I reached the barn. The cows mooed, eager to have their utters milked. Sumter, my chestnut filly, shifted, her nose poking out from the stall in greeting.

"Hello, girl," I responded, her eyes watching me curiously as I entered her stall. She sniffed my hair, her nose tickling my neck. "This will be our little secret." Reaching up to the saddlebag hanging on the tack wall, I stuffed the pistol inside, eager to be rid of it.

I scooped a handful of oats from the bag outside the stall. "A reward for your silence."

I would be ready to defend myself next time.

3

A SOGGY MAN ON A SKINNY, BROWN HORSE

1863 JULY 4, SATURDAY

The eve of the wedding dawned in a warm, putrid, suffocating mist ... a mist that eventually turned to rain, attempting to wash away the gunpowder lingering in the air. Yet, the heat of the day made it feel like a boardinghouse laundry. Sleep evaded me once I hid the revolver, and I was left exhausted, emotionally and physically. Of course, I blamed the wedding festivities, and thankfully, Anna let me alone even as she shot me concerned glances.

We closed ourselves in the house, windows shut tight, keeping out the smoke, drizzle, and Rebel shouts polluting the air. Mother, a ball of nerves, remained in bed. Elizabeth paced the house like a trapped feline, uncharacteristically annoyed by her small cousins. Our houseguests maintained some preoccupation—Aunt Martha took a natural employment in leading the wedding preparations, and Pa led the men into town to see how it was faring under Rebel occupation. The hubbub in town, our weary houseguests, my concern for Union victory, and my imminent nuptials weighed heavily on me. Each quiet moment left unoccupied was assaulted by images of last night, Ethan's hands and his breath in the dark.

Hiding from Mother's sisters, Aunt Martha and Aunt Agatha, I secluded myself in a corner of the kitchen. The humming of our cook, Fanny, the knocking of the butter churn, and the sizzle of grease over the fire quieted my mind. I occupied my hands by wrapping ribbons around the bouquets and nosegays for tomorrow. With each wrap of the ribbon, my mind flashed back to Ethan. Ethan in the dark, his arms like a vice. Ethan in the dark, pushing me to the ground. Ethan laughing. I shook my head as if to shake the images from my mind and sought to focus on the floral arrangements.

The porch door slammed and Harold stormed in, dripping wet and beaming.

"They're gone! Every one of those damn Rebs left in the night! Cowards!" Harold exclaimed, grabbing Fanny and hefting the woman off her feet.

Fanny laughed. "You're soaked to the bone!"

"The battle's over, Fanny. The Rebs retreated with their scrawny tails between their legs."

I set the bouquet on the table and rushed to find Pa. Harold led Fanny in a jig across the kitchen, both of them laughing with glee.

"It's a glorious victory!" Pa announced from the parlor.

I could hear the ladies chatter in exaltation.

"Finally, we have a general worth fighting for!" Cousin Anthony exclaimed.

"Casualties will arrive soon," Uncle Eugene explained. "From what we heard in town, the injuries and death toll are mounting."

I halted outside the parlor, wondering if Robert was there. Anna stepped beside me, Elizabeth's hand in hers.

"God rest their souls," she whispered.

We exchanged concerned glances. My chest gripped my heart, as if to stanch the bleeding that was imminent. The battle in Gettysburg was over.

—

The shade of the veranda was cool as water dripped from the eaves. I wrapped the shawl tighter around me to ward off the ice water in my veins. As soon as the news arrived, Fanny packed up baskets of food, cloth, thread, and needles to be taken to the Penn Common infirmary. Mother's nerves were taut, and she insisted on staying home. I invited her to sit on the veranda with me, but she complained the weather aggravated her head.

With my lack of enthusiasm for wedding planning, I found myself avoiding Mother, and with that, I felt her drawing away from me, creating a wedge between us, a formality growing in its place. I could feel her displeasure coming off her in waves. Perhaps it was the behavior of all mothers before giving away their daughters? A way of guarding the heart? I was jealous now, as I heard her and Elizabeth talking inside the parlor. Elizabeth was reading one of Mother's favorite Psalms while she rested.

I shook my head, trying to release my envy, instead thinking of Robert's little sister, Katie. During my last visit, his pa and stepmother were too deep in their spirits to notice my arrival. When I found Katie down by the creek alone, I was angry. She was small for her four years, frail, and dirty. She twitched like a nervous doe when I approached her. I could not fail Robert now when he was off fighting for our country.

With the Montgomery gumption I'd earned from my mother,

I stormed to the house, leaving Katie in the shade of a shrub, and pounded on the door. The woman, Susan, opened it with a dark scowl on her face, demanding I state my business. As soon as I said my name for the whole house to hear, Mr. Moore limped to the door.

"I know who you are," he said, sternness in his voice. "Robert wrote to me."

I was surprised. "He wrote to you? About me?"

"I don't agree with a word he said. Katie needs no charity from you! We take care of our own 'round here."

"Sir, your daughter was alone at the creek, unwashed and unfed. She is four, sir! No child her age should be left unattended. I promised Robert I would aid in looking out for her."

"Robert had no right to make you promise to look out for *my* daughter. She's my responsibility. Susan does her best by her, but her employer gives her long hours. My lame leg here can't keep up with the li'l wild thing. She loves the creek. And she always comes home when she's hungry."

I tried to persuade them to allow me to do more. Clothe her, give them money to help—anything—but in the end, they refused all and ordered me to leave them be. I had failed Robert. I had failed Katie.

What was I supposed to do? Would it even be appropriate to return? And what of Robert? Was his regiment in Gettysburg now? He had been silent for far too long, and I did not know if I would ever learn about his fate. After my wedding tomorrow, I might never hear from Robert again. I could feel the hope draining from me into the damp ground. Any strength I had left, shedding from my shoulders.

The afternoon was waning. The sky dimmed as if God was lowering a shade over a lamp. A soggy man on a skinny, brown horse trod down the road from the northwest. His head was bowed beneath his forage cap, shielding his face from the rain. He was soaked through. His blue, wool jacket, heavy and dark. Gold insignia glinted in the rain, and I knew at once he was a Union soldier. My heart leapt as I ran from the veranda, my shawl falling behind me, the rain soaking me as my feet fell on the drive in a rhythm that called *Robert, Robert, Robert.*

I wanted to call out to the man, but I could not see his face. The closer I came, I knew my heart had only hoped. I was wrong. This man was not Robert.

Hearing my feet on the drive, he looked up. I halted in my steps. His tanned face was haggard beneath whiskers. Dark circles framed his deep-brown eyes, bloodshot from fatigue and smoke. Despite the rain, he removed his hat in greeting, brown hair falling across his brow.

"I'm looking for Miss Ella Coburg," he said in a hoarse voice. A tired voice, used to yelling above the explosions.

"I'm she," I managed to speak.

The soldier cleared his throat again. "Sergeant Major John Mathis of the 118th Pennsylvania, Company K, Miss Coburg."

I gasped at the recognition of his name. All those months of silence from Robert, I had reread his few letters to the point I could recite the words. He was only mentioned briefly, but I knew.

I stood stock-still while the soldier dismounted his horse with natural ease. He approached and grasped my hand in a strong hello. My hand warmed at his touch. A brief tingle ran up my arm before he released me, plopping his hat back on his soaked hair.

"Apologies, miss, if this is an inconvenient time, but I must speak to you urgently. I've traveled all night from Gettysburg and must return before I'm missed. Is there a place we can sit out of the rain?"

The rain was forgotten while I stood there. Only then did I realize I was shivering as the rain soaked through my bodice.

I nodded my head, unable to speak, while fear gripped me. I

gestured to the back porch. Sergeant Major Mathis took his horse by the reins and followed me. Passing the front of the house, I could see Mother's head above the settee through the window. She appeared to be asleep now, and there was no sign of Elizabeth.

Taking a seat at the top of the stairs on the covered porch, I offered a place beside me. I waited while he tied his horse to the railing, gathering my skirts around my legs, more for comfort than to give him room to sit.

Sergeant Major Mathis sat rigid and avoided my eyes. He looked bone tired and yet completely alert and ever-vigilant. I wondered then if this was what war looked like on our men.

Mathis licked his cracked lips and rubbed the stubble on his chin. "Robert was shot, Miss Coburg. His leg needed to be amputated."

I breathed a sigh of relief. The fear faded to annoyance and anger. I squared my shoulders. Robert had not so much as written how he was faring the last few months, leaving me to worry, and now he sends his friend to tell me he lost a leg. There are far worse things to worry about than a leg! He should be thanking his lucky stars he was alive! As quick as I was to anger, my shoulders sagged at his expression. He had more to tell, and my anger could not shield me from it.

"He also took a shot in the abdomen. There was a lot of blood, and the surgeon says his chance of survival is grim. I swore I would find you and deliver the news. He wrote a letter." The sergeant major reached into his breast pocket and brought out a damp, folded piece of paper.

With trembling hands, I opened the letter.

Ella,

Please forgive me for not writing. I lie here now, dying. I wish for you to know I have loved you since childhood and will love you in the grave. I selfishly prayed every day for our reunion, but I know it must never be so. I know it may be more than I can ask of you at this time, but please continue to look after Katie. I wish for her to have you as a Benefactor as her future is stark without me. This is the only paper I could forage and will not be able to write her. Please tell her what I have written here. I wish you many blessings in life.

Love,

Robert

He was dying, and I was not sure our love was strong enough to overcome the bleakness of my or Katie's future. The sergeant major looked at me, his tired eyes filled with grief and concern. My watery eyes went back to Robert's words. I, too, had selfishly prayed for our reunion. I had taken his silence for resignation these past few months and now knew he still loved me. I was heartbroken and desperate. Desperate to escape this rushing train. How could I marry Ethan tomorrow knowing Robert was dying … alone?

"How—how much longer, do you think …?" I could not say the words.

He shook his head. "I don't know."

I shoved the letter into my skirt pocket and stood up. "I'm coming with you."

"Pardon?" He rose, surprised by my sudden movement. "You can't come to Gettysburg. It's a war, miss."

"You don't know me, sir, but I have my mother's grit and my father's stubbornness, and I am coming with you. Stay here. I'll fetch food and some necessities. When was the last time you ate?" A sudden burst of energy coursed through my limbs, a plan and purpose

27

fabricating in my mind.

Mathis stared at me, his mouth agape. Dusting the front of his coat, he shut his mouth, then said, "I reckon it was three days ago."

I gave him a nod and gestured for him to stay, rushing into the kitchen. Fanny and Anna started at my sudden presence. They both gawked at me, taking in my wet dress and my face.

"Whatever's the matter?" Anna worried.

"Fanny, a half-starved Union soldier is on our back steps. He needs food. You can either keep him on the steps or invite him into the dry kitchen, but he needs sustenance. When he is done eating, direct him to the barn."

Fanny, sensing the urgency, went right to the cupboard to take out a plate.

Anna followed me out of the kitchen to the hall, grasping my arm.

"What's happened?" she demanded, a sound of panic in her voice.

I hushed her. "Come with me."

Anna trailed me into Pa's study and closed the door behind us. I sat down at his desk and pulled out a sheet of stationery. Anna waited as I penned a note.

> Pa,
>
> I have known my duty to obey and marry Ethan Harris, but I cannot marry him. He is a cruel and heartless man, full of evil intent and ambition. He has threatened me on numerous occasions, and I feel as though he is set on ruining this family. If you love and respect my wishes, you will not have me marry Ethan. Our betrothal must dissolve, for in truth, there is another.

My love for this man has been honest and true. Robert Moore is an honorable man, fighting for the Cause. He is below our station, and Mother may argue he is not worthy of me, but I know that you, of all people, will recognize status as not being a mark of worth.

I must go and be by his side, God willing, in his last moments. With great regret, I leave without saying goodbye. I am sorry if I am a disappointment to you and Mother and our family. Please tell Ethan I cannot marry him. I expect he knows why.

Your loving daughter,

Ella

"Anna," I said while she stood guard at the door. "Please bring Pa to his office as soon as he returns home. I cannot risk anyone else coming across this note."

I paused, looking at the diamond-studded engagement ring Ethan insisted I wear. An extravagant piece I often hid in my skirts. I pulled it off and set it on top of the missive.

Anna followed me out of the study and past the parlor. Mother snored softly, sound asleep. In my bedroom, with no time to change into my riding habit or gather belongings, I told Anna about the sergeant major's news and the letter from Robert—and that I could not marry Ethan. She helped me out of my hoop skirt and shoes, trading it for a gingham skirt and sensible boots. I caught my reflection in the mirror. My face was flushed, but my emerald eyes were bright with purpose and determination.

I tied my straw bonnet under my chin, while Anna and I ducked beneath the rain to run to the barn. No one was in sight, not even

Harold. My heart pounded in anticipation. Mathis, finishing a piece of bread, stood at the barn entrance, his horse by his side.

"Are you certain of this, miss?" he asked again as I approached him.

"Yes." I marched past him into the humidity of the barn, Anna quick on my heels.

Sumter whinnied.

"Good afternoon, girl," I said, reaching a hand over the stall. She nudged me in greeting. "Anna, can you help me saddle Sumter?"

"Sumter?" Mathis raised an eyebrow.

"She was purchased from Southern refugees at the start of the war, and my father joked she should be named after the fort that started it all."

As I put on the bridle, Anna, as short as she was, could not seem to get the saddle blanket over the horse's back.

"Please, allow me." Mathis took the blanket from Anna.

The sergeant major was quick to help. As he was putting on Sumter's saddle, I finished attaching the reins to the bridle. I hefted the saddlebag from where it hung on the wall and reached in to pull out the Colt revolver. The metal was cold and formidable in my hand. Glancing up, Anna and Mathis both looked at me with question and apprehension.

"A woman needs a way to protect herself," I explained.

Anna knew this far too well. Mathis just averted his gaze.

Arming myself, the revolver sagged in my pocket, feeling as heavy as Robert's letter against my leg. Anna took the saddlebag back and returned it to its hook. We did not want to slow ourselves down with unnecessary baggage.

"She's ready for you." Mathis patted Sumter on the rump.

Despite his obvious fatigue, his hands were strong and steady as he helped me mount.

"Be careful, Miss Ella," Anna begged, grasping my foot with her hand.

Mathis mounted his own horse.

"We won't stay on the main road," he informed. "The roads are teaming with troops and the retreating enemy. It'll be dangerous for a young woman, whether I accompany you or not. We'll travel the backroads. The route is longer but will be the safest."

"Then we must be on our way," I agreed. Anna squeezed my foot as a final embrace.

Mathis led the way out the barn and toward the driveway. I did not look back to see if Anna followed, but I could sense her presence nonetheless.

Rain plodded down around us. Clopping hooves hit the wet road. Horse breath left clouds in the mist. A weight lifted as soon as we reached the road. I knew this was what I was supposed to do.

"Ella!" Mother's voice pierced through the falling rain. I turned back to see her on the front porch. "Ella!" she called again, but this time, Anna was by her side, urging her to stay.

"We must keep going," I told Mathis, who also stopped to look back.

Mother pulled away from Anna, who ran after her into the rain.

"Mrs. Coburg! Ma'am!" Anna called.

"Ella Mae Coburg!" Mother scolded. "Where are you going in this weather? And without a riding habit?"

A scoff bubbled up my throat, but I kept it trapped.

"Is that all you worry about, a riding habit?" The laughter was left boiling in my gut. "For goodness' sake! Mother, men are dying, and you are worried about proper *attire*?"

"Don't you dare speak to me thus! Tell me what is happening?

Where are you going?" Her eyes were glazed in her laudanum haze.

Anna caught up to her, but Mother shook her off.

"I'm going to Gettysburg. The man I love is dying, and I must go to him," I proclaimed, my temper still rising, no longer caring if Mother knew the truth.

"Gettysburg?" Realization dawned on her face.

"Come, ma'am," Anna soothed. Mother allowed her to take her arm. "I'll explain everything."

I turned Sumter away from her. Away from Woodhue. And followed Mathis onto the muddy road.

—

The rain subsided, but the humidity wrapped us in a suffocating embrace. We had ridden for hours now, but Mathis assured me we had traveled only a few miles and had several more to go. After we stepped off the roads and turned into the woods and valley, the land seemed to roll onward.

Grass rippled over the hills. The gusts were a relief from the thick air. The trees bent and whined with the wind. Birds chorused an evening song, singing their last farewell of the day. Rabbits scurried for cover at the sound of our approach. We rode on in silence, neither one of us knowing what to say.

As dusk approached, Mathis slowed his horse, trailing off into the woods, where several boulders stood among a copse of trees.

"We will need to camp here for the night," he said as we pulled off the trail. "The boulders will shield us, but we cannot risk a fire."

"No fire?" I was soaked through and shivered.

"Rebs are retreating, and Meade's troops will be going after them. There may be deserters too. There usually are after a large battle. I will not risk your safety."

I studied him then. He dismounted from his horse, tethering

the reins to a tree. He took hold of my waist, hoisting me from the saddle and lowering me to the ground. I was curious about this man, older and harder looking than what I remembered of young men, including Robert, who set off to war. He reminded me of his horse, tired and damp, but with legs corded with muscles strengthened from marching. Mathis and his horse had seen battle and death. I couldn't help but wonder what war did to such creatures.

He unsaddled the horses and cleared a grassy area for us to rest near the boulders. We exchanged glances, yet neither one of us knew what to say. Each time our eyes met, I could feel heat rising from my neck, embarrassed he caught me admiring his face—his strong brow, his warm, brown eyes, his straight nose, and his wide mouth. I briefly wondered if I'd find a square jaw beneath his dark beard if I ran my fingers through it.

Mathis laid down the saddle blankets on the cleared patch of grass and gestured for me to sit. Night came quickly beneath a shade of thick clouds. I untied my hat and placed it beside me. Embracing my knees, I gathered my skirts around me, hoping to ward off chill and nerves.

"Are you cold?" he asked, sitting down across from me.

"No, I'm fine, thank you," I said, not wanting his concern. I pulled my coat tighter around me.

"Here," he said, taking up the other saddle blanket from the ground and handing it to me. He found a place for himself beside a boulder, grass and leaves matted down to form a natural bed. My cheeks burned at this handsome stranger's nearness.

"How did it happen?" I asked, not ready to rest. Dread coated me like oil, but I had to know. And I desperately needed to think of anything other than the consequences waiting for me at home.

Mathis fidgeted and then sighed as he leaned against the stone.

He lifted his hat to scratch his forehead, his brown hair now wavy.

"Are you certain you want to know?" he finally asked.

"Please," I begged.

"We were given orders at a place called the Round Tops to carry wounded to the rear. We had been fighting all day, bullets raining down on us. There were heavy losses, and I chose a few of my best men, including Robert, to accompany me. I thought they would be safe there. We didn't know we would have to retreat ..." I waited patiently for him to continue. He watched the horses graze while he gathered his thoughts.

"We had to leave them—all of the wounded. I did not realize until we recouped that Robert was not with the others." His Adam's apple bobbed. "It wasn't until late in the night that we were able to return to the wounded. We were too late for so many of them, and there were wild hogs everywhere, scavenging. Thankfully, I heard Robert yell at one that rooted at him. Otherwise, I'm not sure I would have found him in time.

"I stabbed that pig through with my sword before we were able to pull him out. It wasn't until we'd finished bringing the survivors to the ambulances that I realized his injury. I had seen so many like it before ... I knew he'd lose it. We just didn't know he had a bullet lodged in his side, either, until much later. They had already amputated by then. That's when he asked for me to bring you his message."

Mathis lowered his gaze, needing a moment before he could continue. We sat in silence. He looked back at me, his glossy eyes searching mine. I struggled to find the words. Words I could use to console him.

"I knew it was the least I could do, after bringing him with me. He was my friend and a fine soldier."

"You saved him. Thank you." I wanted to reach out to him, to clasp his hand. To comfort him.

"You should try to sleep. I'll wake you when it's time to leave."

Lying down on the scratchy horse blanket, I closed my eyes, willing myself to sleep. Even with my eyes shut, I could feel the heaviness of his presence. Even when my mind painted images of Robert lying among the wounded, surrounded by hogs, I knew if I opened my eyes, I would still see him sitting there.

4

GETTYSBURG

1863 JULY 5, SUNDAY

Drifting into consciousness, I puzzled at dueling sensations of hard and cold beneath me and firm and warm behind me. I wondered where I was and then remembered we were in the woods. Something heavy rested across my waist. Not wanting to wake up yet, my brow furrowed. The weight shifted, and my eyes sprang open.

At some point in the night, Mathis and I had gravitated toward each other. His muscled chest pressed against my back, his arm wrapped around me, and his warm breath stirred the hairs at the nape of my neck. I remembered Pa telling me once that if I ever came across a rattlesnake to hold very still and back away slowly. I did that now, not wanting to disturb Mathis, to preserve some dignity. If I thought about it too much, I selfishly wanted his warmth. Gradually, so as not to wake him, I extracted myself from his embrace and went a few yards behind the brush to relieve myself.

Mathis was rousing when I returned to our blankets, rubbing the sleep from his eyes.

"It got colder than I thought it would," was all he said as he shed the blankets and left to take care of himself.

Heat rose to my face. He knew what he was doing! I had never slept with a man before, especially one who was a stranger to me, but I found it … *comforting*. Shame clenched my gut at the untoward thought. The thought I should not have when I was on the way to Robert's deathbed.

—

"Whoa!" Mathis pulled up on his reins and brought his horse to a halt. Sumter and I stopped beside him.

A ragged man in blue came out from behind the shadow of a tree. His hair was damp, and his beard was overgrown. His face still soiled from gunpowder. His eyes jerked to and fro, nervous as a deer.

I gripped the reins tighter, causing Sumter to stomp her foot in protest. My hand went to my pocket, feeling the pistol still there. Mathis signaled me to be still.

"Deserter," he whispered. "I will not fault a man for wanting to survive."

We eased past, watching each other with caution.

When we were far enough away from the deserter, Mathis said, "I want to apologize if my account last night disturbed your sleep."

"I asked you to tell me." I shrugged. I avoided telling him I fell asleep thinking of wild hogs and hoping there were none in the vicinity, so instead I said, "You have a way with words."

Mathis shifted in his saddle. "I'm sorry. My father always told me I had an overactive imagination that would only cause me anguish. I wanted to become an author once, after I read Thoreau's *Walden Pond*. I was set on it, in fact, but then circumstances led me here."

"A shame. You have a talent for storytelling. However, your father must be proud of you fighting for the Cause."

"Perhaps he would have been."

I bit my lip at his use of past tense. "I'm sorry."

"Don't apologize. He has been gone a few years now. Consumption."

We rode in silence then, neither one of us knowing what more to say. The sun was peeking through the clouds but not quite enough to dry the earth. My bodice and skirt were mostly dry, but my shift clung uncomfortably underneath. I sagged in my saddle from fatigue … and hunger. Panic rose, tasting like bile. I feared we would reach Gettysburg, and it would be too late. Mathis sensed my uneasy silence and stole moments to glimpse back at me.

"He'll still be alive," he reassured me, but I wasn't sure he believed his own words.

Gettysburg's streets were clogged with horses and wagons, uniformed men, and civilians trying to repair damaged property. People rushed past, as if to stanch a wound before it bled out. The roads were muddy, whipped up by wagons and horses, making it almost impossible to pass. Women wearing aprons carried baskets of cloth and bandages toward a busy camp infirmary down the road. Soldiers walked or, in some cases, limped by and were greeted by townsfolk offering them bread or water. We continued down the road, maneuvering away from those on foot and wagons stuck in the mud.

One soldier, with a thick, brown mustache and missing his cap, thin hair plastered to his head, greeted the sergeant major.

"Mathis!" he called. "We've been looking for you. We feared the worst."

"I had some business to attend to," Mathis explained.

The soldier peered at me. "Oh, good afternoon, miss," he said, tipping his imaginary cap.

He glanced back at Mathis with a sly grin and gave him a wink.

"Honestly, Anderson!" John exclaimed, shaking his head. He chuckled.

It was the first time I heard him laugh. Dimples popped out on his cheeks, making warmth bloom in my chest. The soldier walked on, waving a prissy hand goodbye in mockery.

"Pardon him. After some time in the army, you, too, would lose your manners."

I smiled wryly, hoping I'd get to hear that laugh again.

We halted the horses in front of the infirmary. Sumter pawed the ground. The smell of blood, rotting flesh, bodily fluids, and an unidentifiable, strong, zesty odor stung my nose and eyes. Injured men lay on the wet ground or, for the lucky few, on wool blankets. Hundreds lay moaning and weeping with pain. I could have never imagined this sight. The blood drained from my face, and my eyes blurred. I regarded Mathis for some comfort or explanation of this horrific scene, but he did not look at me. His expression was hard and intense, as though he was about to burst in anger. Anger for the lives being wasted by war.

Mathis dismounted, then assisted me down. He handed the horses' reins to another soldier, ordering them to be sent to the barracks. Mathis held on to my arm, and I was grateful, for fear I would fall to my knees. He led me through the maze of wounded, dying, squalling men. Some appeared dead already, but no one tended to them. There were no blankets to pull over the rigid corpses, to give them respect in death.

We walked through an endless landscape of casualties. My eyes went over every face we passed, searching for Robert and hoping to see any familiar face, but they were all strangers to me.

One man grabbed at my skirt's hem, blithering; only blood bubbled past his lips. I thought I made out the word *please* as he clawed against death's grasp. His eyes were wide in panic. The bandage wrapped around his head oozed, and one arm was left in a mangled, bloody pulp. I stared at him in shock. There was no one to ease him into the afterlife.

Mathis nudged me forward, away from the tormented man. Little could be done for the thousands writhing in pain … nothing but wait for them to die or survive another day.

Nurses sat beside the men they could reach, dressing wounds and scribing letters from those in their final hours. Exhausted but determined, the nurses moved from one invalid to the next.

I followed Mathis, ducking beneath the flap of a medical tent.

"Don't look," Mathis cautioned, pushing me past the surgeon's table. Bile rose in my throat at the sound of a saw grinding against bone. He walked beside me, blocking the view, but it did not keep me from seeing the pile of black and bloody amputated limbs. I swallowed, willing myself not to vomit.

The strength of his hand at the small of my back steadied me, turning my focus back on looking for Robert. Cots lined the tent, each one occupied in different stages of recovery.

"Private Moore?" Mathis asked a passing surgeon. With no time to reply, he jabbed a thumb over his shoulder.

The direction was all I needed to find him, to pull away from Mathis and go to him. His eyes were closed and his mouth ajar. Stubble and gunpowder shadowed his graying face. Soaked bandages wrapped around his abdomen. A sure sign of fatality.

I fell to my knees beside him and grasped his hand, pressing it to my cheek.

His cold fingers twitched and his eyes fluttered open, connecting with mine. A knowing smile curled his lips, as if he knew I'd come.

Robert wiped my cheeks. "Don't cry," he said in a hoarse, tear-strained whisper.

"Oh, Robert." I didn't realize how much I had missed him until this moment.

He needed to know I chose him.

Leaning over him, I pressed my lips to his. His lips were cracked from heat and wind, yet still warm. A surge of hope rushed through me. Now that I was here, I'd fight for us both. Death would not win easily.

"Ella ..." he started, breaking our kiss.

"I love you. I'm not marrying Ethan," I blurted, reminding him of our parting words all those months ago. "I never could have gone through with it."

He gave me a sad smile.

"I'm here now. I won't leave you," I promised, taking off my straw bonnet.

I laid my head on his chest. Robert's heart stuttered under my ear. My hope faltered. He buried his face into my hair, and we held each other and wept.

—

An older nurse knelt down beside me, setting down her basket of bandages and lye soap.

"How's he managing?" she asked, her voice kind and pleasant. She studied his wounds and listened to his troubled breathing.

"Still alive."

Her lips pinched while she unwound the soiled bandage. "You're a Coburg daughter?"

"Yes," I said, surprised. "How … how—"

"I'm Mary Fisher. I worked with Doctor Cooper in York."

"You're from York?" I asked, shocked.

"Lived there all my life."

"And you are now here in Gettysburg. Why?"

"For duty, for country. As you can see, they need every able hand."

She peeled back the sodden gauze. Blood still oozed from the perfectly round bullet hole. I can see how they might have missed it during the initial inspection. Now with each breath, more blood pooled on his stomach.

Robert grimaced in his unconsciousness as she pulled the bandage out from under him.

"Here." She handed me a clean, linen bandage before proceeding to sanitize the wound.

"Can you tell me—honestly, please—if he will survive this?"

She gestured for me to help her wrap the new bandage around his abdomen. "Tightly now."

When we were done, she took my hand. "I fear he will not survive, Miss Coburg. The liver bleeds."

"How … how long?" I choked out.

"Pray, Miss Coburg. Pray that death is quick and merciful."

The fresh bandage was already blooming red. She released my hand, lifting the blanket to reveal the right leg that ended in a stump. A strong, zesty aroma hit my nose, even before Nurse Fisher peeled back the dressing. Something looked very wrong. The skin was black and rotting, and dark, gray-green streaks ran up his leg from the sutured stump, tracing his veins.

"I don't know what the doctor was thinking operating on him," she said. "This may kill him faster than hemorrhaging."

"What is it?" I asked.

"Poison in the blood. I can wash it and put clean bandages on it, but I don't think it will make a difference."

"Please, do what you can," I pleaded.

She sighed and confirmed with a nod, but her eyes shone with sympathy, dunking and wringing out a soapy rag from her bucket.

Robert howled when it touched his raw wound. He eyes sprang open, staring above him, while she washed the stump. He clenched his teeth, and sweat beaded his brow. I bit my own cheek, keeping myself from crying out.

"Grip my hand," I told him.

My bones crushed in his grip, as if he would break them, but I did not care. Robert's pain was far worse, and it hurt to see him this way. Finished with her ablution, Robert sagged into the cot. Any strength he had left now drained. By the time she was done redressing his leg, he had fallen back asleep.

"Please, is there something we could give him for the pain?" I begged.

Her face was stoic as she watched his jagged breathing, as if counting his breaths.

"I'm very sorry. We don't." She squeezed my shoulder. "If *you* need anything, please let me know." As if to say whatever was left was meant for the living. A forlorn smile tipped her lips before leaving us to resume her rounds.

For hours, as the gray light faded into dusk, Robert and I were left alone. I wiped his brow and held his hand, his grasp fading with the light.

He slept until lanterns were lit to invade the tent's darkness, brightening the way for the surgeons and nurses.

His hair damp around his face and his lashes wet, he whispered, "I'm sorry, my love."

I bit my lip to stop the tremble. The color in his cheeks was turning to a gray-orange tint, and his lips were tinged purple. Sweat rolled down the side of his face, chilling him, causing him to shiver. The heat radiated off his skin, and I knew the poison was now coursing through his veins.

"I brought you some food and coffee," Mathis announced behind me.

John stood with a steaming tin cup and a bowl of stew, a piece of bread resting on top.

His face fell when he saw Robert. "What is it?" he asked.

Mathis kneeled beside me, setting the coffee and stew between us. Robert turned his head to look at us.

"Ella," he whimpered, his eyes pleading with me. "I don't want to die."

My heart broke. The poor boy who lived on the creek bottom … the boy who once admired me from afar … the boy I grew up with, who eventually stole my heart, was dying.

"Hush," I whispered. "I promise I'll not leave you. I'll stay right here."

Robert inhaled, a vain attempt to fill his lungs. His exhale sputtered. He looked at Mathis. "My friend."

"Moore," John said, his eyes intent on Robert.

"A promise," he whispered.

John hesitated for a moment, then said, "Anything."

Robert placed my hand in John's. "Take care of her for me."

"But Moore—"

"Take care of her. She needs protection."

"Robert," I pleaded. I shook my head, tears brimming. "I'll be fine. Please, don't worry. Why must we make promises now?"

"Promise, Mathis." Robert stared intently, his words strained.

"Promise me!"

Mathis nodded, relenting to Robert's last wish. "I promise."

"Thank you." Robert's shaking settled, surrendering to exhaustion.

—

It was muggy and damp. There was no relief from the agonizing moans disrupting the night. Horrible, gulping moans—moans that could leave anyone sleepless, that could wake the dead.

I nibbled on bread and watched Mathis smoke his cigar beside the tent opening. Smoke plumed around his head. Why did Robert make Mathis promise to look after me? Why did he think I needed protection? Protection from what? Would he even be able to keep his promise? We were strangers to one another, only united under Robert. With Mathis remaining with his troops, he could very well face the same fate as Robert. Why make a promise no one could keep?

The bread caught in my throat. How could I return home? Surely, Ethan will be waiting for me to fulfill our commitment. Mother and Pa would be furious with me after bringing them such shame and worry. Cold, nauseating fear seized me at the thought of what may be waiting for me in York. I struggled to breathe. My hand flew to my throat.

Mathis hurried to my side, bringing the coffee mug to my lips. I let the smoky liquid go down, dislodging the lump. It was hard in my chest, and I gulped for air, my eyes stinging.

"Are you all right?" Mathis's brow furrowed with concern.

"He's ... dead. I can't ... go ... home." I gasped.

"He's not dead yet," he told me, shaking his head.

"He might ... as well be."

He took my face in his hands, staring into my eyes. His eyes were intense and dark. "He's not dead. He's not. Robert still lives." He turned my head for me to see Robert, asleep, his chest rising and falling. But he was still dying. "Even when he is gone, he will still be with you. He'll be with you … always."

Mathis dropped his hands from my face and sat back on his haunches, surprised and embarrassed by his own reaction.

Searching his eyes, I wondered who he was, how he came to be in front of me now, what motivated him now.

"I wish … the war … was over." Tears fell easily now.

The muscles in his jaw flexed as he clenched his teeth. "There will be an end. There is always an end. I just hope I live to see it."

We sat in silence for a moment, both of us alone in our sadness. I sniffled, and Mathis handed me his handkerchief.

"One day, these memories—these memories of this war—will remind us of the pain and grief we endured, but it will also remind us of the bravery fought against injustice and to preserve our nation. That is what we'll tell our children and our children's children will tell their children. America will forever be reminded of these times, both beautiful and ugly, propelling every injustice to be righted and every recompense to be resolved."

I shuddered a breath, listening to Mathis's impassioned words. "Is that why you fight?"

Mathis gave a wan smile, pinching his cigar in his teeth. "Someone has to. If not for us, then for *them*." He lifted a hand, gesturing to all the cots filled with wounded and dying, to the battlefield torn and bloodied, to the world where men and women lived in grief and sorrow and chains.

—

"Miss Coburg! Wake up!"

I opened my eyes to see Mathis. When I realized I had fallen asleep, I started.

"What—what is it?" I asked, looking at Robert.

Robert's eyes cracked open. "I saw her," he murmured. "I saw her."

My heart pounded in my ears. "Who, Robert? Who did you see?"

Robert took in a long, shaky breath through tremulous lips. "My mother."

My hand went to my mouth. Robert's breathing was shallow and gasping. His lips quivered as if he was suffering from the cold. The moon lit his face through the tent opening, giving him a pale glow, making him look almost ethereal.

"I love you," he whispered.

"I love you too." I clutched his hands, willing him to stay. "Oh, Robert."

Robert's eyes were glazed, the light dimming as he looked at me. "Forgive me ... take care of Katie. Ella, please ... make sure ..." Shallow gasps parted his lips. "Make sure ... forgive me ..." he wheezed.

I nodded, knowing there was nothing else for me to do. "Save your strength," I whispered to him, trying to calm him and myself.

"I ..." His voice came out in a breathy whisper.

"Shh. I know. Don't speak," I told him, my hands trembling on his face. "I love you so much. All will be well, Robert."

"Forgive me ... I ... I love you," he said once more, his neck straining to push out the words.

Robert's breath rattled. A long exhale escaped his lips.

I sat in silence, waiting for his chest to rise again.

I waited.

And I still waited.

Teardrops escaped the corners of his eyes, taking the light with them.

"No, Robert, no." I shook my head. "No. Please, Lord. Please, no."

"Ella," Mathis whispered, his hand grasping my arm, attempting to pull me away.

He used my Christian name, but I did not care. I pushed him away. "Leave us!" I gripped Robert's unbuttoned shirt, holding on to him as if to keep him with me a while longer. His chest was frozen in his last breath, his heart silent. Tears rolled down my nose, dripping onto him, moistening his skin beneath my cheek. He was still warm, but he was gone.

I memorized the smell, the feel, the sense of him. Absorbing whatever warmth was left.

5

GOODBYE

1863 JULY 6, MONDAY

"" T ake her. I'll lead you to the nurses' quarters,"
came a soft, female voice.

"Thank you."

Half asleep, strong arms wrapped around my back and
under my legs. He hoisted me up, taking me away from
Robert. Fatigue consumed my body, yet I still grasped for what
remained of him.

"Shhh," he hushed as I emitted a whimper of protest.

Mathis carried me, following Nurse Fisher through
the early morning. Her lantern swayed, casting light across
sleeping forms on the ground. They picked their way across
the field of casualties, many of them still writhing.

I dozed with the rhythm of his steps, his strong, warm
shoulder supporting my head. A cool breeze fluttered loose
hair across my sticky cheeks, sending a chill through my body.
I clung closer to Mathis for warmth.

We walked for what seemed like a mile, the moans of the wounded fading behind us. I opened my eyes to see rows of white, canvas tents in the moonlight. The camp was asleep, except for the crackle of a dying fire, muffled snores, and the chorusing crickets. Mathis stopped in front of a small, clapboard barn. Nurse Fisher opened the door with a loud creak. It was a single, dark room, musty with the scent of old hay. A dozen cots lined the walls. Personal belongings were tucked beneath beds, and hospital supplies were piled high toward the rafters, soft snores emitting from those who found a moment's respite.

"Right here. In my bed." Nurse Fisher gestured to a cot by the door.

Mathis laid me down while Nurse Fisher straightened the blankets around me. She had brought my hat and now placed it beside the bed. My eyelids were heavy and my body spent.

"I'll see her comfortably asleep, Sergeant Major," Nurse Fisher said in dismissal.

He nodded, leaving me to her care. She helped me loosen my corset, much to my relief. My lungs expanded, though my chest ached from grief and sleeping in my stays. She tucked the blankets around me.

"Here," she said, bringing a small flask to my lips. "Drink." The strong corn liquor burned. I sputtered but was then filled with an expanding warmth. "Now sleep," she said, picking up the lantern and leaving the barn. She said something to Mathis outside. The last thing I heard were his footfalls fading into the dawn.

—

"I thought you may still be sleeping," Nurse Fisher said as she approached me on the steps outside the nurses' quarters, a plate and mug in hand.

I had slept for some time, only to awaken to hunger and a need to relieve myself. An overwhelming sense of loneliness and longing kept me from returning to the dark, damp confines of the barn, content to sit on the steps to watch the morning bugle call as officers took roll. I hoped I might catch sight of Mathis in the reveille.

"Will they be marching out?" I asked her, taking the buttered bread and coffee she offered.

"Some will. Others will stay to guard the wounded and bury the dead."

"May I be of assistance?" I was not ready to return home.

Nurse Fisher pinched her lips, considering me. "We can always use the hands, but I must warn you, this can be disheartening work—work that often requires a calloused disposition when there is no hope to give. And this is the worst I've seen since Antietam."

"I want to help," I insisted.

She exhaled a deep breath. "Eat, and you can assist me on my rounds."

———

Mathis stood among the field of wounded amid the mammoth hospital tents. I stopped swallowing bile after the fifth wound Nurse Fisher dressed. Otherwise, I would have retched at the sight of the amputated limbs Mathis carried. His laughter drifted over the warm, putrid breeze while he spoke to two convalescent gentlemen playing cards in the grass. How could these men still smile and jest surrounded by this?

I must have been gawking because Nurse Fisher said beside me, "His company is detailed to bury the remains." She held up the end of a bandage she had wrapped around the captain's shoulder, and I leaned over to snip the excess with my scissors. It made me feel at ease that he was close by.

"Do you have any opium, ma'am?" the captain asked from his blanket.

"The most I can give you is this." She handed him the flask of corn liquor she carried in her basket.

"Bless you!" He took a deep pull before returning it.

"Now rest."

"There is no opium to give them for discomfort?" I asked as we walked away. He had not been the only one to ask.

"There is, but the surgeons are rationing it for amputees."

We continued washing and dressing wounds into the afternoon. Often, we saw blankets pulled over someone's face, signaling for his removal. Mathis gave orders to a few of his men, gathering the deceased into a surmounting pile beyond the tents. I blanched at the thought of Robert left somewhere in a heap of bodies. It made me angry to see such callous disregard for human life, as if war made men disposable.

"We give them dignity where we can," Nurse Fisher explained, seeing where my hardened gaze lingered. "Our resources are thin, and we all must do what we must to survive this war."

For the first time in my life, I was questioning the validity of this war. Both sides were fueled in the fight for freedoms they believed in. I thought of what Mathis said. Were all these men truly willing to sacrifice their dignity and their lives to free Southern slaves? To preserve a nation founded by men who owned slaves? Would it be worth it when it was over? I hoped so because it all seemed a waste, standing in the midst of it.

With her hands on her lower back, Nurse Fisher stretched. "Come, you need a respite, and I need an excuse."

—

It might have been considered a mess hall if it wasn't for the fact that it wasn't in a hall. A large, sweaty man stood beneath the shade of a chuck wagon, doling out bread and poultry drowned in oily sauce. Nurses and soldiers alike lined up to receive their portion, finding a seat on available ground. Nurse Fisher took our plates, and I followed her to a shady patch beneath a pine tree. A young boy, who looked no older than sixteen, walked around with a water bucket and dipper, offering refreshment.

"Thank you for this," I recognized, referring to her tutelage. "I've learned a lot today."

"It's good to keep your hands busy in times of grief and uncertainty. How long do you intend to stay?" she asked, sopping up the sauce with her bread.

"As long as I can keep away."

"Even the dogs of war occupied York. I don't blame you."

Letting the sounds of the camp settle around us, we ate in silence. I dreaded what awaited me at home, hoping the longer I was gone, the less I'd have to face when I returned. That was a lie, but a comforting one, keeping me afloat when I felt like I was drowning.

The water boy stopped in front of us, offering the dipper. I accepted a sip.

Mathis weaved through the "mess hall" patrons, his intent clear as he approached us. I passed the dipper to Nurse Fisher before I aspirated water. We nodded our thanks as the boy stepped away with his pail.

Mathis's shirt sleeves were rolled to his elbows, revealing corded forearms ... arms I had now felt two nights in a row. What would they feel like under my hand? Heat crawled up my neck at the thought. Robert had been gone mere hours, and I was contemplating the feel of another man. Guilt and sorrow were necessary pills to swallow.

"Miss Coburg. Miss Fisher," he greeted, running his fingers through his hair. His hair was dark with perspiration, the ends curling around his ears.

My plate of greasy goose—I surmised it was not chicken—looked suddenly very appetizing in my attempt to hide my blush.

"If you don't need her assistance after your meal, I'd like her to accompany me," he requested to Nurse Fisher.

"Of course. She has been an eager aide, but I can spare her."

"Miss Coburg, Robert's ready. I was hoping you'd join me at his graveside?"

My eyes locked with his. Warm, pleading, full of sympathy, and maybe regret. I found myself setting down the plate and reaching for Mathis's outstretched hand. His hand was rough and dry with dust and calluses, but the warmth and strength in his grip strengthened my resolve.

—

I did not know what to expect, but it was not this. A large oak tree shaded the gaping hole in the ground. Mathis was down in its depths, his head bowed, his shirt clinging to his broad back, as he shoveled the last few inches. He explained it was the least he could do for his friend and comrade in arms, digging the grave himself. He would not dare borrow his men from their duty.

Down the slope, men in shirtsleeves and bare chests labored beneath the intense sun, picks and shovels hacking at the earth. A mass grave for the fallen, Robert included, if it weren't for Mathis.

"Thank you," I told him as he hoisted himself up, setting the shovel beside the dirt heap.

Mathis squinted in the sun, surveying his company beyond us. "None of this seems right. If we could dig a grave for each and every one, and have a loved one in attendance … this is not just for you and Robert." His eyes met mine, dark and intense with anger. I nearly cowered but knew the feeling was not directed at me. "This is for *all* of them."

He did not wait for my reply, nor did it seem he needed my words. Robert's body lay sewed into a borrowed bedlinen. I did not know if I should offer my help, or if he even wanted it, so I stood still. Tears welled in my eyes, taking in the last of Robert's form. I missed him already. Mathis pulled and rolled the shrouded remains, and I cringed when it landed in the earth with a thud.

"Sorry about that, Moore." He grimaced. "I know you'll like this place beneath the tree, though. You can watch over our brothers from here."

His words were thick when he said "brothers." I smacked a hand over my mouth to suppress my sob.

—

"Did he speak of me?" I asked Mathis while we stood in companionable quiet before the fresh grave. I wiped my nose with the edge of the apron Nurse Fisher loaned me.

"He did. Often."

"What did he say?" I needed to know. Anything to comfort my aching heart, to ease the longing.

"He missed you terribly and wished the world had given your love a chance."

I bowed my head, looking at the hem of my skirt brushing the grass blades. "Did he tell you how we left things—before he enlisted?"

His gaze seemed to burn against my profile. I let it, welcoming the subtle discomfort.

"He told me you're betrothed."

I looked up then. Those warm, brown eyes sad and compassionate. "I'd be married now," I confided.

"Will you go back? To marry, I mean." Mathis leaned on the shovel, his toe crossed over his foot. Why did it look like he was always studying me, analyzing me? He licked his bottom lip, and my eyes drew to his mouth. "If that was too forward, I do apologize."

I shook my head. "I will not be getting married."

We stood in silence for some time, the clouds passing over the sun, stealing the warmth of the day.

I dropped to my knees, pressing my hands into the loose soil where I imagined Robert's still heart to be.

Goodbye, my love. I wish our story had ended differently.

Mathis knelt beside me, a concerned hand resting on my back. Comforting. "Are you well?"

"I'm not ready to leave him. To go back to York." With the well of tears now dried up, malaise filled me. "I'm just so tired, John. I don't know how I'm going to be able to go home." His name slipped naturally off my tongue but he did not correct me, nor did I apologize for the presumption. We had known each other for two days, but it already felt as though I had known him a lifetime. Perhaps it was the grief and longing. Perhaps it was something else entirely.

6

An Errant Mind

1863 July 7, Tuesday

"There you are."

I raised my head from the bandage I was rolling to see John—Mathis—dip his head under the tent's threshold. Rain dripped from his hat, leaving dark splotches on his shoulders. He took in the lone table and baskets piled high with medical supplies.

"Nurse Fisher insisted I rest, but I don't think she believes in idle hands," I quipped.

The sight of him filled my belly with mirth.

I had slept poorly, Robert's frozen gape and Ethan's chilly grasp haunting me in my sleep. Nurse Fisher had taken one look at my dark circles and pale face and led me to a tent shielded by the downpour. The tent was stocked with donated cloth, ready to strip and roll.

"It seems she expects you to be here all day." He removed his hat, shaking off the water.

One basket was filled, and I was already beginning on the next. "I won't deny you, John, if you're offering to help." I had said his name again. This time, I bit my lip, flustered. "I hope you don't mind?"

John set his hat down on an untouched pile and crouched to sit beside me on the ground. Taking the bandage from my hand, his fingers feathered over mine, his mouth curved. "If I may call you Ella?"

A flush crept up my neck, sweat gathering beneath my arms. He had said my name in the turmoil of losing Robert, but hearing it now sounded different—like confectioners' sugar on his tongue.

"You may," I said in a breathy whisper.

His smile grew, dimples deepening at the edge of his beard. If I were a swooner, I might very well have fainted.

"Robert would've wanted us to be friends." He added the bandage to the basket.

At Robert's name, guilt soured my stomach. John was his friend. A friend he trusted. He had asked John to protect me, to look out for me, and here I was, admiring his dimples. Was I this fickle? Robert had barely been in the ground a day, and my body was betraying me. Responding to John's nearness.

I picked up another piece of cloth, slicing it with scissors. Nurse Fisher knew the necessary method to prohibit idle hands, but not to occupy errant minds.

"I was given permission to take leave tomorrow. I will escort you home before our company moves out." His arm brushed mine as he picked up a strip of cloth. I must have blanched because he asked, "You don't wish to return home?"

I exhaled deeply. "I'm dreading it." All I could do was breathe through each punctuated statement. "The reunion will not be a sweet one—the rebellious daughter running off to a sweetheart's deathbed—

leaving them to manage the repercussions of a broken engagement. I'm certain I'll have to face my parents' wrath. And I fear my former fiancé will not handle this well." I quaked, thinking what Ethan might do. "Then there is Robert's father and sister. I'll have to tell them. And how will I ever fulfill my promise to take care of his sister?" It was overwhelming.

John paused in his work, taking both of our dressings and setting them aside. His knuckles lifted my chin to look into my eyes.

I melted into the ground.

"I understand more than you know, but you won't have to face it alone."

"You understand?"

He nodded, dropping his hand. "I fled from home too ... before I enlisted. I had left Vermont without a word to my mother and walked all the way to Pennsylvania to enlist with those who didn't know my name."

My eyes widened. "Why did you leave?"

"There was some trouble. It was best for everyone I leave—"

"But not tell your mother? I'm sure she was dreadfully worried." I bit my lip. My mother must be beside herself.

"She was. I've since written to her, and the rest of my family, apologizing for the grief I caused them. But it was too late to make amends with others."

"Your father?" I recalled him sharing that his father had passed.

"My father and a friend of mine. His name was Robert too. Well, we called him Robby. We were supposed to enlist together." A shadow cast over his face. "I suppose that's why I attached myself to your Robert."

Wanting to comfort him, I reached out, laying a hand on his arm. I wondered what it felt like, and now I did not want to let go. Muscles flexed beneath my touch, warmth penetrating through the damp wool of his jacket. If anything, it only made me wish his arm was bare so I could determine whether his skin was soft or rough.

"He didn't enlist?"

I knew before he said it.

"He died before the war."

"I'm so sorry, John. Will you go home when you have a furlough?"

He shrugged, pulling his arm away to resume rolling. It was like a door slammed between us, his open, happy face now drawn and downcast. "It's best for everyone I stay away," he said again. He heaved a heavy sigh. "But it's not best if you stay away from your home. You are needed there. If not for your family, then for Robert's."

"I know. I intend to keep my promise, even if it's hard," I insisted, anything to bolster my mettle.

"And remember, you won't be doing it alone." A wry smile barely reached his eyes.

7

REPERCUSSIONS

1863 JULY 8, WEDNESDAY

Woodhue lay silent in the twilight, the sky's golden hue blazing the receding, black clouds. Every window was alight, making the stars appear dim in comparison. The smell of roast ham and fresh-baked bread drifted through the open door, cooling the house for the night. My heart surged at the sight of home, and my stomach growled with hunger. The closer we approached, however, the tighter my nerves clenched. I was not prepared for what awaited me.

I sidled Sumter up to Mathis's mount. For a silent moment, John eyed me as I mustered the courage to go inside.

"Please, let's just be still for a moment."

John nodded, leaving me to my thoughts.

We were both soaked through, having ridden through heavy rain since the early morning hours. Sumter shifted beneath my weight and gave a headshake. She was the only one eager to return home. I was not ready to face any of this. Part of me wanted to turn back down the road. I could follow the army, take on the occupation of nursing. Anything to avoid this.

But we were here now. Inhaling deeply, I squared my shoulders.

"I'll take the horses to the barn," John began, "to give you time with your family. Do you want me …"

Yes, I wanted him by my side, but I had to talk to Mother and Pa on my own. And he needed to tell Mr. Moore about his son. John had packed his saddlebags with Robert's personal effects to return to him.

"You go ahead to the Moores. I'll be well enough. You'll be welcomed to rest here for the night. I'll make sure of it."

He gave a curt nod. "That's appreciated." Shadows cast over his face. He dismounted, coming around to Sumter's side. His hands wrapped around my waist. My skirts were weighted down with moisture and the revolver, and I felt every inch of John's body brush against mine as he lowered me to the ground.

I wanted to ask him not to go, to hold my hand while I endured my consequences, but we both had separate obligations tonight.

John did not seem to release me easily either, one hand remaining on my waist while he took Sumter's reins.

"Thank you for everything, John. I owe you a debt of gratitude for allowing me to say goodbye to Robert. I will forever be grateful." I hoped this wasn't goodbye.

The whites of his eyes flashed, blinking in the dark, busy scrutinizing and pondering. "I'm glad I could fulfill his wish before he was gone." He stepped away then, and I felt the absence of his heat drench me like the cold rain from earlier.

—

Mother came rushing from the dining room, her skirts rustling. Her arms wrapped around me, pressing her wet cheeks to mine. I didn't know until that moment I needed my mother's embrace. I buried my face into her shoulder, taking in her scent—bergamot and apples. The grief burning inside me tumbled out.

"Hush, you are home now. Hush," she soothed, her thumbs swiping beneath my eyes. "You are home safe, darling. Hush now."

"I'm so sorry," I managed to say.

She nodded. "There will be time to discuss everything later."

Mother examined me from head to toe, making sure every part of me was safe and sound.

"You're soaked!" she exclaimed. "Anna!" she called.

Anna rushed down the hall at Mother's call, her eyes like huge saucers. Fresh tears rolled at her comforting presence.

"Take Ella upstairs. I'll inform Fanny to put on a pot of hot water. She needs a bath and supper."

With a purpose, Mother moved into action. Her job was to take the helm and right the ship.

"Yes, ma'am." Anna wrapped her arm around me, and I leaned into her soft warmth.

—

Robert's last letter, the one John had delivered a few days ago, sat open on the vanity in front of me. My room smelled of vanilla-scented soap and roast ham. I brushed out my damp hair, losing myself in my stroke count. I almost felt human again, as tired as I was. Fresh undergarments and a warm dressing gown made all the difference.

Now late, the room was bright with gas lamps. Anna's face was as white as my chemise when I explained everything that had happened. She gathered the skirts and bodice from the floor but stopped. Letting the soiled clothing fall, she held something heavy in her hands—the pistol. I confided what drunken Ethan had attempted.

Her fingers tracing *JPH* on the ivory grip, she did not ask questions but tucked it in the trunk beneath the dowry quilt.

With what food I could consume, I gazed out the window, waiting for the imminent confrontation with Mother and Pa. A bright moon peeked through the high clouds.

Mother looked tired when she and Pa came into my room.

"We concluded speaking with Sergeant Major Mathis," Pa explained. He was here? A thrill coursed through my body. "He told us about Gettysburg … about Robert Moore and his wishes."

Pa's eyes were creased with lines. His brow furrowed with concern.

"We read the note you'd left on your father's desk," Mother interjected.

"I'm so sorry. I just could not go through with the marriage. And I know leaving—leaving you both to deal with the guests and with Ethan—was selfish."

"Ethan did not take it well." Pa confirmed my fears. "Your mother was greatly concerned."

"Not only was I worried, but I was *mortified*, Christopher!" Mother exclaimed, unwilling for her husband to put words in her mouth. "Embarrassed to notify our guests the wedding was canceled and to listen to idle gossip about my own daughter!"

"Adellia!" Pa rebuked, gritting his teeth. "Remember yourself. Recall our agreement?"

"Yes, Christopher, but she's an adult now. She must know the consequences."

Pa gave her a pointed look, silencing her.

"I'm so sorry to put you through this." A sob broke from my chest.

"We know you are." Pa cleared his throat. "Now, I'm afraid there is more we must discuss."

Mother took my hand, her palm sweating.

"Concerning Ethan." Mother's gaze hardened on Pa.

Pa itched his chin. "When Ethan heard you were gone, he came straight here," Pa explained. "Your mother told him everything. She told him about the note, about canceling the wedding, about Robert Moore, about everything."

I sucked in a breath.

"Don't fault your mother. She did not know he'd ... Well, when I arrived home, Ethan was in a rage. Your mother was terrified, not knowing what to do. Not one of us could pacify him. It took your uncle Eugene, Harold, and myself to escort him off the premises."

"It was distressing." Mother shuddered at the memory.

Pa ignored Mother's comment. "Mr. Pocket came to fetch me later when Ethan was found drunk in the tavern, slandering your name and talking nonsense. We dragged him out of there. It turns out he knew about your relationship with Robert long before his proposal."

The ham rolled in my stomach.

"Ethan threatened Robert. He threatened to ruin his father, leave his baby sister to fend for herself if Robert did not leave you alone. When Robert did not heed his warning, Ethan paid him to enlist. Told Robert he would turn his father in to the authorities for harboring a runaway slave, his sister would be taken and sent west on the orphan trains. So Robert took the money and—"

"He wouldn't!" Robert's words came back to me. *Forgive me*, he had begged. He had practically pushed me into Ethan's arms when he left to enlist.

"I don't know what he did with the money, but he took it and enlisted," Pa said. "Mr. Pocket confirmed it. Ethan received draft papers and paid Robert to substitute. Since then, Ethan has put himself in the way of trouble. Thus, Mr. Pocket and I have devised a plan for him to leave Pennsylvania."

"What kind of trouble?" I struggled to make sense of all Pa was divulging.

"That's nothing for you to worry about at the moment. Mr. Pocket and Ethan have made arrangements to travel out of the state, and I'm to close Etherton Estate and continue firearm production for the troops, per Ethan's contract with the army."

Mother shook her head, aggravated with Pa. Fire burned in her eyes. Pa was not telling me everything.

"Ethan and Mr. Pocket are leaving tonight. I'll take the sergeant major with me to ensure it," Pa explained. "We must let you sleep. Your mother has invited the sergeant major to stay the night."

"He's still here?" My heart leapt.

"Yes," Mother said, frustrated and weary. "It's late. We'll speak with him in the morning."

"Everything will be put to right," he said. "Good night, daughter."

I suffered a smile for Pa, and Mother kissed my forehead. "Good night."

Once in the hall, Mother and Pa exchanged harsh whispers.

"You'll ruin this family!" Mother's words were sharp enough to cut iron. "You did this."

"Adellia!" Pa chided.

"No. Do *not* follow me, Christopher!" Mother's heels clicked as she marched down the hall, her bedroom door slamming behind her.

A beat later, Pa's own heavy footsteps walked away. What had Pa done?

8
WIDOW'S WEEDS
1863 JULY 9, THURSDAY

I entered Pa's office, where he and John sat waiting. The sergeant major's beard was trimmed and his wet hair brushed back. His uniform was cleaned and pressed, and he beckoned me to sit beside him, a soft smile like balm for the soul. Pa, on the other hand, looked haggard, his eyes shadowed with exhaustion as though he had not slept.

"The sergeant major accompanied me last night. He understands the threat Ethan poses to you and Robert's family." Pa rubbed his temple. "He did not go quietly, but he's gone now."

Pa took a sip of coffee to fuel his words.

"There was a business deal Ethan and Pocket contracted, and I must protect you and our family from it. If the authorities were to discover this scheme, we could all be seen as accomplices to treason. Just knowing this could see me hanged."

I heard an audible gasp. It must have come from me

because John's brow furrowed and his eyes were liquid fire when I looked at him. His jaw flexed and his knuckles turned white as he clenched his fists in his lap.

"Any further information could endanger you, daughter. He conceded to leave, but … Ethan will be back. His pride and greed will force his return. He has a reputation and a fortune to protect. He won't let the law or us stand in the way."

I attempted to digest his words. A business deal I could not be privy to? Accomplices to treason? I thought back to all those times I'd witnessed Ethan and Mr. Pocket conspiring. Was he part of some Rebel spy ring? Was he profiteering? What was he doing?

"I cannot let you stay here, where he knows he can find you," Pa said.

"What do you mean?" My heart pounded in my chest.

"Sergeant Major Mathis told me the promise he made to Robert, and I think we came up with a plan to keep you safe. This, I'm hoping, will not be a permanent solution but only until the situation is stabilized." What he meant by *stabilized* worried me.

"On the four o'clock train, you are to travel to St. Albans, Vermont to stay with my mother." Mathis's voice was hard. An edge I had not heard from him before.

His mother? I'm sure my eyes went wide with surprise because he nodded, a silent understanding he was sending me to the place he had escaped.

"Mr. Harris will not be able to find you there," he continued. "It is a small town near the Canadian border. Far away from the war. I'll send you with a letter of introduction explaining the circumstances and the necessary details. My mother will welcome you."

I sat dumbfounded, as if I were floating away from my body, viewing this exchange from above. I was to be sent away? Away from my home? Where Ethan couldn't find me? To live with strangers?

"Your trunks and luggage will meet you at the station this afternoon." Pa pushed a train ticket across the desk. "From York you will travel to New York, then to St. Albans."

"Alone?" There was only one ticket. I knew John had to return. His regiment had to pursue the enemy. But could Pa not escort me?

"I need to stay here," Pa explained. "I'm protecting you and our family, and you have to trust we are doing our best. Your mother has reluctantly agreed, under one condition. You'll need to dress in mourning. This war has left many widows. No one will bat an eye at another widow traveling alone."

Widow's weeds? I was to pose as a widow? As Robert's widow? My heart felt hollow and stiff in my chest, achy with grief. He had been my one constant since we were children, until this war and Ethan tore us apart. Anger filled that open cavity, boiling up. Ethan was forcing my exile. And Robert damn well let him when he took that money and enlisted … and then held me to a promise to care for his sister? I wanted to scream and curse! How dare these men manipulate me to their will? Katie was as much a victim as I was.

"What about Katie?" I asked, exchanging looks with Pa and John. They were both fulfilling obligations, but what of my commitments?

"Katie?" Pa asked, puzzled.

"Robert's sister. I promised Robert I would look after her. I can't do that from St. Albans."

"What about her parents?" he asked.

"Her father and stepmother are neglectful. She is mute, and they do not seem to be able to properly care for her. She may be in as much danger as I am. I must take her with me. Robert would have wanted it."

"Away from the only home she knows? No, that is out of the

question." Pa shook his head.

"This is all for the best," John piped in. "I assure you, you must be kept out of harm's way. St. Albans is the only answer at the present."

I could not help it, I shot John a glare. He was taking a side—the one where I was not given a choice. John's mouth curved down, but his eyes lit up like a lantern as if ignited by my daggers.

I turned my scowl on Pa. "I will go, but please let me petition Mr. Moore and his wife to be Katie's benefactor? I could take care of her as Robert wished."

Pa steepled his fingers beneath his whiskered chin. "You are young and unwed, without the means to care for a child."

"I will be dressed as a widow. No one will assume the worst. Please, Pa. Ethan may see her as collateral, or a way to still get to Mr. Moore. Robert would have wanted her safe. I must take her with me. At least let me ask—"

"I suppose my mother and sisters can help," John interjected.

I flashed John a grateful smile.

Pa groaned, pinching the bridge of his nose. "Very well, but if Mr. Moore denies her traveling with you, you must accept his decision."

I nodded in acquiescence.

Pa looked at John. "Could you excuse us for a moment?"

"Yes, sir." He gave a curt nod before he strode from the study.

Pa waited until the door closed quietly behind him.

"This breaks my heart, Ella. You are my eldest child, and I feel like we are losing you."

I could detect Pa's pain on his aging face, his moist eyes. I never recalled seeing Pa cry. Not even when my brother, Christopher, passed away. His tears broke me.

"Your mother and I love you very much. Your safety is our utmost concern." Pa dabbed his eyes with his handkerchief. "We have discussed even sending Elizabeth to live with your grandmother, but your mother is hesitant to have her leave when she is still so young. I will need you as far away as possible if Ethan returns or if authorities are involved."

"What's going to happen, Pa?" I knew there was more he wasn't telling me. Pa handed me his 'kerchief.

"I fear grave trouble may be coming … you must be strong now. You have your mother's gumption and my tenacity. I know you will do what's right. I should have never given Ethan permission to marry you."

"What?"

"I thought I was doing well by you and our family. I should have known it would only cause us anguish." Pa glanced at the painting of our young family on the wall. "I made some poor decisions—selfish decisions. Decisions I thought I had to make to prove my worth to your mother, her family, and people like the Harrises."

Pa got up out of his chair and came beside me, helping me rise from my seat.

"Now, now," he soothed. "Gather your wits. You have much to face today, and you will need all the fortitude you can muster."

I took in his smell, trying to memorize the hints of coffee, cigar, wool, and ink.

—

The afternoon breeze drifting off Codorus Creek dried my cheeks. I had no strength to dry them myself. My arms hung limp at my sides, a handkerchief balled in my hand. John stood at my side, while Mr. Moore handed me Robert's Bible and the letters I had written him. He said he had "no use for them," just as it seemed he had little use for Katie. She was missing again, and we waited for his wife to fetch her.

"Found her." Susan Moore ushered her forward by the scruff of her neck. "She was hiding in the chicken coop."

Her frock clung to her, and the sleeves reached just below her elbows. She stared ahead, her little jaw stiff, her brow furrowed, feigning older strength than her four years.

I squeezed my fists, angry to see so much hurt in a little girl. What more could I do? Could I keep my promise to Robert? It seemed impossible now. Mr. Moore was not keen on the idea of me helping care for his daughter, let alone take her to Vermont. I was furious at Robert too. We loved each other, and he pushed me into Ethan's arms. He left me. He left his sister.

Mr. Moore's mouth was firm, his face etched by years of hard living and grief.

"I could give her all Robert would have wished for her," I explained, trying to maintain my composure. I knew I was asking too much of this man. A man who had lost his wife, his son, and now may lose his daughter. "But she'll need to come with me today."

Mrs. Moore looked stunned, as she reached out to lay a hand on his arm. "You're enlisting, Moore," Susan reminded him, brightening.

"Sir?" I was surprised.

"Yes, Miss Coburg, it's my obligation to enlist after Robert sacrificed his life. Rather, it's a necessity. I can no longer stay here either, it seems. Mr. Harris has made that clear."

Ethan was ruining lives in his wake.

"He knows what I've done."

"Slavery's abolished, and you can no longer be held for giving safe haven to a runaway."

He leaned on his cane, an old injury he must have received in the Mexican War. He had already gone to battle … must he return? He most certainly would not survive another war. Katie would be left an orphan.

Mr. Moore lowered his voice, exchanging looks with John. "I took a bounty hunter's life protecting that young man." He shook his head in regret.

"You may be the answer to our prayers. You should take Katie," Susan interjected.

Mr. Moore grimaced. "I don't know what will happen if Mr. Harris decides to turn me over to the authorities. He took the money. All of it. The money he paid Robert for his substitution. Only to keep me quiet." His jaw clenched. "Good riddance! I've no need of his dirty money."

Robert had given his father the money in hopes of providing for them? And then Ethan took it back! But Ethan's threats ... would Ethan turn an old man in to the authorities? Would he involve the authorities, risk being charged with treason himself? I did not know how much Mr. Moore knew or how much I should share. I couldn't put him or Katie in unnecessary danger.

"He has threatened all of us. He is the reason I must leave for Vermont today," I said instead.

"Then you must take her," he said. "Robert would have wanted you to protect her, and I cannot keep her safe. Katie?" he called for his little girl.

Katie peered up at her father.

"I'm going to need you to go with Miss Coburg. You're going on a nice trip with her to Vermont," he explained. "What do you say to that?"

She bobbed her head vigorously. "Yes, yes."

I startled at her words, and her father started chuckling.

"She started speaking after your last visit, Miss Coburg. Only a few words here and there, like *yes*, *no*, *bread*, and *papa*, but she will be speaking full sentences before we know it."

I smiled down at her tear-stained, dirt-tracked face. Robert would have been joyous to hear her speak.

John interrupted, "We must be going. The train leaves upon the hour."

Katie came and took my hand. I gripped it, relief washing over me.

"Papa?" She looked up with questioning eyes at Mr. Moore.

"I'll see you again, little Katherine." His voice cracked, stooping down to embrace her. "Miss Coburg will take good care of you while I'm away." Mr. Moore straightened himself. "Take good care of my child, Miss Coburg."

"Yes, sir. I intend to keep my promise to Robert—and now to you."

Mr. Moore gave a wane smile.

"Thank you," Susan spoke for her husband, who leaned against her.

—

Four large trunks sat on the station platform. Harold was the only one from Woodhue at the station. I had hoped Pa or Anna would send us off, but alas, they would not. My anger flared at Pa's absence.

"Your father would've come if he could," Harold said, handing me a money purse, "but some business required his immediate attention. He insisted I give you this allowance 'til he can send more."

"Thank you, Harold … please, tell Pa, thank you."

"Will do, Miss Ella," he said.

I wrapped my arms around him. Harold jolted a little, surprised by my sudden embrace, and patted my back.

"Now, Anna wished for me to let you know she put some of Miss Elizabeth's old dresses in your trunks for Miss Katie."

Anna assumed Katie would be coming. She had more faith in me than I felt like I had in my little finger.

"Tell Anna, thank you."

I willed myself to step away from him, my last connection to Woodhue. John and Katie stood waiting by the trunks. I approached them, fiddling with my black skirt with apprehension.

"I have something for you." My heart did a funny, little skip. He took a note from his coat pocket. "For Vermont."

The note for his mother. So, this was goodbye.

"You were a good friend to Robert, and now I can say you are a friend of mine. Here, you may need it more than me." I handed him Robert's Bible from my embroidered travel bag.

"I mustn't." John took it hesitantly.

"Please, I insist."

He looked at me with deep sadness. He knew it was goodbye as well. For him, it could well be the last.

"Ella …" He took a step forward and grasped my hand.

He leaned over me and my breath hitched. It was as though his eyes pierced my soul.

"Everything will be well," he said, but his words were wooden. I willed them to be true.

"Thank you for everything, John."

His jaw tensed and his throat bobbed.

The train gave a high-pitched whistle.

I wanted him to say something profound, something comforting that could carry me to the uncertainty awaiting me, but instead he said, "You and Katie best be off."

I pocketed the note in my bag and watched as two men loaded the trunks.

"I suppose we must board." Katie accepted my hand.

We turned toward the train, but then I spun around to look back, a pinch in my gut. John stood with his hands in his pockets, watching us.

"Will I see you again?" I asked.

"God willing."

"Write to me?"

"It would be my honor …" He hesitated, searching for the right words. His face flushed under his broad-brimmed hat. "I'll send you a missive as soon as I know where I'll be."

The whistle blew once more, and the conductor called for all to board.

Katie and I followed the passengers onto the train and were shown to our seats. She plopped herself down on the plush cushion. With a jerk and a squeal of steam, the train lurched forward. It was as though my skin were peeling from my bones, being ripped away from my home as the train left the station. John's figure became smaller and smaller, and I feared I was leaving something I'd never get back.

9

THE MATHIS ESTATE

Someone on the train called it "Rail City," the hub of the Vermont and Canada Railway. But it was distinctly more of a village than a sprawling town, for the characteristics of an old trading post still lingered. Farms and country cottages surrounded the outskirts, connected by roads and covered bridges over brooks, leading to Lake Champlain or the Green Mountains.

Men and women alike did not shy from staring at Katie and I as we disembarked. Looks of sympathy and curiosity followed us. You'd think they'd never seen a young widow, especially in these trying times. I bowed my head, hiding the embarrassment and panic that my lie would be discovered.

I asked the station clerk if he knew the way to the Mathis estate, and he directed me toward the Franklin County Bank across the street. "Ask there," he simply said. I nodded and left his brusque countenance behind.

At the bank, I found a tall, educated-looking man who appeared to be in his early thirties. He reminded me of what a professor may look like, although I had never met one. He had sharp features that drew your attention behind his small spectacles. His face was clean-shaven with ruddy cheeks. I told him I had just come into town, and I was hoping he could give me directions to the Mathis home. His eyes grew wide, looking down at me as if I were a child who had no business asking such a question.

"I'm married to the eldest Mathis daughter, Margaret. The name's Cole Smith. May I ask what business you have with the family?" His tone was not coarse, but it was direct.

My confidence this was the right decision deflated. "A friend, Sergeant Major John Mathis, arranged for us to stay with the Mathis family for a time. I have a letter of introduction here for his mother."

A warm smile split his face, despite his curious gaze. "John, eh? How is the ol' sport?"

"Well, last I saw him was in Pennsylvania."

"We heard about Gettysburg. He came out unscathed?"

I nodded, though I did not think anyone was completely unscathed. "They may be in pursuit of the enemy now."

Mr. Smith peered down at Katie, who hid in my skirts. Dipping a pen in an inkwell, he wrote down directions to the Mathis estate. "Do you have luggage?" he asked.

"At the station."

"I'll have it delivered for you." He handed me the paper as he showed me to the door.

"Thank you, sir."

"Welcome to St. Albans, Mrs. ..."

"Ella Coburg, and this is Katie."

"Mrs. Coburg and Miss Katie," he said, bowing his head in

farewell. I blanched at the title, but I did not correct him.

Our walk into the country didn't look anything like Pennsylvania. York County had not been as wooded or as shady as Vermont. The land was picturesque, as though I had just stepped into an oil painting. Rich, green foliage and wildflowers of every imaginable color stretched beyond my vision. Katie's eyes were as round as saucers.

As if the trees parted at its will, the Mathis home stood firm and proud when we rounded the bend. The Greek Revival brick house was massive with white columns holding up an entry portico. The structure's magnificent and chimerical beauty inspired awe, reflecting a time of tradition and civility before the war commenced. I hesitated at the huge, polished door embedded with stained-glass windows. The door opened, and a rather large golden retriever rushed past, bounding down the steps. Katie pressed her little body into my side.

"Moses!" a brown-haired woman with bony features yelled. "Pardon him. May I help ye?" She was dressed in simple homespun. By her accent, I could tell at once she was Irish. Her voice made me long for Anna.

Moses sniffed around us and wagged his tail as though we were long-lost friends. Katie gripped my skirts, squeezing closer as I shooed the dog away. The servant woman looked at us skeptically.

"Is Mrs. Matilda Mathis home?" I asked.

"She is. May I ask who's callin'?"

"A friend of John Mathis. I have a note of introduction for her."

"Wait here a moment." She disappeared into the house. I could hear jovial voices and laughter.

Silence abruptly descended on the house, and then a woman's heels on the floor hurried down the hall. A plump, middle-aged woman dressed in a fashionable, dark dress opened the door. She looked at us curiously, yet excitement danced in her eyes.

"I'm Matilda Mathis," she confirmed.

"I'm sorry to intrude." Nerves caused my stomach to flip, but I kept my shoulders straight with Katie at my side. "I have a letter here from your son … it should explain everything."

She examined me from head to toe. I wanted to shrink, wondering what she thought of this stranger standing before her in black, knowing her son.

She took the note without a word and opened the letter. Her eyes moved back and forth, reading each word, growing wider as she moved down the page. She looked up at me only once while she was reading. Her face held concern and surprise.

"Oh, you poor dears. I can't ever imagine why he did not telegraph. Now"—she paused, searching for words—"it seems you have been thrust in quite the predicament. I trust my son has made the right decision in sending you both here. You are safe here, Miss Coburg." My shoulders sagged in relief. "You may stay as long as necessary. Now, we will have time later to discuss this arrangement further, but for now, you and the little one must be hungry, and you must meet the others. I'm sure you both need to rest."

She did not hide her perplexed look, but she didn't ask any questions. John had detailed everything in the letter, except for the possible treason Ethan was involved in. I was thankful for that, wanting to protect Pa. I was relieved I would not have to lie to her, but at the mention of meeting the others, I wondered how much I should reveal.

She spoke rapidly as she led us into the spacious home. Hushed voices floated from the parlor. She hurried us past the open doors. I could feel heads turn our way as she led us down a long hall of polished hardwood floors with rich-colored rugs. At the end of the hall, the kitchen door swung open, revealing a cozy, cement kitchen.

Introductions were made to Louise, the cook, and Thad, an elderly liveryman, who was eating his dinner at the table. Thad stood and gestured to us to sit down as he cleared his place. Appearing like magic, Louise placed steaming dishes in front of Katie and I.

"Here, my dears. Eat, and then you must meet the others." Louise gestured at the food, her eyes sympathetic.

Hungry, we thanked her and began shoveling food into our mouths. Mrs. Mathis stepped out while we ate, only to return to lead us to the parlor.

"They are privy to the necessary information," she explained. "Please know, we would do anything for John. You are both welcomed here."

The moment Katie and I stepped into the doorway of the fashionable, cherry wood-furnished parlor, the chatter ceased. Three young women sat beside one another on the settee. The Mathis sisters were not beautiful, but they were indeed pretty, with dark-brown hair contrasting against magnolia-white skin. Their deep-brown eyes were bright with intelligence and humor. The younger one, who appeared to be close to my age, looked plain compared to her two older sisters. A smile spread across her face, making her eyes sparkle supplementary to her sisters'. A boy about sixteen sat lazily in a high-backed chair beside another young gentleman, who was straightening his tie.

Mrs. Mathis made introductions. Her eldest daughter was Margaret Smith, married to the banker. She stood to shake my hand and resumed her seat. The middle daughter was Nora. She was a head taller than I and clasped my hand with a firm handshake. The youngest sister, Irene, did likewise, and requested I call her Renny like everyone else. The boy's name was Seth, and he bounded out of his seat like a jackrabbit, eager to shake my hand. Landon Greene was the young gentleman who was introduced as Renny's beau.

With all the introductions complete, they offered me a seat. Right then, I knew I was where I needed to be. They welcomed us with open arms, inviting Katie and me to a place in their family, no matter how temporary it may be.

10

PRESSED FLOWERS

I n those first months, I walked on deerlike feet, afraid I might do or say something to warrant offense. In leaving the only homes Katie and I knew, I was like a ship lost at sea. Ignoring my reserve and Katie's shyness, they showed grace and kindness. No one asked why I wore mourning clothes or how Katie came to be my ward. I assumed Mrs. Mathis explained the circumstances. She asked few questions of me, mostly about John. Her silent observation when John and I started exchanging correspondence left a ghost of a smile at her lips.

Although we were surrounded by the Mathis family, I was an island. I could not help the guilt I felt in thrusting this burden upon Mrs. Mathis and her children. The longing and sorrow I felt for the loss of Robert, and then my home, left me homesick. I wrote John as much.

"Remain stalwart," he replied. "The woman I met in

Pennsylvania was brave and determined. I know you can face this trial in the same vein. Do not worry about my mother and siblings. It sounds like they are taking this all in stride. Nora writes that you and Katie are a pleasant distraction from her own worries and believes you will be fast friends. Seth is grateful you have given our mother purpose, taking the attention off him for once."

His encouraging words bolstered my resolve, but I worried about the speculation cast upon Mrs. Mathis and John. With the help of Kay, the maid who greeted me upon my arrival, I dyed all my dresses black. Donning mourning would keep the judgment at bay, while neighbors acquainted themselves with Katie and I.

The Chisholm family, dear friends of the Mathises, were particularly welcoming. Clara, who was closest in age with Margaret, was a twin—her brother also fighting in the South. I was told her brother, Brett Chisholm, was a very handsome, young man, matching his sister's beauty and charm. According to Nora and Renny, Brett was a shameless flirt. They were regular callers and even came for supper on my birthday. When Renny discovered the date of my twenty-first birthday in early October, she insisted on hosting a party with cake.

"It brings a smile to my face to hear of Renny arranging your birthday party," John inscribed. "I have enclosed a gift for you. Wildflowers picked near our camp." Pressed flowers were folded among the pages. "The yellow one particularly reminded me of you." My heart soared at the sweet purple, white, and yellow flowers.

He did not talk of war in our letters, though I asked him how the troops fared. I had to stumble upon a letter he wrote to Seth to learn of the conditions and morale.

"If I never lived through another Virginian summer, I would die a happy man," he wrote. "Skirmishes prevail, but it's the swampy heat and mosquitoes that tear us down, not the Rebel bullets. For the first time in *a long time, I crave the coolness of Vermont autumn. Five deserters were executed a week ago, four of whom were foreigners drafted to the Cause. They were discovered attempting to recross the Potomac. These occurrences seem to be increasing. Our troops are plagued with malcontent. Many of them are draftees and substitutes now. Very few volunteers remain. Our company has been despondent, solemn from the awfulness. Our officers issued an order of peace, forbidding noise and levity, in remembrance of these men.*

"*It's been days since I commenced this letter. Seth, I pray to God this war ends before you are of age. I tell you, brother, my heart is still pounding after the surprise we had. The sun rose brilliantly this November morn', and we finally had a break in the heat. Rations and ammunition were low, but we were content to wait patiently for supplies. If we had only known the rail lines and telegraph lines had been cut. I had stepped out onto a hill to survey the land, only to find the enemy en masse waiting in the valley. Without hesitation, I ran to give the orders, calling all stretcher-bearers and ambulances to the front, knowing we could not win this one. My men were the first ones struck. We ended up firing from a ditch, waiting till the enemy was upon us so as not to waste a shot. It was in this fight that I came face-to-face with a boy in Gray. He had to have been no more than fourteen. I thought of you, and it pains me to think it could have been you facing my barrel. So close have you been to the fate of this boy. I knew if you had been allowed to follow me, just as you had done that one night, you, too, would be lying on the ground.*"

After having read the letter, I knew I had to appeal to John to take a furlough. Just as he'd encouraged me in my absence from home, I attempted to urge him to come home. To visit his family and set aside the past. His reply surprised me.

"*More than anything, I wish to gaze upon your beauty.*" My whole body flushed. "*I spoke of this briefly with you in Gettysburg, but I do not believe I am welcome home. I have not been under my mother's roof since my father sent me away. I have not stepped foot in St. Albans since Robby was killed."*

Killed? I had yet to hear what happened to Robby Chisholm, but I often heard the Chisholms reminisce about Robby and John's camaraderie. There was always a sour tone when Mr. and Mrs. Chisholm mentioned John. Mrs. Mathis seemed remiss to ignore cutting comments, often changing the subject. No one spoke of what had caused John to leave.

"I send you my fondest thoughts and prayers. This war may one day conclude, and when it does, I hope I may still find you safe, and dare I dream—waiting for me."

A thrill shot through me. Was he daring to dream of a life with me? So many emotions whirled in my mind. Elation at his sweet talk and our care for one another. But there was also an overwhelming sense of guilt and fear. Guilt that I was taking advantage of John and the Mathises' kindness, and that I was somehow betraying Robert's memory and the love we'd shared. And fear that if I opened my heart again, I would lose. I did not think my heart could handle another loss.

11

A Derailed Train

A fresh dusting of snow covered the windowpane in the parlor, and everyone was warming by the blazing hearth. Katie sat at the window, staring out into the dark, watching the falling snow. The parlor was cozy and warm. Lamps illuminated the room. Mrs. Mathis hummed as she crocheted a blanket for Margaret, who'd recently discovered she was expecting. Renny lay on the blankets and pillows by the fireplace, reading Dickens. Nora sat beside her mother, crocheting, while discussing the campaign in Virginia with Seth. We all wondered how John was faring this winter. I sat at the rolltop desk, composing a letter to John.

I reread his words, hoping the heat of the fire hid my crimson cheeks.

"I was promoted to lieutenant after a recent battle, though it feels undeserving. I would be prouder to have you on my arm than the insignia it now bears.

"Our winter camp at the fort is lonely, but your letters keep me warm. We do our best to occupy ourselves with games and music. A group of officers invited a bevy of ladies to the camp to dance with us, but I was content to remain in the shadows, observing the choreography. Though I've been told I have fine feet, the lady I'd rather share a dance with was not present."

Bang. Bang. Bang.

I jumped at the sound of the loud knocking at the front door.

We stalled in our occupations. Kay's heels clicked in the hall as she rushed to open the door.

"Who could be out in this weather?" Mrs. Mathis pondered.

An icy gust breezed into the room. Familiar voices came in through the cold night—Thad, Cole Smith, and the Smiths' liveryman, Buckley. The three men stepped into the parlor.

"Cole?" Mrs. Mathis stood from her seat, her face growing pale in the firelight. "Is it Margaret?"

"Margaret is well. We came for a different matter."

"Nothing's worth tromping in this weather," Seth grumbled.

"The train derailed a few miles down the line. It's quite a mess. The local press is having a field day because the governor is on it … and so is your son," Cole stated.

"My son?" Mrs. Mathis's hand touched her lips.

John! Blood pounded in my ears.

"John's on the train," he confirmed.

"Impossible!" Renny exclaimed, sitting up. "He's in Virginia with Meade."

"Not anymore. He's coming home for Christmas and wanted to surprise everyone. Alas, with the derailment, the surprise is inevitably ruined." Cole fiddled with the hat in his hands.

"Well, well," Mrs. Mathis whispered.

John was coming home. John was coming home. My heart beat the rhythm of the words.

"This certainly is a surprise." Nora's voice rang with laughter.

"Sure is!" Seth exclaimed.

Mrs. Mathis, shaking herself from her shock, asked, "Is everyone unharmed? On the train, I mean."

"Oh, yes, everyone is safe. They are digging out the train as we speak. He was supposed to come in this evening. Buckley was to take me to the station to fetch him and bring him home by suppertime. When we reached the station, we were told of the trouble. The train will be delayed till morning, at the least."

We all exchanged excited glances.

Mrs. Mathis spoke, her eyes glassy. "I suppose we will be making a trip to the station tomorrow, now won't we?"

"Oh, yes!" Renny blurted.

Everyone spoke at once. I imagined the cacophony of voices was what the Mathis home used to sound like when the Mathis children were younger.

"He's going to be home for Christmas!" Nora exclaimed with excitement.

"He'll have to tell me all about the campaign," Seth said with enthusiasm.

"Now, now." Mrs. Mathis's motherly voice rose above her children, giving Seth a stern look. "We won't bother him too much about the war. It's been too long since John was home, and we'll just be thankful he's here."

Tingles ran up my spine at the thought of seeing him.

12

HOMECOMING

1863 DECEMBER 24, THURSDAY

T he shrill whistle blew, and the brakes screeched to a halt. Steam hissed and filled the bitter air. Light flakes swirled around us. People bustled everywhere. Faces shone with excitement and anticipation to see their loved ones. Katie clung close to my skirts as people pushed their way toward the train, searching for familiar travelers.

"Come on!" Seth beckoned us to push closer.

"Well, let's not smother him," Mrs. Mathis cautioned, taking hold of her son's coat sleeve.

"Please, Ma," Seth pleaded, flashing his dimples.

She heaved a heavy sigh. "Very well, go ahead. We'll stay here, out of the way of this chaos."

Seth kissed his mother on her plump cheek and hurried off through the crowd, pushing his way toward the large iron engine. Soldiers and civilians poured from the cars. Loved ones cried with joy and grasped their visitor or returnee. Those who were wounded or ill dismounted the train on stretchers or crutches. The crowd cheered as the charismatic Governor John Gregory Smith exited his personal car. Governor Smith commonly traveled to and from Washington to conference with President Lincoln and Secretary Stanton for his valued war counsel. He shook people's outstretched hands as he walked toward his wife and children standing at the end of the platform, decked out in their holiday finery.

Then we saw him. His teeth flashed as he stepped off the train. At once, I realized how much Seth and John looked alike, their smiles nearly identical, as Seth pulled him into a hearty embrace.

"There he is!" Nora pointed, bouncing on her feet.

John's brown hair was longer than I remembered, tucked behind his ears. He was taller and broader than his gangly younger brother, but the resemblance was uncanny. The same charming dimples and sparkling eyes flickered with fervor. They exchanged words, Seth pointing in our direction. John's eyes followed, landing on us, connecting with mine. His smile broadened and my breath hitched.

Seth hoisted John's bag, following him as they weaved toward us.

"Son!" Mrs. Mathis opened her arms to John and buried her face into his shoulder.

John patted her back. "I'm here now, Ma."

Gathering her emotions, Mrs. Mathis stepped back from her son and examined him. "Your hair is so long! And you have a beard! You look much older than I remember."

"I'm glad I trimmed it before I left. Otherwise, you would have *never* recognized me."

She caressed his cheek. "I will eternally recognize my own flesh and blood."

John scooped Nora and Renny in his huge embrace, squeezing

them.

"My little sisters!"

"Merry Christmas, John!" they both chimed.

John's eyes caught mine. I lowered my eyes, my cheeks reddening, feeling his perusal. Katie was looking up at me with a questioning expression, and I took her hand.

He released his sisters and came to me, his eyes examining my face.

Fidgeting under his gaze, I said, "Merry Christmas, Lieutenant Mathis."

John's smile faded, and I immediately wished I had not used his new rank.

"Merry Christmas, Miss Ella." He bowed his head.

His lips quirked as he knelt beside Katie. "Now, how are you?"

Katie sunk her face into my skirt.

"Do you remember me, Katie Moore? I was your brother's friend John."

Katie peeked out, giving him a tentative smirk.

"Attagirl! You've grown since I last saw you. I see Miss Ella and the Mathis women are taking good care of you." Her face bloomed pink, and she escaped back into the folds. John chuckled and stood. He looked at me once more, but feeling timid, I avoided his gaze.

"Ready to go home?" Mrs. Mathis asked.

John turned away from me and nodded at his mother. "I'm ready."

Mrs. Mathis took her son's arm. "Praise the Lord, my boy is home," she said in an audible whisper.

In the family cutter, Mrs. Mathis insisted John sit beside her, putting him across from me. I found the winter scenery outside very interesting as we rode home, unable to meet John's attention. My skin tingled with his proximity. I had never been known for shyness, but seeing John after all our letters made me nervous.

The Mathis women chattered, filling John in on the weekend's holiday festivities. Seth said something about how the war was affecting Christmas this year, and Mrs. Mathis gave him a stern look, shutting him up. John opened his mouth to respond to Seth when Mrs. Mathis changed the subject.

"Clara Chisholm has been moping around ever since Brett went South. When I saw Clara this morning, I told her you were coming home. She perked right up," Mrs. Mathis said. "She is quite looking forward to seeing you, John. In fact, we invited the Chisholms over for your welcome home supper. I hope you don't mind, but I took the liberty to tell them you would call on Clara this afternoon and bring the whole family back with you for supper."

John rolled his eyes. "You always 'take the liberty' to do as you please. Yes, Ma. I suppose I can call on her. Will the Chisholms be all right with that?"

"Time heals wounds, John."

With a heavy sigh, he conceded, "I suppose so. I ran into Brett the other day in Woodford. He seemed well. It was nice to see a familiar face. I barely recognized him at first. He must have grown a foot since I last saw him."

"Clara will want to hear that." Mrs. Mathis squeezed her son's hand.

"He was with Bradley House and Owen Childe." He turned to Nora.

Nora brightened. "Oh, how is he?"

"Bradley is doing just fine. He, of course, looked tired as all get-out. But then again, I'm sure we all look that way."

John's blue uniform was clean, but faded. Dark circles shadowed his brown eyes. The whites of his eyes were bloodshot. I remembered how red they had been in Pennsylvania, irritated from gunpowder, smoke, and fatigue. His eyes flickered toward me and I blushed, pivoting back to the window.

—

Always cheerful, Margaret Smith was the prettiest of the three Mathis sisters. Since discovering she was expecting, she seemed twice as exuberant, especially now that she had passed the early stages of sickness. Given that Margaret was married and kept her own house, I had spent little time with her, unlike Nora and Renny. I soon realized, however, through the duration of the evening, that she was close friends with Clara Chisholm, making it her duty to place John in her circumference.

While Margaret was pretty, plump, and warm in all the right places, Clara was beautiful with a thick mane of chestnut hair, a narrow waist all women pined for, and an ample bosom. Her fiery, blue eyes flickered coyly with each playful pout of her bow-shaped mouth. A sharp pang of jealousy shot through me seeing how easily she drew John's attention. Her charm and vivacity even caused young Seth to fluster.

Discomfited, I withdrew to a settee in the upstairs hallway. The words I had exchanged with John over the months were filled with a growing intimacy and affection, but now I was confused. I had hoped we could resume our last correspondence, but now, in each other's presence, I felt awkward.

Heavy footfalls sounded on the landing, and I looked up from where my sweaty palms crushed my dark skirt. John stepped out from the shadows. I was thankful for the dim lamps, hoping he did not see pink stain my cheeks.

"I was looking for you," John said. "May I?" He gestured to the space beside me.

I nodded, not trusting my voice. He took a seat, resting his hands on his thighs. The air seemed to heat and electrify around us, taking me back to a tent in Gettysburg where we rolled bandages.

"I was unsure about returning home," he confided. "I didn't know if I'd be received, but it was your words that gave me pause. Thank you. I'm glad now."

His little finger reached out as if he contemplated touching me. I smoothed my skirts, wiping the moisture from my hands.

"I'm glad you came home too, John. And that you're received."

"I wasn't sure how the Chisholms would greet me, but it appears I am forgiven."

"You needed their forgiveness?"

"Robby's death could have been avoided. I didn't realize how much I needed their forgiveness until now. But let's not talk about that."

We sat in silence for a moment, but it was not an uncomfortable silence as I'd assumed.

"I'm certain the rest of the community will be pleased to see you at Governor Smith's Christmas party tomorrow."

John scoffed. "That remains to be seen. Ma will insist I attend."

"There will be dancing," I prompted, but I immediately bit my lower lip, hoping I was not too presumptuous.

His eyes flickered to my mouth. "Will you save a dance for me?"

Heel clicks jarred my attention. "The parlor was becoming quite loud," Margaret announced.

I had been transfixed on John, not hearing Margaret and Clara approach.

John gave Margaret a smirk. "What a nice idea we share," he said to his sister.

"Yes, it's incredible how much we think alike," she teased.

"Now, John." Clara grinned. "I heard Mrs. Mathis just received a crate of leather-bound books from your father's collection at the law firm."

"Is that so?" John arched a brow, bemused.

"Would you like to go see which one's came in? I know I would."
Did she really?

John vacated the settee, taking Clara's arm. Envy scoured my insides, making me want to slap Clara's arm away from him.

Once gone, Margaret turned to me. "Would you like some spice cake? It's a family recipe."

Margaret did not wait for my reply, looping her arm with mine and leading us downstairs.

"It's so good to see Clara and John back together again," Margaret said.

I flinched. "Back together again?"

"Yes. It has been too long for both of them. Clara isn't getting much younger, and neither is John. They have gone through so much, and settling down would do them both some good. This furlough may be John's last chance." Margaret studied my puzzled face. "You do know they have been sweethearts for years, don't you?"

John and Clara? It stung to know he omitted the relationship from our communication, yet was that something I had a right to know?

Margaret patted my arm. "That's all right." She continued to talk about John and Clara's history together while I ate my cake. Their fathers were law partners in the firm, naturally bringing the families together. It made sense when John asked to court Clara, but when Robby died—Margaret mentioned in hush tones—it caused a rift in their relationship. He left without a word to anyone.

"What happened to Robby?" My curiosity piqued, but I wondered if I was betraying John's confidence.

"He was killed. The Chisholms were absolutely destroyed by his passing." A shadow crossed over her face, her eyes darkening. "John did not say a word to any of us before he disappeared. We didn't even know he'd enlisted until he sent a letter to Seth months later."

"And he hasn't been home since?" I asked, wanting to confirm all John had shared with me.

She shook her head. "He's refused all our pleading until now. I hope this furlough mends what was broken for him, especially with Clara. She still cares very deeply for him. If my brother had any sense at all, he would propose before he leaves."

The cake hardened in my throat. I swallowed, tears springing to my eyes. John was spoken for, promised to Clara. That putrid guilt swarmed me. Here I was, inserting myself into his life—his family's life—and I was allowing our intimate correspondence and private moments. Was I just lonely? Was I using John to comfort my grief?

"Excuse me." I put down my plate. I needed to be alone. I didn't belong here. Margaret did not stop me from walking away.

Passing the closed office door, a muffled conversation drifted into the hallway. Clara's voice was quiet and somber, and John's carried a stern edge. I didn't intend to eavesdrop, but my feet stopped just the same, my ears pricking at their words.

"You have no right, Clara. Don't make Robby's death an excuse. You have no idea what it's like to watch someone die and be unable to stop it. I've seen too much of that. Our courtship never lasted for a reason."

"John, please, I love you. I've always loved you."

"Clara, enough. Stop."

"Don't you love me too?"

Silence. I held my breath.

After a moment, Clara whispered in realization, "Oh."

Her heels clicked on the wood floor as she came toward the door. I hurried past, not wanting to be caught eavesdropping, but it was too late. Clara's face was pale and tear-streaked. She kept her head down, and I pitied her embarrassment. John followed behind her, raking a hand through his hair.

His eyes found me in the dim light, heaving a sigh.

"How much did you hear?" he asked, an eyebrow raised in question.

"I—I'm sorry, John," I stammered. "I didn't mean … I was only walking by …"

He looked resigned, exhausted. "She needed to know."

"John," I took the hand that dangled at his side, but he withdrew it from my fingers and walked away. Making me feel even more alone.

—

Holding Katie after a long day was like coming home. She was the one constant I could depend on. Her cherubic, sleeping face, her soft-brown curls splayed across the pillow, made my heart glad.

It was impossible not to look at Katie and think of Robert.

His gray eyes twinkling with laughter. His lips curving in an impish grin. The boyish playfulness I had known since childhood when he wagged his brows in a knowing gesture. I had seen Katie make the same expression, the pang of longing crashing over me.

Tears came unbidden and trickled down my cheeks. I closed my eyes, hoping to squeeze the tears back. But having my eyes closed only punctuated and illuminated the memories—dead and dying scattered on the ground at Gettysburg, Robert lying on his cot, trembling with pain and fever, Robert saying goodbye one last time. The memory morphed to John. John kneeling beside me. Swearing his promise to

Robert. Taking my face in his hands. His back muscles rippling as he dug Robert's grave. Those arresting eyes that seemed to see me, to make me feel ...

"Ella?" John's presence darkened the doorway.

I started, sucking in my sob. I brushed the tears away from my cheeks.

"I'm sorry," he apologized. "I was passing in the hall and heard ..."

I put a finger to my lips, nodding to Katie.

His shirt was untucked, and his sleeves were rolled to his elbows. He ran a hand through his disheveled hair.

"Sorry," he whispered sheepishly.

I tiptoed from the room. John backed up into the hallway, allowing me room to close the door softly behind me.

"I thought you retired for the night," I whispered. I could smell the whiskey wafting off him. He was drunk, and I knew now the danger it presented. He needed to go to bed.

"I had, but then I needed another drink ... a nightcap."

"We should be quieter." The rest of the people were silent in their rooms.

John shuffled on his feet.

"You should probably go," I told him.

John huffed. "Go?"

"Go back to bed."

"You still love Robert?" he blurted.

His question surprised me. "I—I—I will always love him."

John's brow furrowed, his eyes dark and penetrating, flickering in the lamplight. He surveyed me from head to toe. "You aren't a real widow, Ella. Why do you feel the need to dress like one?"

The sting of his words was induced by liquor. I didn't feel like I needed to explain. I moved around John. His hand shot out to grip my arm.

"Now, my mother, she is a real widow. She was married and had children of her own and then lost her *lovely* husband to consumption. What a man, my father. Now, if I didn't know you and saw you were wearing black and had a child, I would think you were a widow. Thank God you are smart enough to wear black. Otherwise, seeing you with a child and no husband, *Miss* Coburg … well, only assumptions would be made."

The insinuation he made was exactly why I did it, but I had not expected him to throw it in my face.

"How could you say such a thing to me?" I hissed, wrenching my arm from his grasp. "Robert was an honorable man. Never in a million years would he … which you should know since you were his friend. He was man enough never to break a woman's heart." I should save my breath. I jerked my arm from his grip. "As for you, I'm certain you have done enough heartbreaking for one night—and enough drinking. You might as well retire while you're ahead." I wanted to ask him if he was in love with Clara. Jealousy fueled my anger. But fear won out. I did not think I wanted to know.

He harrumphed, his face becoming an emotionless mask in the shadows.

"Fine by me." He shuffled off, leaving me to storm to my own room.

How dare he? His sharp words were a slap in the face, making me realize I did not know John at all. Miffed, I tossed and turned in the bed, playing every possible insult and rebuff I wanted to throw at him.

13
CONFESSIONS
1863 DECEMBER 25, FRIDAY

Governor Smith's ballroom was alive with vibrant colors. Garlands and red ribbon hung along the wall and gathered at the center of the chandelier-lit ceiling. Women in silk and velvet gowns, from red to the palest blue, floated around the room. Men in fresh-pressed uniforms and suits conversed, drank, and danced with the lovely ladies of Franklin County. Music from the ten-piece orchestra filled the air, inspiring sprightly footwork and twirling skirts.

My eyes scanned the ballroom, seeking his figure. John had been avoiding me all day, and still he was nowhere to be seen. I had a few choice words for him.

Couples waltzed across the dance floor. He was not there. Food was piled high on tables lining the perimeter. Guests lingered, flirting and sipping punch in cut-crystal glasses. But John was gone. He had disappeared. I considered excusing myself, wanting to search the curtained alcoves, but then thought better of it. If his way of handling conflict was disappearing, then so be it. A little voice scoffed at me, knowing very well I yearned for our confrontation.

Mrs. Mathis insisted I sit beside her and the other matrons. Dressed in my own best dress—a black crinoline—it was better I blended in with the rest of the St. Albans' widows.

"Ella." The deep timber of his voice at my ear sent shivers down my spine.

"John." My face flushed, and all the words I had wanted to say to him evaporated.

He stepped from behind me, sidling up to my chair. He looked down at my feet. They peeked out from under my skirts, still tapping to the music. John gave me an amused smirk. My lips curled in an attempt not to grin and encourage him.

"May I have this dance?" he asked, holding out his hand, searching deep into my eyes. He stood composed, his back straight. His hair was slicked back, his beard clipped short, revealing a strong jawline, and he smelled rich of cologne and cigar smoke. My breath caught.

The matron chatter stilted, waiting to hear my reply. Mrs. Mathis was the only brave one to respond to John's outrageous gesture.

"John Mathis, Ella is in mourning," she chided, loud enough for the other ladies to hear. "Surely—"

"And too young and beautiful to be doing so," John interrupted. "It is her decision …"

"Yes." The word tumbled from my mouth. He took my offered, gloved hand, and I did not divert my eyes from his as I stood. The heat of his hand in mine going straight to my cheeks.

"I declare!"

"The gall of your son, Mattie!"

"And the fastness …"

The ladies gasped and fluttered.

As soon as I was out of hearing distance, I would be the topic of discussion, but I did not care. Tonight, I would let John lead me with the music.

Eyes followed us to the dance floor as we took our place beside the others. I felt selfish, not caring about the gossip that would ensue or how my reputation would stand after tonight. All I wanted was to dance, to feel John's arms around me.

"I'm sorry for my behavior last night," John said, whirling us around the floor.

"It's Christmas, John. Could we just dance?"

We did not say a word, only feeling the thrum of the orchestra. His hand splayed across my lower back. The heat of it scorched through my gown's heavy fabric. He was not boastful when he said he had fine feet. His other hand gripped mine, his strong legs—legs spent years marching and riding—pushing into my space, leading us through the steps. My chest heaved. I did not know if it was the exertion of the dance or John's proximity, but I felt powerful with his hands on me in front of everyone.

Too soon, the song concluded. John bowed and I curtsied.

"Thank you, John." My voice strained as I caught my breath.

Another gentleman stepped toward us. "May I—" he began.

John's jaw ticked, his eyes flashed in warning, and he pulled me close.

"Another round?" he asked me, his eyes possessive.

A lively dance, a heel-toe polka, struck up. John took my hand again, his other firmly around my waist.

"Hold on." He grinned. With my free hand, I held up my gown. We left the other gentleman in our dust, soaring across the floor like two birds chasing each other to the sky.

Dance after dance, I reveled in the feel of his arms around me.

"This is scandalous, John," I murmured.

"Let them talk." His whisper was hot in my ear.

We glided along the floor, never tiring or stopping to catch our breath. The lively dancing slowed, and we paced ourselves as a plump woman stepped beside the musicians. The instruments still played while she introduced the song.

"This is a ballad that was suggested by a recent incident. On the battlefield of Gettysburg, among many of our wounded soldiers, was a young man, the only son of an aged mother. Hearing the surgeon tell his companions that he could not survive the ensuing night, the young man placed his hand upon his forehead"—the woman put her black-laced mitt to her forehead—"talking continually of his mother and sister, and said to his comrades assembled around him, 'Break it gently to my mother.'"

Her address of the song came crashing around me. The strength I felt dancing in John's arms was dashed. She began with her soprano, her hand placed on her bosom.

Through my lashes, John peered at me with concern. Was he haunted by the same thoughts and memories? Winded, I now felt how my toes pinched in my shoes.

"Thank you for the dances, John. It's nearing ten. It may be best for me to take my leave. Katie will be waiting up for me." I stepped out of John's reach.

He did not stop me from leaving him on the dance floor.

Finding Nora and Renny, they both knew it was time to leave. Mrs. Mathis, her face crimson, was more than happy to depart the matrons' tittle-tattle. I cast a glance over my shoulder. Our eyes connected over the glass rim of his drink. A fire bloomed in my belly, and I no longer cared what they thought.

—

Unable to sleep, I wrapped my dressing robe around my nightgown and pulled my hair into a loose plait. Katie was asleep when I returned, but I could not rest without peeking in on her to ensure she was safe and well.

My mind reeled with the words John and I exchanged yesterday and the feel of his arms around me as we waltzed. Closing Katie's door, I listened to the sleeping house. Soft snores drifted from bedrooms. Shuffling and crackling sounded downstairs. Like a moth to the flame, I was drawn to the stoking of the hearthfire.

John's eyebrow raised when I entered the parlor. "Still up?"

His heated inspection of my night clothes made me feel naked, yet brazen.

"We created quite the scene this evening." I smirked.

His dimples popped. "Another reason I shouldn't come home. I always find some way to embarrass my mother."

I cringed with guilt. "We shouldn't have done that. Your mother has been immeasurably generous, allowing Katie and I to stay here— we're strangers—and not once has she made me feel unwelcome. But I'm afraid we're a burden. It was selfish. We'll only bring unwanted attention, dangerous attention, to you and your family."

The bell chimed on the grandfather clock. The dongs echoed throughout the quiet house. It was no longer Christmas.

John gave a loud sigh, placing the poker back with the fireplace tools. He picked up a glass of amber liquid from the mantel, downing the last drops before setting it down again. His eyes pierced mine, searching for something.

"I'm sorry about what I said yesterday. I was not myself and I didn't mean—"

I held up my hand to stop him. "You did mean it. No one can be anything but honest when in their cups."

He shook his head. "I hurt you. It pains me to know I hurt you. I know none of this can be easy for you—away from your home, hiding from Ethan, responsible for Katie, and among strangers."

"It hasn't been easy, but you know that. I shouldn't be wearing mourning. I should be dancing with all the other young ladies like I did tonight. Instead, I'm hiding, surviving, doing what I can to get through this, just so I can go home."

"Still, it wasn't right—"

"I know you didn't mean to hurt me."

John looked away, running his hand down his face. "I don't like who I was before this fu—before this war. Apparently, being home summons demons I've tried very hard to shed."

"You're forgiven. I know this can't be easy for you either."

We stood in silence, listening to the crackling fire.

"I don't have much time before I leave in the morning. I hope we can just enjoy these last moments of Christmas. But there is something I must say …"

His eyes found mine, urging me to speak, pleading with me to ease his own discomfort.

"Then tell me," I encouraged.

His deep-brown eyes softened.

The air between us sparked and popped like the flames in the hearth. He took a step toward me.

"The first day I laid eyes on you—the day I came to your home with the news of Robert—I was caught off guard. There I was, delivering his message, and all I could do was stare at you. You demanded to come with me. And I thought you were the most beautiful woman I had ever seen. I was jealous of Robert, seeing you determined to go to him, to cry and mourn for him. He was my friend. You and I both lost him. Yet selfishly, I wanted you for myself."

My breath caught and he stepped closer. I took a step back.

"You were so brave in Gettysburg. Brave even still, leaving your home, taking charge of Katie, while you're doing everything in your power to protect everyone. Selflessly thinking of me and my family by wearing black. And still you seem to grow impossibly beautiful."

"John." His name came out a breathy whisper.

"Ella," he growled.

He kept charging forward, my feet carrying me back until I collided with the wall beside the hearth. He braced his hands against the wall, caging me in, as if to keep his fingers from wandering. Blood pounded in my ears.

"With every word you wrote me, I found myself falling, tumbling. Consumed with the need to be yours and you to be mine. I've fallen in love with you. I didn't know it could feel this way, but ..." His brows pinched. "I love you so much, it hurts. It's a fire that will consume me if I can't touch you."

I gaped, taken aback by his words, my mouth opening and closing like a fish. My body felt hot, too hot. My heart felt like it would burst from my chest.

From stomach to knees, his body pressed against me. I felt him. Hard, muscled, and burning. My body hummed but I stood rigid, too reluctant to reflect on my own emotions. Too afraid to be hurt, to surrender completely, to lose anyone I cared for—to love—again. All I could do was absorb the desire coiling between us, readying to strike.

"You're so damn beautiful. Those emerald eyes arrest me."

He leaned toward me, resting his forehead on mine. Closing our eyes. Steadying my heart.

His breath skated across my parted lips.

I willed him to kiss me, pressing myself more firmly against him.

He cursed under his breath before his lips crushed mine, our teeth clashing. The kiss was demanding, the whiskers of his beard rasping against my skin. His tongue flicked across my lips, and I wanted to taste him. I opened for him. Our tongues caressed, explored, tasted. He was a robust flavor of tobacco and whiskey. A smoky sweetness I wanted to devour, to drink until I was satiated.

He leaned into me. I could feel our willpower crumbling. I had never felt anything like this before, not even with Robert. This all-consuming need to feel someone, to let someone know all of me.

John's hands scraped down the wall. I wanted him to touch me. I wanted to touch him. My back nearly arched off the wall, begging for him. His lips never left mine.

His hand cradled my neck, his fingers tangling in the loose braid at my nape, his thumb stroking my cheek. A tingle ran through me.

"John," I breathed, pleading. Needing more. I reached for him, running my hands down his chest, feeling the muscles tense beneath my fingers.

His lips scorched a trail down my jaw, down my neck. The rough scrape of his beard exfoliating. His other hand gripped my waist, pressing me into him. No petticoats or hoop skirts separated us, only our thin layers. Heat from our bodies and the fire engulfed us. I felt his growing arousal against my stomach, but I was not mortified. Pride warmed my chest. I did this to him. His hand roamed the curve of my waist until his fingers wrapped around my breast. My breath hitched and I felt like liquid, my center pulsing with each gentle squeeze of his hand.

My fingers did their own exploring, threading through his hair, holding him there as his lips continued their journey across my collarbone, leaving a moist trail toward my breasts.

The parlor filled with our panting, the flickering shadows dancing across the walls. My frustrating mind hooked on to the fact that we were doing this in his mother's parlor, under her roof, in the dark while everyone slept.

I shouldn't let this continue. I'd be taking advantage of the situation, of his mother's kindness. I couldn't let John do this—not when I did not know what tomorrow would bring, what could happen with Ethan, what could happen once John returned to Virginia. This was never a permanent solution. I would return home eventually.

John just confessed his love for me and here I was, giving him hope, when I didn't even know I had the right to give it to him. My body screamed with desire, the need to consume, while my heart cracked.

"John." I pressed him back. "We shouldn't."

John froze, straightening to look down at me, his chest heaving.

He took my face in his hands. "I know you must be surprised. I've never felt this way about anyone either. But after all our letters, the dances we shared tonight, I just thought ..."

He didn't understand my hesitancy. "It's not that. With everything, I just don't know if we should ..." I was struggling to find the words. "Your mother—"

"What about my mother?" There was an edge to his tone.

I averted my eyes, not wanting to see the naked hurt in his, and not wanting him to see the disquiet in mine. He had made himself vulnerable, and now rejection was his unwarranted payment. A rejection I didn't want to give him. It was safer this way, though.

"Is it Robert?" he asked. "You told me you still love him." John released me, running his hand through his hair. Frustrated, his voice rose. "I'm competing for your love with a damn ghost!"

I flinched as though he struck me, hurt coursing through my body. I backed away from John, moving toward the parlor door. His expression fell as he realized what he had said.

"Oh, I'm so sorry, Ella. I meant—"

"Don't. You keep saying things you don't mean." I snapped. He knew my secrets, he knew the threat I was hiding from. He just apologized, yet he still did not bite his tongue. "And what of your love for Clara? Do you still love *her*?"

"Of course I don't love her. I know that now. I've never felt this way toward anyone. You're the one I want."

"You can't confess your love for me and then curse me and your dead friend in the same breath!"

He winced, his eyes becoming flint.

"Perhaps I've imbibed too much again," he said stonily.

I shook my head, disappointed. "You're more sober than drunk, John."

I turned on my heels, not wanting to see the broken look on his face, leaving him in the parlor. I had to give us distance because if I stayed a moment longer, my resolve would fail and I would surrender myself wholly to him.

Collapsing on my bed, I willed my heart to slow. My body ached with the unsatiated need. A need he coaxed from me. Skin tingled where his beard branded my skin. My lips were still warm and swollen from his kisses. I wanted him so badly, it was excruciating. He infuriated me, he tested me, yet he made me feel beautiful, wanted, and powerful. Like I was strong, like I could get through this crisis. I was falling for him, and I knew that would only bring sorrow. War, death, and threats were still very much our reality. Were we all bound to lose? I did not think I could survive another loss. And this time, his claws were embedded in me. It would rip me apart.

14

SICKNESS

1863 December–1864 January

"Miss Ella?" Kay's bubbly voice sounded as she shuffled around my bedroom, filling the porcelain washbowl with steaming water and poking the crackling logs in the fireplace. "Miss Ella, ye best be out of that bed. Mister John will be leaving in a moment. He's on his way out, he is. Ye need to get out of that bed if ye want to say goodbye."

I stretched and yawned, the memory of last night floating back to me. My body flushed, recalling the feel of his mouth and hands. But it was a tourniquet to my heart. John was leaving. I had walked away from him, and it made me physically ill.

"He wants ye up to say goodbye to him before he leaves to catch his train. Please, Miss Ella, do get up. And the misses want a word with ye as soon as Mister John has left, so not to embarrass ye further."

I quailed, knowing I had disappointed my hostess. Her

words caused my head to throb.

"I don't feel well. I don't think I will be able to get out of bed today." Maybe it was a coward's move. "Tell John goodbye for me and extend my apologies to Mrs. Mathis. I have such a splitting headache this morning."

Kay finished draping fresh towels beside the washbowl. "But Mister John is leavin' an' won't be back for I don't know how long—however long this war has to last."

I grimaced at her mention of war's uncertainty.

"Tea, please," I rasped. A swallow sent a thousand tiny knives down my throat.

She hesitated, looking at me with concern, before skittering from the room.

Gray light from the early morning sky filtered through the window. Heavy sheets of white flakes drifted down. The cold floorboards penetrated through my wool stockings when my feet hit the floor. I shrugged a shawl over my shoulders and tiptoed to the window. My body screamed at me, my joints aching.

Spruce trees were dark silhouettes, weighed down with heavy snow and ice. Paths I had walked through the summer and the fall were now covered in a pristine, white blanket. My breath fogged the crystallized glass, and I wiped it clear with my shawl.

Thad rode around the house on his brown stallion, pulling two chestnut bay horses beside him. The beasts' brown, muscular legs sunk in the snow. A drift had yet to be cleared, covering the front steps. Thad dismounted his horse and plowed through the snow to the front door, disappearing beneath the portico.

Was I making a mistake letting John leave without a word? For all the strength I wished to portray, I was frightened. What if this was the end? John was returning to his regiment. To fight and to, what …

get himself killed? I dreaded the thought, pulling my shawl tighter around me. I sniffed. My heart lurched with yearning, fearing this would be the last I'd see him.

I desperately wanted to run downstairs, throw myself into his arms, and never let go. My limbs itched with the need to follow him—to Virginia, to the ends of the earth. As if I could hold on to him and protect him! I shook my head, knowing it was irrational. I had responsibilities here … Katie to think about and a family to eventually go home to.

Thad returned with two leather-clad bags, which he strapped on to the saddles. John shuffled through the snow, hunched against the snowfall, to his horse. His collar was turned up to ward against the chill, his hat pulled low. Seth followed behind him, his lanky body matching John's steps, bundled in a gray, woolen coat and a black, felt cap. A knitted scarf wound up to his ears. They both mounted their horses with ease as though they had been born to it, and I suppose they had. Thad mounted his horse and turned it away from the house, into the wind and snow.

Desperation clenched my heart. My throat constricted. My hand went to the windowpane, wanting so badly to reach out and touch him, but I couldn't do anything as their horses waded toward the snow-packed road. He was leaving for good. If he did survive the war, would I be gone by the time he came home? Would Ethan still be a threat?

The horses turned the bend.

I waited, dreaming he might come back into view, galloping through the snow to the house, pounding up the stairway, flinging open the door to my room, pulling me into his embrace, and pressing his body against mine as he had done last night. But all I saw were hoofprints vanishing in the accumulation.

I was a coward. For if I were a brave girl, as John claimed, I would have been downstairs saying goodbye with all the others. More than anything, I was scared to see him go. I was afraid for him and afraid for myself. An overwhelming sense of foreboding coated me like the falling snow. Waves of nausea broke against me. Something was coming, and we had just made ourselves exposed, vulnerable to pain and suffering. And there was nothing I could do to stop it.

15
LETTER OF INTENTION
1864 WINTER

I confined myself to my bed. Kay brought delicious food to tempt me out from under the warm blankets, but I couldn't eat. Katie came knocking on the door once, wanting me to read to her, but I couldn't even find the motivation to enjoy a storybook. Kay shooed her away, telling her to be a good girl and play in the nursery.

Every so often, I thought I heard the sound of voices and the jangle of the horses' harness. Eventually, Seth and Thad came home on top of their mounts, John's empty horse trailing behind them. I stood before the window for a long time afterward, hoping to see his shadow coming down the lane, but knowing I may never see him again. The cold penetrated my body, and I crept back into bed, my heart heavy.

As the day wore on and the sky grew dark, the weather worsened, and fatigue settled into my bones. By nightfall, I could not get out of bed. My head pounded, my mouth tasted sour, and my tongue was thick and dry in my mouth. My stomach throbbed with hunger, but I was too nauseous to eat.

For days afterward, I battled fever. Mrs. Mathis kept Katie away. Other than the care of Kay and Mrs. Mathis, I was left alone to fight it. In my dreams, I cried out to John. I cried out to God to protect him. And I begged God to give me the strength to face Ethan when the time came—because I knew there would be a reckoning.

———

My bed and clothes were boiled, the rest scrubbed clean. It was scarlet fever. Thank goodness no one else contracted it.

I, too, was scrubbed clean.

My hair was damp, making me shiver. The fire in the hearth and the heated bricks beneath the mattress did little to warm me. I shivered throughout my sponge bath, my eyes pinched, not wanting to see my jaundiced skin. Kay assured me my skin color would return, that the infected skin would peel away to new skin. A piece of skin had peeled from behind my ear, making me shudder with the unpleasant feeling.

Humming, Kay waddled into the room with a tray of warm chamomile tea, toast, and the recent post.

"What are you so gleeful about?" I asked, somewhat annoyed by her happiness when my head still pounded.

"Why, have ye seen the sun this afternoon?" She gestured to drapes covering the window.

"No, the shades have been closed," I grumbled.

"Well ..." Kay hastened to the drapes and pulled them back, making my eyes squint from the brightness. "It's mighty pretty, shining down on the pearly white snow. So glad that storm is over."

I pulled the blankets tighter around me and turned my head away from the blinding sun. "Maybe we should wait for the sun awhile longer."

Kay came to my bedside, her hands on her hips. "Ye will enjoy the sun as it lasts. It will do ye good, it will. And I won't hear any complaining either."

"Yes, Kay."

She left the room, smiling to herself, glad I obeyed her commands. Kay was always quiet and gentle, but there were moments when she would bark orders like a sergeant.

Still squinting, I took up the two letters. I fumbled opening the envelope. Mother wrote, her elegant, scrolled handwriting emphasizing her disappointment in my "boisterous" and "reckless" conduct at the Christmas party, reminding me I'm a guest in the Mathis home. The guilt and shame I already beat myself with came anew. She and Pa were praying for my health and asked me to return her letter with a report of my well-being. She ended the letter with news on Ethan. Last they heard, he was near Fredericksburg, Virginia in league with a Rebel officer, but there was no other news.

I gave a sigh and set her letter down, picking up the other letter—from John.

My blood quickened. Gulping, I broke the seal. It was a brief message, scrawled with a hurried hand.

> Dear Ella,
>
> I must begin this letter with my extended apology. My forwardness was uncouth and only caused you discomfort, and I apologize. I guarantee you that my intentions were true and honorable. I should have warned you what was coming, but my actions came as a surprise to myself as well. You have a way of arresting me. Still, I do not regret telling you how I feel.
>
> You are continually in my thoughts. Not only is the reason for this letter an apology, but I also want to inform you of my true intentions and to tell you who

you are to me. I can assure you this is not a letter of love. I cannot compare this letter to all our other correspondences. For those were love letters, even if you did not realize. I've loved you since the first day I laid eyes on you, which is the truth. I promise you I do not confess my love to dishonor Robert's memory, nor do I wish to replace him in your heart. You constantly infuriate me and make me madly jealous. I want you more than I ever wanted any other woman, and I could wait for you forever, if I must. I tell myself that I will have you, and I ask you now, could you love me too? I drive myself mad thinking about this. I've felt for no other as I feel for you.

At the present moment, I am on the train, returning from my furlough, leaving my home and family, and leaving you. I will post this at the next depot. I hope you are well and that I have not caused you too much grief. I apologize once again for my behavior. Please forgive me.

If you wish to write a reply, please send to our winter encampment, Camp Barnes in Beverly Ford, Virginia.

Patiently waiting,

John Mathis

I shivered and pulled the comforter up to my chin, dropping the letter on top of Mother's. To find the words I wanted to say to him, to speak them aloud … I was falling in love with him.

16

RAINFALL

Ews reports heralded General Ulysses S. Grant's new leadership. With the spring thaw, nearly the whole Upper South was under siege or occupied by Union troops. Anticipation this war would finally be over spurred us on.

I shuddered, knowing John was in the thick of it. I had yet to find the right words to send him, attempting letter after letter—all which were thrown into the fireplace to burn. Instead, I avoided the task. Now fully recovered, I threw myself into caring for Katie and helping with wedding preparations for Renny and Landon.

Watching them exchange vows while Landon stood in his soldier blues, eyes shining, made me admire their bravery. My lips tipped down, feeling regretful. Where was the gumption Mother instilled in me?

—

"Rain pours all the livelong days, never ceasing. It penetrates my body and my mind, and I wonder what I am doing here? Who longer cares whether I live or die, or whether I am lost in the shadows of some great skirmish?"

Renny and I huddled around Nora by the parlor fire, while she read her letter from John.

We said goodbye to Landon Greene this morning. Renny had yet to cease crying, and her brother's words did not help. Nora made us swear we would not retell John's words to their mother. It would break her heart. As soon as Mrs. Mathis left to call on the Chisholms, Nora gave us both a knowing look, whipping out the letter from her pocket.

"All I had to live for is no longer tangible but elusive beyond my credence."

My silence caused this. His loss of hope.

"I wonder what will become of us once this war is over and we no longer fight this never-ending battle? What will become of us once we have run everyone into the ground?

"Once I was bold and believed in the Cause, abolishing slavery, and preserving the Union. A noble cause. Now I question whether the Cause has been worth the thousands of deaths. And still, people remain in bondage! I am desensitized to killing and no longer flinch as bullets tear through Rebels and comrades alike.

"Nora, of any of our family, you have understood me the most. My bosom sister. I knew I could confide in you and not feel your judgment from states away.

"I'm sick of fighting. I put man after man into the darkness of the earth—men like me, who are brothers, sons, husbands, and fathers. Men who will never return home. Children who will never see their fathers, and wives who will never feel their husband's kisses. All that keeps me from slipping into some dark place is a fading hope of coming out of this alive.

The blood has not, and will not, wash away the sins of our Fathers. These atrocities will follow us and stain the ground."

Nora paused to wipe away a tear. Renny was already weeping into her handkerchief.

"My dear sister, I dread the end of this war, the outcome that awaits. With all my heart, I wish not to make my family pity me or hold sympathy for me, but I no longer feel the need to fight for a Cause that murders, rapes, and plunders. This feels like penance for the debts I must pay. Debts that piled up before this war began. There is no relieving myself of this burden I've carried since the day Father disowned me. Forgive me for the harm I caused you all. Pray for me, for I have never had the will to pray. God has forgotten me. Pray my soul will be carried Home if I am to perish on the battlefield.

"Read this letter to Seth (he needs to hear it), but tell Ma nothing. I have already caused her such grief throughout the years, and anything further shall depress her. I am sorry for my disheartening words. I wish I could conclude this letter with some happy anecdotes, but I have none to tell. Every day, there is only rain and mud. And in this rain, we march and drill. Our rations have decreased again. It's as if there is nothing more for us and we know this war is drawing to a close, yet there is still so much more to be done. Our only hope now is that General Grant will pull us through. Many are confident victory is on the horizon, but many of us are tired and weary and wish nothing more but for this war to end. Pray for me. Your loving brother, John."

We sat in stunned silence. Renny let out a short sob, then covered her mouth with her handkerchief. Nora leaned back in her chair and pressed the letter to her lips. Her eyes were distant in contemplation.

"I don't want this war to go on any longer," Renny whined. "It should end before any more men die, before Landon and John are killed."

I stood from my seat. Nora and Renny shot me a questioning look. I had to do something.

I stormed from the parlor.

The war and my rejection did this to him. Why did I walk away? Why didn't I go to him the morning he left? I should have allowed him to have me and love me as much as he wanted. Give him hope of life after the war. A reason to fight. Instead, I allowed fear and remorse to steer me away from him.

In my bedroom, I sat at the vanity. My head swam. From the top drawer, I retrieved paper. Many times I had attempted this, but now I dipped my determined pen into the inkpot, and words poured from my heart onto the paper.

Dear John,

Nora shared your letter with us. I should have written to you weeks ago now. Too much time has gone by, and I must say what has been burdening my heart since Christmas night. I should have told you then. Many days, I feel I can run, carrying myself to Virginia until I reach your arms.

My dearest John, I did not realize how much I love you. I wish I could go back in time and retrace my steps. I was terrified. I thought if I could deny my feelings, blame my responsibility to Katie, and honor your mother's hospitality, the burden I placed on you and your family ... I would be protecting you all and protecting my heart. But instead, it pains me so deeply to know that I injured yours. Please forgive me. I love you.

Now, I beg you. Fight. Do everything in your power

to survive this bloody war. I will remain in St. Albans, in your mother's house, even once the threat is gone. I will wait for you. My last strand of hope is that you will return. Hold on to that hope, John. I pray to God you will come back to me. I pray I am not too late. I pray this letter reaches you. I pray you are still alive.

With all my love,

Ella

I signed my name with a trembling hand, praying this would reach him in time. Fumbling with my hat, I tied it beneath my chin and pulled on my gloves. Lord, if anything happens to him, I don't know if I could ever forgive myself. My heart thumped in my ears as I ran down the stairs to the foyer. Nora sat beside Renny, comforting her. They both glanced up as I dashed out the door.

—

Dinner warmed our bellies. Nora and Renny sat silent at the table, staring at their plates. Mrs. Mathis talked about the Chisholms and some odd town gossip, oblivious to the mood. Seth interrupted sporadically with his side comments. As soon as Mrs. Mathis paused to take a breath, he jumped in to tell us what happened at school with his friends.

"How could you?" Mrs. Mathis admonished. "The poor man gets enough with you four."

"Ah, Ma, Mr. Gates isn't a *poor* man. We treat him right finely." Seth's eyes gleamed.

"And I can see he has taught you proper English as well," Mrs. Mathis retorted.

"We weren't awful to him, Ma. We only put his chalk in the water bucket, and he never found it. No harm done. But you should have seen how he walked around the classroom, scratching his head and saying, 'Oh, dear me, what have I done with that chalk?' It made it rather difficult to continue our lessons after that."

"You better hope he never finds that chalk, young man, or you should expect punishment this afternoon," Mrs. Mathis told him, taking a sip of her tea.

"He won't find it. The chalk will be melted in that water by the time I get back, and besides, one of the little boys will fill it with fresh water after dinner." Seth grinned as he helped himself to a second serving of apple pie.

"Slow down, or you'll make yourself sick."

"Ah, Ma, you worry too much."

"It's a mother's prerogative to worry about her children."

"I'm not a child." Seth glared, setting his fork down. "Another year and a half, and I'll be able to join John in the fight."

"You're *my* child. And God willing, I'll never see the day another son of mine marches off to war. Now finish your dinner and hurry back to school. If your father were here, I would have him take you out to the barn and give you a good whooping. God knows you need one."

"But he's not here," Seth snarked, shoving one last bite in his mouth before hurrying out the door before his mother could react.

"Seth Mathis!" Mrs. Mathis called back, but he was already gone. Releasing a heavy sigh, she pushed herself away from the table and left the dining room.

"We should have made him stop." Renny frowned. "He knows he hurts her feelings when he reminds her Pa's gone."

"He wants to fight, and Ma treats him like a baby. And I don't think he'll ever admit it, but he misses John," Nora reasoned.

"We all miss John. That's no excuse for ill behavior. And Ma treats him like a child because he acts like one."

Heavy silence settled over the dining room while we finished our pie and tea.

"Oh, it pains me to keep secrets from Ma," Renny whined. She dropped her fork and rested her chin in her hands.

"It would pain us more if she read John's letter; we would never hear the end of it. I hid it safely in my secretary. She'll never find it."

"I hope not."

Nora squeezed her sister's hand. "Don't worry your dear head about a thing. I have it all handled." Her eyes twinkled with laughter. "Now, if only Mr. Gates finds that chalk and gives Seth a beating. Ma's right. He needs one badly to deflate his big head."

Renny giggled.

"There's a telegram for ye, Miss Ella," Kay interrupted.

I perked up. "Did you see who it's from?"

"I believe from your family. It's from York, Pennsylvania."

Home.

I retreated down the hall to the sideboard table in the foyer where mail and telegrams were placed each day.

Dated April 13, 1864

To Miss Ella Coburg,

Your mother is very ill. She asked you come home. Necessary precautions have been made.

Pa.

I found where Mrs. Mathis had retreated. In the parlor, she looked up from her sewing.

"Is something wrong, dear?"

"My mother's ill, and she asked for me to come home."

"Oh, your poor mother. Is it safe for you to return?"
"My father is taking precautions."
"Then you must go."

17

GOLDEN STRINGS

1864 APRIL 17, SUNDAY

With Katie left in the care of Mrs. Mathis and her daughters, I traveled home. But this was not how I imagined my return to be. Pa and Harold met me at the York–Wrightsville station. Pa's face was drawn and pale, and I knew Mother's condition was declining.

"Robert's father died of typhoid last month," he divulged when we settled in the carriage. His voice was despondent.

I did not expect Mr. Moore's death. My mind never even considered it.

"His wife brought adoption papers she had a lawyer draft. She hoped you might one day consider adopting Katie, making her your own once you wed."

"Pa ..." I didn't know what to say. I thought of dear, little Katie and how much she needed me—how much I needed her.

"I know it's a lot to ask of someone so young and yet unmarried. I am leaving the decision up to you, daughter. But

I can give you the papers to hold on to until the time comes."

If John responded right away to my letter and was willing to take my hand, then I could adopt Katie and she would belong to me—to us. A surge of hope rose in me.

Pa took my gloved hand in his. "Think about it. You have time to make such an important decision." He released a deep sigh and adjusted the tie at his neck. I could tell there was more Pa wished to tell me, hope falling and simmering into nothing.

"What is it, Pa? What's the matter with Mother?"

"She isn't doing well, dear. Your mother has been ill for a long time now, longer than anyone ever realized. She is an extremely strong woman and rarely complains. Her headaches are worse than ever before. She is in constant pain. Unfortunately, the pills stopped working last summer, around the time you left home. The doctor suspects it's a cancer of the brain."

"Oh, Pa, no." I swallowed my tears, wanting to be strong for him. "I should have never left home."

"Don't bring that guilt upon yourself. That's the last thing your mother would want." Pa continued, "There is nothing left to be done but wait. The doctor has given her a much stronger dose of laudanum, and she sleeps most of the time. I know she is in pain, but she is too strong and stubborn to cry out." His lips tipped in a brief smile.

"Oh, Pa, certainly she will not leave us."

"Before you see her, I must warn you. She is struggling to see and speak, but she needs to see you, Ella, before she dies."

"Pa, please don't say that. She won't die. She mustn't. She knows we need her."

"A lot of things have changed since you left York. There is not much more we can do. For now, it appears you will be safe at home. At least for a short time."

I had to be Pa's stronghold now. Just as Mother had been for over two decades of marriage. Of course, no one could fill Mother's shoes. I never felt that I lived up to her expectations. I disappointed her more times than pleased her.

Lord, please give me the strength Mother possessed. Allow me to be the pillar my family needs me to be.

—

Silence drifted over Woodhue. It was not the silence of peace, but a cease-fire. I could feel death hovering and waiting. Drapes were drawn, blocking out the light. An eternal night.

I imagined my return so many times. A sweet reunion of joy and happy tears. Instead, Anna embraced me, her own eyes weeping, greeting me in hushed tones. Full of sympathy and regret.

I followed Pa upstairs. Doctor Cooper greeted us as he came down the hall. I thought to ask him how Nurse Fisher fared—I often thought of her in the aftermath of Gettysburg—but his face stalled my words. He looked tired and concerned.

He took Pa's arm, gripping it in comfort. "You should go in right away. I'm going down to the kitchen for some food and coffee. It's going to be a long night." His eyes flitted to me. "Now stay tranquil and quiet when you go in to see her. I needn't have her worry any or have her heart strained."

Pa gave a brisk nod and dragged me past Doctor Cooper. A soft moan drifted out from Mother's closed door, quickening Pa's steps. He pushed through the door, releasing me to rush to Mother's bedside. My feet froze at the threshold.

The room was dark and stuffy. The smell of medicine and sweat was powerful. Mother looked tiny in the bed, buried beneath layers of blankets. Her face was as white as her pillow. Her hair, like golden strings, splayed across the sheet. Gray lips pinched in pain, hollowing her cheeks. Her eyes landed on me, and I gasped. The brightness had already faded, leaving a dullness shadowed by bruised rings.

"Daughter," she croaked through parched lips.

"I'm here, Mother." None of this seemed real. Pa beckoned for me to come closer. "Don't worry. I'm home now."

Moisture gathered in Mother's eyes and misted my own.

"I'll give you a moment," Pa whispered. He leaned over to kiss Mother on the forehead before leaving us alone.

"You shouldn't be here. But ..." She wheezed. "I needed to see ... my girl ... one last time."

"I love you so much. Please forgive me—for everything."

She shushed me. "Forgiven. Just thankful," she whispered, closing her eyes.

I grasped her hand, bringing it to my lips. To touch those fingers that gently caressed me through my childhood. To smell her skin. The aroma of sweet apples. I breathed in, memorizing the feel and scent of her.

Anna came in from the side door and walked to my side. My eyes blurred.

"Let's let her sleep. Come, ye should get some rest too. There's food in the kitchen." She helped me to my feet.

She guided me into the drawing room beside Mother's room. Faces looked up at me with a start as I entered. Pa leaned against the wall with Elizabeth, who breathed in jagged sobs, in his arms.

"Oh, Sissy," she bleated, clinging to Pa.

Aunt Agatha sat beside Grandmother Montgomery. Grandmother was as I remembered her—rigid, her face drained of color and emotion. Her wrinkled hands, adorned with diamond and ruby rings, clutched her shiny, mahogany cane. Within her large, black bonnet, her shrewd eyes and beaklike nose protruded. She prided herself on her appearance, her black, silk dress cut to the curves she still managed.

Through thin lips, she upbraided, "Why in heaven's name are you wearing that mourning dress, child?"

My mouth fell agape.

"Don't look at me like a mute, dearie. Have you married, and has your man been shot by a Rebel bullet? I don't recall you ever having a wedding. In fact, if I remember correctly, a certain wedding was canceled at the last moment because a certain bride had run off to Gettysburg to nurse some poor boy while he died. You left your mother distraught with anxiety and humiliation. No wonder she's dying before her time!"

"Mother!" Aunt Agatha put a hand to her heart.

"Don't say a word more to my daughter, Mrs. Montgomery." Pa spoke sternly to his mother-in-law for the first time in his life. "She did no harm. She merely loved a man. We don't punish children around her for simply loving someone. And don't you dare guilt her for her mother's condition."

"Humph! I don't recall speaking to you, Christopher. I never did approve of Adellia marrying you, and I can see why I shouldn't have allowed it. Her children were never disciplined accordingly."

"For goodness' sake, Mother—"

"Not a word, Agatha. You haven't done your best by way of marriage and child-rearing either. I thought I raised my daughters better than this. I only wish my eldest daughter would have disciplined her children more in accordance with their status and rank in society."

Pa took a step forward. "Adellia loves her children very much, and I expect civility while you are in this house. Not another word of disrespect, madam, while my wife is lying in the next room, dying. I will escort you out of my home if need be."

"She's *my* daughter. Don't speak to me as if I do not know the direness of the situation. Mothers are supposed to die before their daughters!"

"Please!" I broke. I ripped my black bonnet from my head, throwing it to the ground. "I can't bear another word." I stormed out of the room, leaving stunned silence in my wake.

—

"Oh, Mother, I have tried very hard to be the woman you wished me to be. I really have. I never meant to disappoint you." My voice strained with emotion.

Mother grasped my hand. Her hand was featherlight in mine.

"Proud," she croaked. "Proud of my girl. You are … who I want … you to be."

Tears stung my nose and escaped my eyes. "Why didn't you tell me how ill you were? I would have returned sooner. Please don't go yet. I still *need* you."

"Find a loving husband. Someone … like your father."

"Oh, I will, Mother. I will." I thought of John, hoping my letter reaches him.

"Don't bury your heart … with the one … you lost."

"I know, Mother. I've made many mistakes, and I've been so scared. I still need your guidance."

Her lips cracked into a sleepy smile. "You know … what to do. You … are my … daughter. Strong."

I wiped my eyes and returned her smile.

Mother breathed in a short breath, and her face flinched with pain. "Your father," she said, trying to catch her breath.

"Yes, Mother. What about Pa?"

"Tell him … lay me … beside … my son."

"Oh, brother Christopher. Yes, Mother."

Mother's eyelids grew heavy, and she closed them for a short interval. "I love you," she breathed.

"Oh, I love you so much, Mother."

"You know ..." Her words faded off into the silence and her face relaxed.

I lay my head down on the bed, kissing her hand, pressing it to my wet cheek.

18

THE WILDERNESS

1864 APRIL 18–MAY

Mother's funeral was bleak. Dense fog rolled off the Susquehanna River, covering our world. The parlor was decorated with black crepe, lilies of the valley, and ferns. The coffin lay on a long, rectangular table for the wake. Mother was dressed in a gown of white lace, her golden hair brushed to her waist, her cheeks and lips smeared with rouge to hide death's bloodless color. A bouquet of lilies lay on her breast, tied with white, satin ribbons. She looked as beautiful as I remembered, as though she were sleeping, her face peaceful. I stood by the door and barely noticed the sympathetic touches as people passed Pa, Elizabeth, and me.

Grandmother Montgomery cried broken, horrid sobs while her old valet butler, George, patted her shoulder. Whenever she paused in her wails, she would shoot scalding glares at us and harrumph before proceeding her cries. Aunt

Agatha sat beside her mother, staring into her lap, embarrassed by her dramatic antics.

The funeral procession parted the thick fog to the graveyard. I stood in a daze, barely noticing the hymns led by the homely reverend, while Mother was lowered into the ground beside my brother.

When the last goodbyes were whispered, Grandmother Montgomery trudged toward us, her valet and Aunt Agatha on her heels.

"Stop, Mother," Aunt Agatha called after her.

"Christopher Coburg, you should be ashamed!" She shrugged off her daughter. "Look at the mess you created! Your house in disarray, the stress you caused my daughter killed her, and you are letting her daughters run rampant. My granddaughters deserve better than this. I suggest you find a husband of good standing for this flair of yours." She pointed at me. "And hand Elizabeth over to me. I'm returning to France in a couple of weeks, and I will raise Elizabeth. She will be more respectable and less high-strung than your eldest girl. Or if you prefer, I will take her as well, and *I* can find a suitable husband for her. It seems you are incapable of doing so thus far."

I pulled Elizabeth to my side, protecting her from the onslaught.

Aunt Agatha gripped her mother's arm, but Grandmother Montgomery shook her off, heedless of her daughter's pained look.

"You'll not take my daughters away from me, Mrs. Montgomery. I suggest *you* stay clear of my family, and you close those tight lips of yours."

Pa turned, leading us away.

"How dare you! I'm not finished! If I hear one mishap concerning my granddaughters or your negligence, I'm coming to take both of them home with me!"

"Mother!" Aunt Agatha reached again for her mother's arm.

"Don't touch me!" Grandmother blurted.

Pa and I walked on, not sparing a glance back. Elizabeth looked over her shoulder as I pulled her with us.

"May I go to Paris?" she asked.

"No," Pa said in a tired, but firm voice.

—

A battle broke out in Virginia's wilderness. It was bushwhacking on a grand scale, where all formation and order was lost. Battle lines did not exist in the forest. The newspapers detailed the confusion and chaos. Men fought hand to hand, firing at anyone who posed a threat, burying each other in the brush and trees. No one could tell a foe from a friend.

I begged the Lord would spare John.

By May 6th, news reported our troops scraped by with a shallow victory. Wounded filled hospitals, and scouts searched surrounding areas in hope of finding missing men, many of whom were lost among the tumult. So many were left unrecognizable or taken prisoner.

Days later, we heard Grant was marching toward Spotsylvania, the town where Ethan Harris was last seen. There, Grant attacked Lee's Army. Rumors floated back that our army was suffering desperately to keep its ground, the losses mounting. In the darkness, a mob resembling the one in the wilderness fought a hand-to-hand skirmish. The fighting persisted throughout May. Casualties continued to mount on both sides.

—

To Miss Ella Coburg,

John reported missing. Brett Chisholm wounded. Mr. Chisholm gone to fetch him. Able bodies called to *nurse. Wounded arrive in trainloads each day. Please come if possible.*

Nora Mathis

Pa's eyes were sad and tired while I read the telegraph. "You love him, don't you, daughter?" He did not wait for my reply. "It's best you leave anyway. We lost track of Ethan's whereabouts days ago. The wilderness was chaos. Go back to St. Albans, then when John does return, he has you to come home to."

He squeezed my shoulder in sympathy.

"Come to my office. There are things I must tell you before you go."

19

MISSING

1864 JUNE 1, WEDNESDAY

Pa looked up from the ledger on his desk. The gaslight cast shadows, accentuating the fatigue on Pa's face. His gray hair stood on end, and he rubbed his whiskers. An open decanter sat beside his coffee, and I wondered if that was how he always preferred his coffee.

His lips thinned, seeing me eye the liquor.

"You may need this today more than I," he said, pushing the mug toward me.

I raised my brows. Pa jerked his chin to go ahead, and I brought the mug to my lips. Bitter coffee washed over my tongue, the bite of whiskey hitting the back of my throat. I coughed, then gulped more—anything to give me strength.

"Some people find profit in war, and that is all Ethan saw in it. A way to profit and a way to get what he wanted." Pa's brow furrowed.

I offered the mug back to him, but he shook his head, so

I took another sip.

"I noticed shortly after your engagement that munition orders were missing, and the outgoing shipments did not equate with what our government contract entailed." His fingers fiddled on the desk. "I realized then that my signature was on several forms to individuals not part of our contract. Not Ethan's signature, but mine. In my negligence, I was approving guns and ammunition to profiteers—for Rebels. He was supplying them while supplying our own troops."

The blood drained from my face, and Pa gestured for me to take another drink.

"He can't get away with this, Pa." Anger boiled in my chest.

"He already has, daughter."

"How could he do this to you? You've been nothing but loyal to his family and his father's company."

Pa shook his head. "The Harris men are full of pride, greed, and vengeance. Woodhue was promised to Ethan once, but in spite of that, Mr. Harris gave it to me. He was angry at both of his sons— his eldest for selfishly throwing his life away, and his youngest for his arrogance. Ethan has always been bitter, blaming me for taking what he thought he was entitled to. I don't attempt to understand the workings of his mind."

I remembered something then ... something Anna had told me months ago.

"Emilyn Murphy? Do you know what happened between her and Jeffrey Harris?

"Rumors, my dear. Rumors Mr. Harris wanted to put to bed. He knew Ethan would drain him of what wealth he had left. On his deathbed, he asked me to safeguard his legacy. Ethan discovered some of the fortune was not for him. I put it into the Ironworks, believing Mr. Harris would have wanted it to prosper. I hoped one day Ethan would be worthy to take control of the company. When I'd discovered Ethan's profiteering, he blackmailed me to secrecy. He threatened to ruin me, to turn me over to the authorities—after all, my signature was on the orders—if I didn't turn a blind eye. I did as he said because I was a coward. I worried what this would do to your mother. She warned me years ago not to accept Mr. Harris's money or take claim of the company, least of all Woodhue. But when I finally told her what I'd done, she was more concerned about what this would do to our family's reputation than what Ethan may do."

"She found out while I was in Gettysburg?"

He nodded. "When we found Ethan drunk in the tavern, he was angry and delirious. Saying some nonsense about a curse and that he would end anyone who stood in his way. He threatened right then in the street to shout I was a traitor. Federal troops had pushed the Rebels out and were still patrolling the streets. I was scared. But then, he also threatened your life. He threatened to find you and force you to marry him, or he'd kill you. He was nonsensical and dangerous that night."

I shuddered, taking a large gulp of the whiskey-laced coffee. Red-hot panic washed over me. What was this curse he was drunkenly claiming? It itched in the back of my mind. Had he said it to me that one night when he forced himself on me?

"When Mathis and I had escorted him out of York, he warned he would come back for you. That he would return for me if he learned I betrayed him."

"You shouldn't be telling me this, Pa." I looked behind me at the closed door, worried someone was listening.

"You need to know because I don't know how much longer I can protect you. We haven't known Ethan's whereabouts for a while now. This may all catch up to us—to me. I don't know how it couldn't. I have already spoken to your grandmother about sending Elizabeth to live with her."

"Pa, you can't!"

"I must. She will be safe there. Your grandmother will dote on her. Elizabeth is a vibrant and amenable child. She will do well under your grandmother's guidance."

Pain etched his face, and I knew this was destroying him. I had to relent and make this easy for him, give him some sort of peace.

"Thank you for telling me, Pa. I'll do what I can to protect myself, and I know you'll do what you need to do to protect us. Please promise me something, though?"

"I will try, daughter."

"Promise me that when this war is over—when this is all bloody over—we'll be together again."

He closed his eyes and repeated my words. "We'll be together again ... one day."

I did not know if he was lying to me, but I took him at his word because I wanted to believe him.

20

THE INVALIDS OF THE WILDERNESS

1864 JUNE 4, FRIDAY

Grief followed me to St. Albans. I did not know if there would be word. My hope soared for a moment, seeing Seth meet me at the station. But he sadly shook his head when he read the question on my lips. The sweet reunion with Katie and the Mathis family was overshadowed by the grief of losing Mother, the surmounting casualties, and John missing. Needing nurses, Mrs. Mathis and Nora went to tend the wounded at the hospital, and I chose to help the Chisholms. The hospitals were overflowing. Having the room, they volunteered their home to care for Brett and three others.

When I arrived, Clara's cheeks were flushed, and her curled, auburn hair was falling from its hairnet. Her bright-blue eyes were intense with urgency, and her red lips were pursed with determination.

"Oh, thank God you've come, Ella!" Clara exclaimed, taking my arm and guiding me into the upstairs room.

The scent of raw flesh, blood, iodine, and rubbing alcohol mingled with the stench of urine and bodily waste caused by the merciless dysentery. Gettysburg came crashing back to me, and with Mother's death still fresh, I was hesitant to enter. I pulled a perfume-scented handkerchief from my pocket and held it to my nose.

The room was dim but for the five lamps lit on side tables and dressers. A full-size bed stood at one end of the room, and two single beds were close together against the wall facing balcony doors.

Two men groaned in the full-size bed. Both had dark hair and dirty beards surrounding their parched, blistered lips. A thin sheet and a single quilt lay over them. One was deep in sleep, while the other twitched as if pestered with ticks, a hand touching his face as if to check that his eyes were still in his head.

In one of the twin beds, a pale, curly-haired boy—who did not look much older than Seth, if not for a fleece of whiskers—lay prostrate. His mouth hung open, shallow breathing escaping from his thin lips. He would have looked tranquil in sleep beneath the quilt layers if it weren't for his sallow skin. I had seen it so many times in Gettysburg, in Robert, and knew he was not long for this world.

Clara pulled me close to the other bed where her mother washed a soldier's face. He had light-brown hair, the lamplight bringing out hints of auburn. His face was pale beneath his tan and well-trimmed beard. The boy's eyes were shut and looked as still as the dead, deep in sleep. Mrs. Chisholm turned the boy's face as she washed it, revealing a handsome face marred with a grewsome wound. Stitches crisscrossed the raised, red, jagged cut from his temple to a half inch away from his symmetrical, pointed nose.

"He's sleeping now, but when he wakes, you must meet my dear brother." Clara touched his still hand.

"We'll see, darling," Mrs. Chisholm said. "I fear we should've never moved him from Fredericksburg. He's feverish now."

Clara ignored her mother's remark, instead guiding me to the blond boy to the left of her brother. "A doctor is supposed to come look at him before midnight. We fear he may not live through the night. He hasn't made a noise or lifted an eyelid since he arrived here earlier this afternoon. His name, I'm told, is Private Will Baker. More of a boy by the looks of him."

"What about the other two?" I asked, looking over at the two in the full-size bed.

I followed her over to their bedside. Clara vainly tried to straighten the sheet and quilt over the gentlemen who kept twitching.

"This is Captain Jacob Reynolds. His other arm was amputated yesterday, and we'll have to change his bandages soon. The other is Sergeant Matthew Downs. He has a bad puncture wound on his right side and is missing two digits, but it appears he is healing nicely. Sergeant Downs might even be up and around earlier than all the others, unless he contracts pneumonia or blood poisoning, for which we are keeping a strict eye on all of them. He was awake earlier to take his medicine and drink a little chicken broth, but he went back to sleep before he could finish."

Hours upon hours we sat vigil, alternating our positions at the bedsides. Their conditions neither improved nor worsened. The only change that occurred were the facial expressions as laudanum, which allowed them to sleep painlessly, wore off. All were unconscious as they lay motionless—except in Captain Reynold's case—upon their soiled bedding. I eventually became accustomed to the stench of the room, but I could not shake the fear I would erupt at any moment. Too reminiscent of the soldiers at Gettysburg. The night wore on, and coffee cups were replenished.

By midnight, an unfamiliar physician arrived. He checked each man's wounds. I noticed then where Clara's brother, Brett, was injured. A bandage was wrapped around his torso where a blood stain the size of a grapefruit spread. It reminded me of where Robert was hit, but I did not dare utter my fear to the Chisholms.

"Thank goodness the surgeons in Fredericksburg extracted the bullet in his side, Mrs. Chisholm," the doctor said. "But I fear it was not wise to move him from the hospital there."

Mrs. Chisholm clutched her collar. "I fear the worst ... that you are right, sir."

"The hemorrhaging has slowed, but keep a strict eye on him. We do not want an infection to set in. Be sure to change the bandages in the morning, and keep the wound as clean as possible. That is all you really can do for him, besides giving him laudanum to allow him to sleep."

Clara put an arm around her mother's waist in comfort.

"Now," the doctor said, moving over to Private Baker. He sighed as he peeled back the private's eyelid. Then sighed even heavier as he pressed two fingers to his pulse. "I fear he won't be with us much longer."

"We have already prepared a letter to his family," Clara informed.

"Very good, very good. I'll have someone check on him again at six this morning. If he expires before, send someone to the hospital immediately. We can have a final check of his vitals and prepare him for burial."

With expediency and efficiency, he checked the two in the full-size bed, declaring both must be monitored for symptoms of pneumonia or infection and stating Sergeant Downs was on the mend.

Private Will Baker did not survive the night.

21
LORD, GRANT ME STRENGTH

I closed myself in my room the moment I found respite from the dead and dying. Watching Private Baker exhale his last breath unsettled me, transporting me to Gettysburg and my mother's dying hour. It was all still fresh.

I sat at my vanity, examining my face in the mirror. I was twenty-one and looked as though I had aged ten years. My once-rosy cheeks were pale and dry. My lips were gray and cracked, dark circles shadowed my eyes, and my eyebrows arched into a worried expression that caused lines to pucker my forehead.

The black mourning gown aged me. I was tired of hiding, of feigning widowhood for a boy I would have never married. I was squandering my youth, letting fear and loss dictate. I needed to reclaim myself. I had to do it for Katie. If John never returned home, what then?

—

"What in heaven's name *are* you wearing, dear?" Mrs. Mathis asked, her eyes wide when I entered the dining room for supper.

"A dress," I simpered.

It was a blue organdy, suitable for the summer heat. Shiny, black buttons trailed from the starched, white collar down the bodice. Tucks and folds made the skirt full and becoming to my small waist, and the puffed sleeves made my arms look petite and white. I had released my hair from its everyday hairnet and made Kay, though reluctantly, curl my tresses and gather them at the sides and at my neck in the most fashionable way.

"You look mighty pretty, Ella," Seth said, pink staining his cheeks.

"Thank you, Seth." I beamed, ignoring the look Mrs. Mathis still gave me.

Nora sat across the table from me, an approving smile on her lips. "Ma, doesn't she look beautiful in my new dress?"

"*Your* new dress, Nora?"

"Yes. The one I picked up from the tailor. I daresay the dress suits her better." Nora gave me a wink.

I turned from Nora and looked firmly at Mrs. Mathis. "It has been nearly a year since Robert died, and we never wed. I've been hiding. I just don't think I can do that anymore." I didn't want to explain that I felt I needed to keep wearing black for their sake, when all they had done was embrace complete strangers into their family.

"I know, dear," she replied. "I just assumed you were loyal to that soldier. It seemed *right* for you to wear black—what with Katie and all. I only want to protect you."

I knew what she was thinking. She was thinking the same things John had been drunk enough to verbalize the first night of his furlough. Toting a child around with no husband would lead to speculations. Only Mrs. Mathis was too polite to say it aloud. All I ever wanted to do was deter that kind of unwanted attention and gossip. I couldn't burden Mrs. Mathis with the need to explain the circumstances of her guests.

"You did say propriety was another sacrifice we must make during wartime," I replied.

"Yes, I did say that once, but ... what of your dear mother?"

The kitchen door swung open, and Louise and Kay deposited honey-glazed pork, boiled potatoes, green beans, and bread and butter on the table.

I did not reply to Mrs. Mathis's comment about my dead mother. My mourning period was over.

We ate in silence ... Mrs. Mathis chewing her food thoughtfully, Seth cutting glances at me between bites, and Nora grinning in victory.

Kay rushed back in, her face pinched with worry. "Miss Coburg," she said in a small voice. "The Chisholms sent a servant over to request you immediately."

The blood drained from my face. The boys' conditions were improving; that was the only reason I had left. Something must have changed.

"Lord, grant me strength," I said under my breath.

"You must hurry and change," Mrs. Mathis advised.

"There's no time to change."

Mrs. Mathis groaned. "At least grab a kitchen apron!" she conceded with a sigh. "I sincerely hope it is not their boy."

—

Brett's face was flushed with fever, and his lips were parted by wheezing breaths. His wavy hair stuck to his perspiring forehead. Lamplight made his clean-shaven cheeks glow. If not for the overpowering, sickly-sweet smell of infection, I would have appreciated his handsome, square jaw, dimpled at the cleft of his chin.

I picked up a rag from the water bowl beside his bed. I could feel the heat radiate off his skin while I wiped his neck and cheeks. He was as handsome as his sister was beautiful, the cut across his cheek only giving him a rugged appeal. I had yet to see him open his eyes, but I imagined they were the same azure as Clara's.

When I arrived, Clara and her mother were asleep on their feet, refusing to leave Brett's side. I insisted they eat and rest while I tended to him.

The room was quiet, except for the others' deep breathing. I hummed an Irish air I sang to Katie earlier that morning, when she had woken in tears. It seemed to settle my own nerves. I was not ready to watch another person die.

As I hummed the notes, Brett Chisholm's eyes fluttered open.

His eyes were clear and as blue as the sky. As Anna would say, "Blue eyes that go all the way back to heaven." Unlike his twin's piercing, deep-blue eyes, his eyes were calm and gentle and had a gray light to them. He looked almost awestruck as he gazed at me now.

Through dry lips, he whispered in a deep, gravelly voice, "An angel."

The corners of my mouth curled, trying to soothe his delirium. "No," I said, "I'm no angel."

His eyes dimmed in disappointment. "You must be an angel. I've never seen anything like you before in my life. Am I dead?"

"No, you are still alive."

"Then have you come to take me home?"

"No, I'm not here to take you to heaven." And I decided to humor him. "I'm here to tell you that you have many more years to live."

He scowled. "Must I return to the battlefield?"

"That I cannot answer. I'm not a fortune teller."

"Then I'm glad of it. Angels are far too beautiful to be fortune tellers."

He gave me a wane smile.

"Sing to me that heavenly song you were just singing."

I resumed my humming, while I continued to wipe his face and neck with the cool, damp rag.

His lips parted to reveal straight, white teeth. "Beautiful, just how I imagined an angel would sound."

His eyelids drooped, yearning for sleep. As I reiterated the chorus, his eyes sprang open as if to force himself to stay awake. I wiped the damp rag across his eyes and de crescendoed to a slight whisper as his eyes shut.

I couldn't help but smile. He thought I was an angel.

22

SECRETS

1864 JULY 5, TUESDAY

Nearly a month had passed, and the men in the Chisholms' care were all on the mend. Brett turned a corner, recovering from the infection. The hospital was less crowded, as men either recovered or succumbed, allowing us all to return to some semblance of normalcy.

I had been alone in the house for the past day, while Mrs. Mathis, Nora, and Renny were over at the Smiths' home. A message arrived early in the morning that a healthy baby boy was born. They gave him the name John Mathis Smith. My heart clenched seeing his name written. I wondered what John would have thought about his nephew being named after him.

Alone, Katie kept me busy, but as soon as she was asleep, the house dark and silent, I could not quiet my brain. My thoughts whirled with worries for John. I tossed and turned in my bed. The room was too hot. I dreaded the return of the nightmare I had the previous night. I could not recall the details, but it hovered over me like a fog, tugging at my mind with a sense of foreboding. It made me question whether I was truly safe here.

I huffed and propped myself up on my elbows. My eyes pinned on my cedar chest. The revolver. I needed to find ammunition. No one else was here to protect me.

I went to the chest and opened it, retrieving the Colt. The metal was cold in my hand, and it glinted in the dim moonlight. Flashes of Ethan's angry, determined face on another moonlit night … I shook my head to dislodge it. Wrapping my robe around me and dropping the gun in the side pocket, I tiptoed from my room. The weight and cold metal seemed to burn through my night clothes as it bumped against my leg on my way down the hall.

I knew where to find bullets. A large, crafted gun closet with glass doors stood in the cellar. The house was silent in the dark, but I still listened for signs of the Mathis women's return. Neck hair prickled when Moses barked outside. Sweat broke out beneath my arms. I padded downstairs until I reached the kitchen. Opening the door, I feared I would come face-to-face with one of the servants, even though they had long departed for the evening.

The room was still warm from the cook stove, although a slight breeze escaped from a small window propped open with a cookery book. Glowing coals emitted heat from the hearth. The scent of fish and grease clung to the stuffy air. The air wafting through the window stirred the dry herbs in the low rafters, casting a scent of spice more pleasant than the fish fry.

At the back corner of the kitchen was the cellar. I picked up the candle and matches from the hearth, lighting it. The cellar door squeaked on the rusty hinges. If that did not give my presence away to someone still in the house, the creaking, wooden steps would. The candlelight guttered when it touched the cool air of the cellar.

The cellar was narrow and rectangular. Cedar floorboards covered the dirt floor, and shelves and cabinets were filled with jarred preserves and dried goods. In the far corner, near the outside storm door, was a rack of assorted, aged wine, champagne, bourbon, scotch, cooking sherries, and other bottled liquors. From the ceiling hung a glass lantern, the metal oil dish and handle crusted over with red-brown rust.

Light reflected off the gun cabinet's paneled, glass doors, the shadows escaping as I ran the candlelight before me, revealing several hunting rifles, a couple Colt revolvers, three old muskets, and a tarnished LeMat revolver. I shone the light upon the LeMat, for I heard it mentioned once that the revolver used to be John's.

The cabinet opened with a soft click. Beneath the mounted weaponry were two ammunition drawers. The top drawer held several tin boxes of gunpowder and ammunition. Picking up the middle box, which belonged to the Colt revolvers, I slid open the lid, but there were only four paper cartridges. Their disappearance would be noticed if I took a couple.

A scurrying creak sounded from the rafters, and I held my breath to listen. The darkness on the other side of the cellar door stood still like a yawning cave. Exhaling, I replaced the lid on the box and took up the box of LeMat ammunition. I lifted the lid and saw that it was packed full of brown, paper cartridges. Taking the revolver from my pocket, I opened the revolving cylinder and began loading it, twisting it to load every circular slot. Once it was loaded, I placed it back in my pocket. I gathered two more cartridges in my other pocket and closed the lid. The click of the cabinet doors as I shut them sounded louder in the deafening silence. I was now a thief.

I hurried back up to the kitchen, finding it empty. I extinguished the candle and placed it back on the mantel. The floorboards seemed to creak louder under my feet than I remember. Through the open window, crickets chirped. *Thi-ef. Thi-ef. Thi-ef.*

Holding my pockets so the revolver and cartridge did not bounce against my thighs, I scurried out of the kitchen. Rounding the corner in the hall, I startled seeing Seth tiptoeing down the steps.

He stumbled, the candle trembling in his hand as he regained his balance. His white, button-up shirt was tucked into brown trousers, held up with suspenders.

"You scared me half to death, Seth." I clutched one hand to my collar, closing my robe tight.

A lopsided grin traced Seth's lips. "Likewise. What are you doing down here in the dark?" His eyebrows arched.

"I should be asking you the same."

"You first, Ella."

"I couldn't sleep."

"And?" He looked at me expectantly.

I pinched my lips.

He shrugged. "Suit yourself."

Slung across his back was a small haversack.

"Are you sneaking out?"

In the flickering candlelight, I could see his worried eyes and furrowed brow. "Please, don't tell anyone. I won't tell anyone you were down in the cellar either."

"You knew I was there?"

Seth shrugged again. "I went into the kitchen to grab a few provisions and saw light from the cellar."

He hadn't stopped me then.

"I won't say anything if you won't." His brow smoothed, and his cocky grin returned. He looked so much like John in the low light.

Seth set down the candle on the sideboard and stuck out his hand.

Sighing, I shook it. "Fair enough."

"Follow me for a moment." Seth tilted his head toward the kitchen. Once he closed the kitchen door behind us, he held out his hand. "What?"

"Let me see if you did it right."

"I'm sorry? I'm not sure I know what you mean." I suffered the lie, though he must know what I stole.

"I heard the gun cabinet open. It's obvious by the way you're holding your pockets you have a revolver and cartridge in there."

Seth flourished his hand, impatient, and I relented to hand him the gun.

He inspected the revolver, opening the cylinder.

"Do you want to kill yourself?" Seth chastised, taking the bullets from the revolver.

"No, I was not planning on it."

"Well, you would have if you tried to fire these. These aren't the right bullets." Seth put down the revolver and cartridge on the kitchen table. He rummaged through his sack and took out a Colt revolver and paper cartridge.

"Where did you get that?" I asked him.

"Won it in a bet," Seth confessed. "It's just for protection," he explained. *Protection from what?*

Seth took the bullets from his own gun, replacing them in mine, and gave me the paper cartridge.

"Here." He handed back the revolver. "I can get more."

"Thank you, Seth."

Seth nodded. "What do you plan to use it for?"

"Same as you. Protection."

"Well, promise me you'll let me teach you before you go firing that thing."

"How do you know I don't know how?" I asked, hoping my feigned confidence would get him to leave my secret alone.

He gave me a pointed look. Loading it with the wrong bullets was a dead giveaway. He flashed a grin and turned toward the back door. What was he protecting himself from? I wrapped my arms around myself, feeling naked now that someone knew one of my secrets.

23
A PENNY TOO MUCH
1864 JULY 6, WEDNESDAY

Mrs. Reynolds was not a beautiful woman, but when her pink lips parted, she revealed a broad smile of striking, white teeth and a certain overwhelming charm.

A small, rosy-cheeked boy, dressed in a miniature soldier uniform, sat beside his mother. In Mrs. Reynolds's arms was a bundled sleeping baby, the child's small fists exposed above the blanket. A mass of black hair escaped from the swaddle, curly and soft as feathers.

"Mrs. Reynolds," Clara spoke, guiding me over to the woman who sat in the Chisholms' parlor. "May I introduce Miss Coburg?"

Mrs. Reynolds took a lily-white hand out from beneath the infant's body to grasp my hand in a light shake. "It is indeed a pleasure to finally meet you, Miss Coburg."

"You as well," I replied, taking a seat beside them.

"This is Ulysses Grant Reynolds," she said, looking down at the baby. It had recently become fashionable to name new babies after generals and colonels. "And this is little Jacob."

The boy stood on his short, stubby legs and gallantly bowed like a wee gentleman. Mrs. Reynolds gave a soft chuckle. "His uncle taught him that. Jakey thinks he's a grown-up."

"I'th thwee, ma'am," he said with a lisp, two fingers held up before him.

"Are you really?"

"Yeth, ma'am. I'th thwee. Pwetty thoon, I'll be big enough to be a tholdier."

Mrs. Reynolds made her son sit back down beside her. "We hope the war won't last long enough to see our children fight," she said with a twinkle.

Mrs. Chisholm leaned over to pat the boy on the leg. "Thank heavens, it should be over soon enough."

Mrs. Reynolds turned back to me, a smile still on her lips. "I want to thank you, Miss Coburg, for the kind care you have given my husband. He would have never survived if it wasn't for you and the Chisholm ladies."

My face flushed. I had little nursing skills. "Oh, ma'am, you flatter me. It was by the grace of God. He simply has more use for him than the army does."

She bobbed her head. "Yes, of course. But still, I cannot thank you and the Chisholms enough for what you are doing to help him and the others."

"You're very welcome, ma'am. He was hardly any trouble at all. He spoke only of you and the children."

It was her turn to blush. She took a breath and then said, "I expect you have yet to hear that I will be taking him home when we leave.

We are only here for a couple of days, and then we will return to Milton. I wasn't sure if he was going to be well enough to make the trip, but considering it's not too far and he is regaining strength, I believe he'll be up for it." She looked at both Mrs. Chisholm and Clara. "We'll finish his recovery at home."

"Yes, of course," Mrs. Chisholm replied. "I'm sure you are anxious to bring him home. Would you like more tea?" Mrs. Chisholm asked, picking up the teapot.

"Yes, that would be nice, thank you."

Mrs. Chisholm poured each of us a cup, and we sat back to listen to Clara's melodious song on the piano. The tune was languid, feeling like water trickle over me. I momentarily closed my eyes, and an image of the Codorus Creek flowed through my imagination. For a brief instant, a flash of Robert's face appeared beneath my eyelids, but only as a shadowed face. My eyes sprang back open. I had nearly forgotten what Robert looked like.

—

Before leaving, I went upstairs to the sickroom. The room was hot and stuffy, even with all the windows open to let in the summer breeze. A few unwelcomed flies buzzed around the room, receiving impatient slaps when they came too close.

Brett was sitting up in bed, reading his old Roman book—a favorite of his. Captain Reynolds lay straight on top of the blankets, his eyes staring idly above him, and brushed away flies with his twitching hand. Sergeant Downs sat at a desk brought into the room for his particular use, his back to me as he scratched out words on paper.

"Why, if it isn't the angel herself!" Brett's face brightened, setting down the book, his blue eyes examining me from head to toe.

Heat crept into my cheeks. Ever since he recovered from his fever, he insisted on calling me "angel." He did not shy away from calling me such in front of others either. I had given up denying his flattery every time, and now I relented with amusement.

"Yes, it's me." I laughed.

Both Sergeant Downs and Captain Reynolds looked up.

"Come here," Brett said, "and give your favorite corporal a kiss."

"You're a scoundrel. If your mother heard you speak such—" I leaned over and brushed my lips on top of his head. His hair still smelled like soap.

"She knows how I speak," he teased.

"I'm sure you met my wife?" Captain Reynolds interrupted, sitting up in bed.

"Yes, sir, I certainly did. She is very pleasant. And your children, Captain … they're absolutely precious."

"Thank you. Did she tell you I'm going home?" he asked, shooing away a fly.

"Yes, sir. She said in a couple of days."

He nodded. "You have been mighty good to me, Miss Coburg."

"No need to thank me, Captain. Your wife already did that for you. Emphatically, in fact."

Captain Reynolds chuckled. "Yes, that's like her. She's a very gracious woman."

"Yes, and a very lucky one as well."

"Thank you, Miss Coburg."

Brett grasped my hand. "Ella, why didn't you come and see me yesterday?" he asked, giving me sad eyes.

"Margaret Smith had her baby," I shared.

"Oh, did she? What is it?"

"A baby boy."

"What did they name him?"

"John, after her brother," I told him, feeling as though a certain shadow moved across my face.

Downs stood and came to my side. "What is it, Miss Coburg?" he asked, a concerned look on his face as he gripped my arm.

My face must have given me away. John was not far from my mind. His silence was disheartening. There had been no news of him. With his nephew named after him, as if in memorial, I wrestled with the feeling everyone had given up on him. That he was lost to us.

"Oh …" I patted my hair to hide my face from Sergeant Downs. "It's nothing." I regained composure and looked up at him, forcing a smile. "I assure you."

"Would you like to come with me for some fresh air?" Downs asked.

"Well, I must leave soon. I promised Katie I wouldn't be gone long."

"We won't walk far," Downs insisted. "Humor me. I'm in need of movement."

My eyes darted away from his face to glimpse at Brett, who looked disappointed, and then I turned back to Downs.

"Maybe a short walk, but it is quite warm."

"Here." He picked up a paper fan Clara had left on Brett's bedside table. "I'm certain Clara won't mind."

"Thank you." I wrapped the fan's cord around my wrist, turning to Brett. "I'll come visit you another day when I have more time."

"I'll hold you to that," Brett said, his eyebrows raised. "I cannot rest a day without seeing you."

I patted his arm in reassurance.

"Goodbye, Captain Reynolds. I'll say farewell before you leave for home."

"I wouldn't have it any other way, Miss Coburg. Thank you again for all of your tender kindness."

"You're most welcome, Captain."

"Miss Coburg?" Sergeant Downs said, offering his arm. I slipped my hand around his elbow.

We walked through the grass along the road, shaded by trees and my parasol, neither one of us speaking. Sergeant Downs's head was bowed as he studied his feet at each step, his face calm in quiet contemplation. He rubbed the sides of his mustache with his thumb and forefinger, his other hand rested upon his belt, his thumb looped. Sweat pricked at the back of my neck, despite the fan I waved in my face.

"A penny for your thoughts, Sergeant?" I cocked my head to look at him. He seemed troubled. Anything to avoid my own spiraling thoughts.

He stopped midstep and peered down at me, his eyes quizzical and apprehensive. "I'm afraid I may not even be able to afford these thoughts," he chuckled, stuffing his injured hand into his pocket. Downs seemed self-conscious about his two missing fingers on his left hand, but he worked daily at his desk to regain movement.

I turned away from him and resumed the walk, his long strides catching up with me. We strode along the road beside the Chisholm property. Horses and buggies passed, but we were far enough away that the dust did not blow in our faces.

I breathed a deep sigh. "When do you expect to return to your regiment?" I asked, knowing that was on his mind. He was well enough, and able-bodied men were still needed. With the departure of Captain Reynolds, I knew we would soon say goodbye to all the convalescent men.

"By the end of the summer—either the end of August or beginning of September. We're winning this war, Miss Coburg, so I don't expect too much time is left. It may be over by the first of the year, God willing. My duty requires my return to the front, and my strength increases with each passing day."

"Do you really believe the war will be over by the first of the year?" It was all we heard these days. The siege of Petersburg was proving successful. However, we had all uttered those words before, and the war still waged on.

"Yes, if our armies continue the steady progress, I would be surprised if the South did not surrender. I will return to finish out my enlistment, but I don't believe I will return to Milton once it's over."

"Won't you? Why ever not? Your family is all there."

"Yes, but I think ... well, I—I kind of was thinking of returning here once the war is over. Maybe settle down and start a family and maybe a business." He paused, his eyes searching mine, his hand reaching out to take mine. "Miss Coburg ..."

"Are you unwell?" I asked, worried he had grown faint in the heat. "The heat is too much. Should we return?"

"No. I mean"—he cleared his throat—"Miss Coburg, Ella, I was wondering if you would have me?" He got down on one knee, and I felt the blood drain from my face. "Marry me? I can make you happy. I promise. Before I leave, if you'd like?"

"No ... oh!"

"Well, then, we can wait for when I return from the war?"

My thoughts were wild, searching for anything I had said or done to make him believe I shared the same affection. I leaned against the nearby tree. Sergeant Downs stood from his knees and came to me, his hand still gripping mine as he looked down into my face.

My temples throbbed. I gulped and tried to regulate my breathing. "Sergeant Downs—"

"Please, call me Matthew," he said, clueless to my fumbling.

Nonplussed, he must believe this was how most young women behaved when proposed to.

"Matthew, I can't marry you."

"If it's because of Brett Chisholm … he is young and charming, but a husband he cannot be for you. You deserve more than pretty words and flirtatious smiles."

"No, it's not because of Brett, it's just …" I did deserve more, so did Katie. Brett was flirtatious, yes, but we had formed a friendship over the last few weeks. I should have considered that the others might think we shared a mutual affection for one another. I never put off his attention.

"Oh, how careless of me! I know I should have written to your father for permission, but I couldn't wait for his approval. I'll write one right away if you would like?"

I shook my head. "No, that's thoughtful, but it's all right. I mean, I would need my father's approval, but I can't marry you. I don't—"

"You don't love me," he stated flatly, finishing my sentence.

His hand still gripped mine. His grip growing in intensity, as if willing me to accept.

"There is someone else?" he asked with a bite of accusation.

My eyes flew back to his, feeling pity for him in my rejection but also feeling irritated at his tone.

"I can't lie to you, Matthew. Yes, there is someone else."

"Who? Tell me, I must know."

"It's really none of your concern."

"No, I want to hear it!" He gritted his teeth.

I held my chin up high. "John Mathis."

"I'm daft! I should have known! I see your face every time Clara or Mrs. Chisholm mention him. He is one of the missing from the Wilderness?" He sucked in a breath and exhaled, his facial expression full of hurt. "You must know there is no hope for him. Those reports do not exaggerate."

My chin trembled. His words cut me. "He was taken prisoner." Or so I hoped.

"I have heard no one survives those Rebel prisons. You can't wait all your life for a dead man, Ella. You and Katie need someone, and I could be that someone."

I shook my head, as if to shake out the dark thoughts he was putting in my head. John's face—bloodless, eyes vacant.

"Ella." Sergeant Downs took me in his arms, his tone softening. "I know it's hard to accept. He's not going to return, sweetheart. Start a life with me."

My hands balled into fists at his chest, pushing him away from me. "I will not marry you."

He could not guilt me into choosing him. He could not fill me with hopelessness, break my heart to make room for himself. I turned away from him, leaning my shoulder against the tree trunk. I held out the fan in my hand, as if returning his offered heart, and reluctantly, he took it before walking away.

—

Katie looked up, a grin lighting up her little face. Guilt sunk in; I needed to find a husband in order for Katie to have a father, a mother, and a true home. Sergeant Downs's proposal hung over my head like a cloud, but his quick frustration with my refusal and his stinging words about John confirmed I did the right thing.

I leaned against the doorjamb of the nursery. Katie cuddled a small, calico kitten. "It's one of the new kittens from the barn." She held it up for me to see. "Can I keep it?"

"Well, I don't know. Don't you think its mother would miss it?"

She shook her head. "No, I can be its new mother. Oh, please let me keep it."

I petted the kitten on its head, and a soft rumble reverberated under my hand. "Will you take care of it?"

"Oh, yes, I promise. Please, I'll take better care of it than its own mother. She has six other kittens. Thad said this kitten wasn't eating enough and would probably die. Oh, please, I won't let it be a problem. It'll die without me," she urged with pleading eyes.

I squatted down beside her. "You'll have to promise to take very good care of it, and don't let it make a mess of the house. Otherwise, it will have to go back to the barn with the others."

"I promise! Thank you! Thank you!" she beamed. With a quick peck on my cheek, she ran to a doll carriage where she placed the kitten beside one of her dolls.

I had to do right by her. Those adoption papers were waiting for a family's name, but Robert would have wanted me to find someone we loved and who'd love us in return. Sergeant Downs was not the one for us. My heart ached for her loss and mine.

24
AFTER THE DUST SETTLES
1864 JULY–AUGUST

Tension grew between Sergeant Downs and me, causing me to steer clear of the Chisholms' home, to Brett's great disappointment. Captain Reynolds departed on a gurney, waving farewell to us as he was loaded onto the train with his wife and children. Sergeant Downs was well enough to return to his regiment yet continued to stay in St. Albans, as if stalling for time and waiting for another opportunity to approach me. I avoided him, especially at the summer bazaars and parties, allowing Clara to take up most of his time, while I stuck with Nora and danced with every gentleman who asked.

The only great concern of the month was the invasion into Maryland toward Washington. Confederate General Jubal Early led his forces into the North in order to relieve the pressure on General Lee's Army. Early came close, only five miles away from Washington, but was then driven back to

Virginia on July 13th. However, news was light, with no great battle to be remarked of, except for a few skirmishes in Virginia and in the west, down toward Louisiana.

Then came the siege of Petersburg. We had hoped the war would end soon. Richmond, the capital of the Confederacy, was twenty-some miles away. Our troops had been digging a mine beneath the enemy entrenchments and planned to set explosives, leading from a ninety-foot fuse, directly beneath their lines. Union forces would have the entire city by July 30th. The day came, and four o'clock in the morning approached, but nothing occurred. The fuse went out halfway down the line. Two intrepid men volunteered to relight it. The ground shook like reverberating thunder and a great explosion burst into the air, spreading like an enormous mushroom with fire and smoke.

The explosion rained down rocks, timber, and mangled human bodies. A plume of smoke filled the air and ash floated to the ground, revealing something deeply unexpected. There, in the location of the leveled land between the enemy entrenchments and the Federals, was a crater more than two hundred feet long, fifty feet wide, and about thirty feet deep. Every soldier rushed forward as ordered, charging toward the enemy and thinking they would trample right through them, but our men found themselves trapped against the wall of the crater, enemy fire showering down upon them. Regiment after regiment descended into the crater, and the enemy, who had recovered from the surprise, continued to throw concentrated fire upon our trapped soldiers. Many were killed and others were taken prisoner, hopes disintegrating as the explosion evaporated in the air.

In the early morning hours, Seth and I walked forest trails until we were miles from St. Albans. In the quiet of nature, he showed me how to load the revolver and fire at makeshift targets he would line up against trees, fallen logs, and abandoned, split-rail fences. With each passing morning, my confidence grew and my aim improved. Seth was impressed how quickly I acquired marksmanship.

He kept my secret and I kept his.

"Where do you go at night?" I was too curious to avoid the question after days of watching him rub sleep out of his eyes.

He was rubbing them now. "Ma would kill me if she knew. I promised her I wouldn't after what happened with John."

We stood in the wooded silence, our grips on our guns, ready to fire at our next mark.

"A group of us practice drills and bivouac on a friend's property. We're all itching to fight, and I want to be prepared when it's my turn to enlist next fall."

Nodding, I took aim at the tin can resting on the split-rail. I fired, the tin pinging as it fell to the forest floor.

Seth whistled. "You're a quick learner."

"I won't tell your ma what you're doing. Preparing is all we have control over, and if it helps protect us in the end, then it's all worth it."

"What are you preparing for?" Seth studied my face, waiting for my answer.

"The same as you. A fight."

He was perhaps rebellious, but I was thankful Mrs. Mathis instilled some manners in him as he did not press me to elaborate.

By the end of the summer, I was hitting each target without hesitation. I felt strong and capable; each time, Seth whistled in amazement. He did not pry further, and I never commented on the dark circles under his eyes.

"What happened to Robby?" I asked Seth one day. "John never told me."

"It's why I promised Ma I'd not sneak out anymore." He gave a long sigh. "I promised John I'd never tell, but then … I'm not sure it matters now."

"Don't say that!" I couldn't bear to think John would never return, that it didn't matter.

Seth shrugged. "Who knows anymore? I'll tell you anyway. I think I was fourteen when my pa sent him out of the house. They got into a row. Something about John not wanting the law firm, and his excessive drinking and gambling. I know John wanted to be a writer. I think my pa thought John was wasting his life. They didn't end things on good terms.

"And then Pa died that winter. John didn't even come to the funeral. I was lonely and missed my brother, so I started sneaking out to find him.

"He and Robby would be in saloons or at the Chisholms' home. At some point, John moved into a boardinghouse, and I'd visit him there. He'd teach me card tricks, how to cheat—but don't tell my ma—and he'd weave adventure stories just like he had when I was little.

"I remember that he'd usually yell at me to go home." Seth chuckled, and I softened at his memory.

"At his furlough, I hadn't seen him since the night Robby was killed. I recall following him from the hotel where he had been playing cards with some out-of-towners. I think it was March because there was still snow on the ground, and I kept pestering him with iceballs. He yelled at me that time too.

"But I kept following him all the way to the Chisholms' house, all while he told me to get lost. I think he thought I had, but I trailed him and Robby to the bridge over Rugg Brook. I remember hearing him tell Robby that he was caught, and he had lost all his money. When they reached the bridge, two men were waiting for them. They all argued with each other. One of the men fired his pistol and hit Robby. I ran then, until John caught up with me, making me swear to secrecy … then John was gone and Robby was dead."

"Oh, my God!" My hand flew to my throat. "Were those men ever caught?"

"They were found hiding in Smuggler's Notch. But I'm not sure what became of them after they were arrested."

"No wonder John avoided coming home."

"Honestly, I didn't think we'd ever see him again. He's different now, though. At Christmas, he seemed like the brother I remembered. He wasn't so angry anymore."

"I'm glad he came for Christmas." Not just for myself, but for his family. It may be the only happy memory we all had left.

"I am, too, but I don't think he came home for us … I think he came for you."

Seth averted his eyes, uncomfortable with the heavy emotions settling around us, and went back to priming his revolver.

My heart ached for John.

—

Brett Chisholm was regaining his strength, and although I avoided their home, he and Clara would meet me for a walk down at Houghton Park, a ride along Stevens Brook, or a picnic at the lake. On days Clara had to remain home, the Chisholms would allow me to invite him for a buggy ride. Thad drove us as we talked, laughed, and innocently flirted—such was our relationship. I was a different person when I was around Brett. I enjoyed being in his company. He made me feel young and carefree again. I felt powerful each time Brett winked at me or gave me a sideways smirk, knowing that I held the control.

By August, Sergeant Downs had given up on me, and it was soon announced he and Clara were engaged to be married. A party was held in their honor, and I had no excuse but to attend. I made certain I was on Brett Chisholm's arm, feeling that it afforded me some level of protection. I feared Sergeant Downs would treat me coldly, but he behaved cordially and respectfully. Clara, overflowing with sheer joy and excitement, told Downs to kiss me, and he did so obediently with a peck on the cheek, although we both cringed in the discomfort.

At the end of the party, Sergeant Downs found me alone on the porch while I waited for Brett to fetch my hat and shawl. The sky was already dark, sparkling with glittering stars, and the waxing gibbous, glowing with powdered whiteness. Neither Sergeant Downs nor myself looked at each other but stared into the night sky.

Then he spoke. "Do not think I am marrying her to spite you because I would never mean to hurt you in any way. My only wish is that it is you I was marrying instead of Clara."

"Clara adores you, Sergeant, and I don't want to see you hurt *her*. Be good to her. You're a lucky man to be marrying a woman so beautiful. You should be pleased."

I was relieved when Brett stepped out with my shawl and hat in his hands. I took the hat from him, while he stood behind me to drape my shawl across my shoulders, his hands resting on my arms. I could feel Brett's protectiveness through his firm hands. He shifted from one foot to the other. I knew he could sense the uneasiness between Downs and me.

He cleared his throat. "I'll take you home." The Mathis carriage already left, but Brett had promised Mrs. Mathis he would deliver me home safely after the party concluded.

I nodded and walked away from the house, my hand on Brett's arm, leaving Sergeant Downs in the shadows of the dark porch.

Once we arrived at the Mathis house, Brett accompanied me up the front steps.

When we reached the door, he put a hand to my elbow to stop me. "Something transpired between you and Downs, didn't it?"

The moon cast shadows over his features, the scar on his cheek making him look swarthy.

I didn't want to say anything. I knew it would hurt him and Clara. "No, there is nothing between Sergeant Downs and me." I touched my hand to his smooth-shaven cheek. "Don't worry, Brett."

He took my hand in his and brushed his lips across my knuckles. "Good night, Ella, my angel."

"Good night, Brett."

He released my hand, and I went into the house. Nothing would ever occur between Sergeant Downs and me again. He knew where I stood. My heart still yearned for John. Sergeant Downs would not hurt Clara or betray Brett's friendship. I believed and was entirely convinced my heart would never be unlocked to anyone but John.

25

CAUGHT IN A STORM

1864 AUGUST 25, THURSDAY

The ground was muddy, and water still dripped from the maple leaves and spruce trees as Brett, Clara, Sergeant Downs, and I led our mounts toward the Green Mountains. As soon as the morning dawned bright and clear after last night's rain, Brett was at our doorstep.

Brett never ceased talking, pointing out the different plants and wildlife, naming trails and rock formations. It was called Smuggler's Notch, he told me, because the British smuggled goods from Canada during the War of 1812. Naturally, he teased, it was still used for illicit behavior because of all the caves and siltstone outcroppings. I recalled Seth telling me it was the same place the men who killed Robby were found hiding.

He retold childhood stories, and I was content in listening while navigating the rocky trails. Every once in a while, Clara's high-pitched giggle in response to Sergeant Downs would disrupt, and Brett would roll his eyes, causing me to hide my own laugh.

A pond, smooth and shining in the sun, had been placed by God at the top of the summit. Brett suggested an ancient glacier carved the basin where snow had melted, leaving the pristine small body of water. Fir and deciduous trees stretched out toward the water, shading a shore of shale and boulders. Hills and mountain peaks nestled our riding party.

Brett and I walked along the shoreline while I admired the view. Clara and Downs stayed back to set up the picnic on a flat rock.

"I've never seen anything like it in my whole entire life."

"I'm glad the weather cooperated so I could bring you here," he said.

We walked in silence, until Brett stopped to stare across the water.

"It's hard to believe people are dying when we're up here far away from it all, isn't it?" Brett asked.

I desperately wanted to smooth his brow, to touch his scar that marred his cheek—the wounds war gave him. Before I could stop myself, my gloved hand had reached his cheek, the roughness of stubble prickling through the fabric.

"What's wrong, Ella?" he asked, and I wondered if my own worries left scars on my face.

"It's nothing."

"Are you certain?"

I nodded and took my hand away from his face, but he grasped it in his.

"Now, angels don't lie," he said, inching closer and placing my hand against his chest.

I laughed at the use of the sweet nickname he gave me. "You have a decent heart, Corporal."

"Only decent?" he asked, his eyes crinkling with playfulness.

"Oh, you want me to praise you further, do you?" The momentary seriousness dissipated. "Well, sir, I think you are very egotistical, and you should humble yourself before I retract the compliment altogether."

"You wouldn't do that and wound a poor soldier's self-esteem?" he teased.

"Wouldn't I?" I quipped, turning to walk back to where Clara and Downs were setting up the picnic.

—

The wind picked up. Escaped hairs whipped across my face as we rode home. Brett advised we take another route that should help us avoid some of the wind. He led the way, telling us about the Williamses who used to live off the trail and how they one day disappeared. No one knew what happened to them, and everything was left behind. Some said they were killed and haunted their cabin to this day. But no bodies were ever found.

Clara told Brett to shut up and he teased, telling her she was a "'fraidy cat." Clara argued with him like a child, saying she was not, and Brett never stepped down, telling her she was indeed.

"Besides," Brett said, "that story is just a ghost story told to children so they don't come up here. There are too many bears to worry about."

"Oh, Brett, you're horrible!" Clara exclaimed.

Brett laughed as we continued down the stone- and root-muddled trail. The woods on either side grew to shield us from the wind. Finches rushed away from the treetops, a chorus of chirps.

"They know a storm's coming," Sergeant Downs observed.

"It will be a couple more hours until it hits." Brett seemed so sure of himself.

"I don't know, Brett." Clara fiddled with the reins. "Those clouds appear to be moving rapidly."

Brett shrugged and we continued forward, everyone but Brett glancing over our shoulders. The clouds were starting to choke out the blue sky, the sun having long since disappeared.

Tree branches swayed and leaves rustled overhead, the horses' hooves squelched as they trudged down the slick Notch Road. The wind carried a slight chill, causing goose bumps to run up my back and prickle the hair at my neck.

Brett galloped ahead, leaving us to continue picking our way down the trail. Clara called after him, but he announced he would meet us down the road. We trudged on, never slowing or stopping, but looking forward to where the trail would soon meet the road, leading us to the security of town. Finding shelter before the storm hit was our priority. We were still an hour away from St. Albans.

A few yards down the road, we met Brett, his horse stomping.

A single drop hit the bridge of my nose. Dark clouds gathered above.

"There." Brett pointed to the right, between the tree layers. If you looked closely, past a narrow clearing, overgrown with grass and ferns, there were wagon ruts. "The road to the Williams' place."

"Brett, not now," Clara whined. "We have no time for this. Oh, I just felt a raindrop! We must hurry back before it pours."

"No, we should go see it." Brett's eyes narrowed at his sister. "We shouldn't return without saying we've seen it for ourselves."

"Please, Brett, some other time when the weather is more reasonable. We'll die out here if we're caught in the storm!"

"You're overly dramatic!"

"I am not!" Clara snapped back. "I saw lightning in the distance."

"Ella will come with me. Won't you?" He turned to me, his eyes soft and pleading.

"I don't know, Brett. This storm is coming rather fast. I really don't think we should."

"Suit yourselves. I'll be just behind you all." Brett turned his mount away from us.

"Chisholm," Downs, ever the sergeant, called after Brett as he turned his horse toward the abandoned road. "We can't let you go alone, but we have young women to think of. We can't endanger them."

"Then you take them back. And hurry before the storm erupts," Brett said, an edge of irritation in his tone.

"I'll go with you," I found myself saying, fueled by a need to take care of him.

A flash of concern crossed Brett's face. "You shouldn't, Ella. Go with Sergeant Downs."

"It's all right. You need someone to stay with you." I urged my horse up beside him. "And we will only be a moment."

"May we go now?" Clara droned. "Ella, you don't always have to appease him. And Brett, don't be so careless."

Just then, the clouds to the east flashed, and we all stopped to listen for the echoing thunder.

"Ten miles," Downs announced.

"Brett, please," Clara begged now. "The lightning is dangerous. I will not lose you again!" The truth of her fear was written all over her face.

"You have yet to lose me, sis." Brett's tone turned soft. "Go with Downs, he'll protect you. After all"—he narrowed his eyes on Downs—"he is *your* fiancé."

I cringed and watched Downs's face to see if it would reveal anything. I sensed Brett knew his sister was his second choice.

"Just follow the path for another mile, and you should reach the road," Brett explained. "It leads behind our house a few acres away. You should be home in less than an hour … ahead of the storm. Ella will come with me, and we shouldn't be more than ten minutes behind you. Now don't worry, Clara, you'll be safely home in no time."

Clara bowed her head, resigned to her brother's stubbornness. She slumped in her saddle, tired of arguing with him. "Very well. Let's go, Matthew. We shouldn't delay any longer."

"I'll lead the way," Sergeant Downs told her, eyeing Brett and me with concern, a glint of jealousy flashing in his eyes.

"Be safe," Clara cautioned before they both turned away from us.

We didn't watch them ride away but led our horses down the path. I followed Brett where it narrowed and wound around trees. Trees groaned and wrestled with the wind. Thunder sounded again, closer this time. A drop here and there escaped the tree branches. The horses' ears twitched, listening to the approaching storm.

The trees reluctantly parted, revealing the small cabin. Branches brushed the eaves with each wind gust, as if wishing to hide the house from the suspicious world. A half-rotted porch sloped down from the front door. Soot-hazed windows flanked the door. Wild ivy grew along one side of the house, pressing into a single, broken windowpane. On the opposite side of the cabin stood a large lean-to, assumed to hold horses and livestock.

"It looks less haunted than I thought," Brett observed, then he turned and pointed out through trees at the bluff's edge. "*That* sight is more haunting."

Earth fell away from the bluff, and hill after hill rolled toward the Green Mountains. Black clouds painted the horizon, flickering with light. We stood, watching the storm and listening. Clouds lit up again with lightning. Silently, we counted until thunder groaned, vibrating through the earth.

"We should head back," I said. "That one was close."

Brett hopped down from his mount. "It won't hit for a while yet. Come on," he urged, coming around to my horse, "let's go see what's inside."

Brett pulled me down from the saddle before I could protest, and I clung to him as he steered me toward the cabin. "Oh, Brett, please let's head back now. I don't feel right about this ..."

"Scared you might see a ghost inside?" he teased.

"No, I'm not! Besides, there aren't such things as ghosts."

"There aren't, are there?" His eyebrows raised in question. "Let's just have a peek, then we can head back to the road."

Brett grasped my hand, leading me to the door.

"Come on, it's sturdy enough." Brett stomped his foot on the lopsided porch. Without warning, the board gave a cracking snap, and Brett's foot pierced through.

"Sturdy enough, huh?" I glared at him.

"Well, just not that board. Here." Brett continued to hold my hand, leading me to step over the broken board and to the door. His arm went around my waist as he pushed open the door. It creaked on rusty hinges.

It was one room, shadowed and covered with spider webs and dust. Dried leaves littered the floor and scattered across the few furnishings. Against the far wall was a bed, the quilt wrinkled up as if something had been nesting there. A roughly made cabinet stood against the wall. A small, maple-slab table with four mismatched chairs were set as though prepared for someone to come eat at them. Dusty, gray ash filled a stone hearth.

Shivers went up my spine, and I clutched on to Brett's arm. An abandoned cradle beside the hearth rocked to and fro as if a gentle hand still rocked it.

"It's just the wind," Brett assured me.

I stared at it for a while, as if not trusting an apparition to appear, until I forced my eyes to look elsewhere. A set of stairs jutted out by the bed, escaping up into the ceiling where there was a loft. I stepped in farther, my hand still on Brett's arm, and swiped away a spider web. The discarded items were sad, and I wondered what had become of the family. A chamber pot was left under the bed. A cloth doll hung limply upon a child-size chair in one corner, and the Holy Bible sat, molding and dusty, upon a bookshelf where no books were kept … only discarded cloth, a basket of darning, a pail and dipper, and a hammer and mallet. Everything was left as though the residents would soon arrive home from an afternoon drive. But they never returned.

"This is the saddest, little home I have ever seen," I said, breaking more webs.

"It is a sorry sight, isn't it? Not at all what I expected."

As I examined the house, I brushed cobwebs aside. A broom was hidden in the corner beside the door, and I picked it up to sweep out the leaves through the front door. I didn't know what compelled me to swipe away the dirt; it just made me sad that a family's home would be left to fall apart without them. I swept out the last of the leaves. A sudden chill blew through the open door and broken window. I took up a scrap of fabric, nails, and a hammer and handed it to Brett to cover the broken window.

Then came the rain.

"Shit!" Brett exclaimed.

We looked out the open door. The sky had burst. Rain poured in sheets, obscuring the tree line on the bluff. A horse whinnied. Both of them shifted restlessly and pulled at their reins tied to a nearby tree. A lightning bolt streaked through the sky. Thunder responded, rumbling the earth.

Brett's face went stony and pale. I waited for him to tell me what to do.

He simply said, "I'll have to put the horses up in the lean-to."

"Put the horses up?"

"We'll have to stay here until the storm subsides."

"I knew we shouldn't have come."

"It's too late for that now. I'll see to the horses. Stay in the house and see if there are any spare blankets lying around … and maybe some candles."

He ducked out into the rain, his hat pulled low against the force of the downpour. I closed the door and turned to the room. Water was already dripping from the eaves, leaving wet circles on the dusty floor. I hastened to the cabinet by the table and opened it. Old preserve jars were stacked, and dead bugs lying on their backs littered the shelf. I grunted in disgust and picked up a stack of pie pans to place under the leaks.

Brett was as wet as a fish when he came in. Water dripped from his hat brim, and his shirt was plastered to his chest. Brett had his arms full of firewood he discovered in the lean-to. We silently prayed it wasn't damp, but the discarded matchbook I found was useless. Rain sounded like dirt pellets drumming against the wooden roof. Water continued to gather in random places along the eaves, and I hurried to put down more pie pans. Thunder boomed and the earth shuddered. The storm was right above us now. Lightning lit up the small cabin as bright as day, followed by another rumble.

I looked out the window but distinguished nothing through the dirty glass, water streaming down in rivulets. Lightning and thunder struck again, blasting the cabin with light and shaking the floor beneath us. Brett startled, dropping a log close to his toe. He did not have to explain, for I had heard about the effects of soldiers' nostalgia. The thunder claps must be sending him back to the battlefield.

The storm had darkened the day, and the only telltale sign night was approaching was the protest of our stomachs. There were no picnic leftovers except for an apple, which we both shared. I did not trust the leftover pickled preserves on the shelves. By the time darkness descended, Brett had yet to ignite the firewood. Lightning continued to flash every minute, illuminating the cabin in white light. Brett sparked a flame in the wood, adding more kindling and a couple split logs.

"You better get out of those clothes, or you might as well catch pneumonia," I warned, handing him the quilt I shook out.

He escaped under the loft stairwell.

I made myself comfortable on the rug, before the fire. It was going to be a long night, and I was still hungry.

The last time I was this famished was on my way to Gettysburg. It rained then too. Now, it seemed like a lifetime ago since I'd said goodbye to Robert. I was a different person now, and my memories of him were fading dreams. I could barely remember his face, let alone the sound of his voice and the touch of his kisses.

Instead, there was John. John comforting me. John's strong hands and warm eyes, bright in the gray light of a camp tent. John pressing me against a wall, kissing me, touching me in the dark, while I whispered his name and he said he loved me.

Brett touched my arm. I flinched, taking me out of my reverie.

He held the quilt closed around his shoulders, draping his wet clothes across a chair before the hearth. He leaned over to set his boots in front of the fire, his calves bare. I averted my gaze at the glimpse of his white undergarments.

"I'm sorry. This will not go down as one of my finer ideas." He smirked. "I'm certain Clara won't let me forget it."

"Nor I." I rolled my eyes.

Silence fell over us and we both sat there, staring into the flames and listening to the storm outside.

"What are you thinking about?"

I smiled at him, feeling open and honest. He seemed vulnerable beneath the quilt while the storm threatened to return him to war, and I felt the need to soothe him with my own woes. "My past."

"Ah ... I feel like I know you, but in truth, I do not." His eyes pierced mine, like matching blue flames.

"You're right. I know more about you. Your mother and sister *love* talking about you."

Brett chuckled. "Embarrassingly, that's true. Tell me something. What do I need to know about Ella?"

I considered his question. "Perhaps, if there is anything you should know about me, it is that the last two years have taught me to live in the present. Even if there are regrets."

He reached out to touch my sleeve. "The war will do that to you ... faced with your mortality."

Sadness washed over me.

"Why did you come to St. Albans?"

"I had to, for protection. So I didn't have to live in fear."

"Live in fear?" He intertwined his fingers with mine.

"I'm not sure it's safe for you to know. Not everything. Mrs. Mathis is aware, but I don't think she or the others know everything. John knows, though."

"John Mathis?"

I nodded. "It was his idea for me to come here. I was a stranger when I arrived. I still feel like I don't belong." I shrugged.

"You belong here." He squeezed my hand.

I gave a wane smile. "Thank you, but I don't. Not really. I've felt so guilty about burdening the Mathises, putting them in this impossible position. John encouraged me and helped me see that I can make a life here."

One I might have made with him if circumstances were different.

I released a long sigh, collecting myself. Then I told him. I told him about Robert Moore and how we would have never been, but I was determined to have him. I told him about Ethan Harris, and how bitterness and my need to please my parents led me to accept his proposal.

"Ethan Harris is a dangerous man. I would not have survived that marriage. Somehow, he discovered the relationship between Robert and me. I learned later that Ethan had paid Robert as his substitute, threatening me and his family if he did not take the enlistment. He is a jealous man and a prideful man. He does not give up easily."

I went on to tell Brett about John riding all the way from Gettysburg, despite being worn from battle and risking discharge, to find me and deliver Robert's letter. How I put my complete trust in him, and he brought me to Robert's deathbed. I told Brett the promise I made to take care of his sister, Katie, and the promise John made to take care of me.

"My pa has learned other incriminating evidence against Ethan since then. John helped him convince Ethan to leave the state. He has since disappeared over Rebel lines. No one knows where he is now." I did not know how much I should confide in Brett. I trusted him enough to share this much, but I also needed to protect Pa.

"You and Katie should be safe here. We are so far north, the war and Ethan won't touch you here." Brett scowled, his face fierce.

I appreciated his protectiveness. Brett cared about me and was a true friend.

That's why I felt like I could tell him.

Looking down at my hands, I said, "During John's Christmas furlough, he told me he was in love with me."

"He did?" His brows shot up. "Did you tell him you loved him too?"

"I'm *still* in love with him, but I'm not sure he knows. I wrote a letter, but I don't know if it ever reached him. No one has received a letter from him since."

"Why didn't you tell him when he was here?" Brett asked, his face earnest.

"I was scared. I didn't even realize I truly loved him until that night, and it terrified me. I didn't want to disappoint Mrs. Mathis after she had done so much for Katie and I. But more than anything, I didn't want to be hurt again. I was still healing from the loss of Robert and my home. I was confused. Now, knowing that he is reported missing and possibly even dead, I regret rejecting him that night and wish I could turn back the clock."

"Sadly, it does not work that way. We lose, we grieve, but eventually, we must keep marching."

He was squeezing my heart, telling me to move forward. Brett's eyes were urgent, as if wishing me to forget, flickering in the firelight.

His hand went to my cheek, stroking up, threading his fingers through my tresses and letting pins fall.

"You have the most beautiful hair I've ever seen." His face leaned toward me, burying his nose into my hair. "I almost expect it to smell like honey." His breath tickled my ear. "But I'm pleasantly surprised it smells of lavender."

I could hear myself breathing as he moved his face, his cheek pressing against mine, and his arms encircling my back to embrace me. The blanket parted, revealing his broad chest.

"Do you think … do you think you could ever make room in your heart for me?" he asked tentatively.

I didn't reply; he knew. I bared my soul to him already. John had my heart.

But we were both lonely and needing affection.

His hand left my hair, and instead, he cupped my face, searching each other's eyes. Asking permission. Asking to fill a void. I found myself nodding. Brett's lips brushed mine, and I couldn't stop my eyes from closing. It was a sweet kiss. A kiss meant to soothe. I wanted this, and I found myself leaning toward him, urging him on. The softness turned demanding, and I could feel his breath enter my mouth.

I did nothing to stop him, but my eyes inched open, as if waking from sleep, watching him trail kisses along my jaw and down my neck. The scar marred across his chiseled cheekbone was more severe in the firelight. My fingers feathered across the pink, jagged skin. Shadows flickered in the room as lightning illuminated the sky, and the orange flames danced across his features. His hands moved across my back, holding me tighter against him, his flesh burning through my riding habit. Brett's mouth moved down my neck to my collar. He unbuttoned the top button, his lips moving to my collarbone, then he unbuttoned the next button, revealing cleavage. He began to push me back against the floor, his lips coming back upon mine, hungry, and my elbow hit the floorboard.

Reality came crashing down, and I put my hands between us, pushing against Brett's chest. This didn't feel right. The void was still there because John wasn't here.

"I can't do this, Brett." This wasn't fair to Brett. I tried to catch my breath. "I'm sorry, but I just can't." I was worried he would be angry.

Brett guided us back up. He ran his hand through his hair and brought the blanket about his neck, his cheeks crimson.

Gathering his knees beneath the blanket, he said, "No, it's all right." He didn't look at me.

My fingers fumbled with the buttons. "This shouldn't have happened." If we were to arrive home in the morning, after being alone together all night, assumptions would already be made. I wasn't about to let that happen, not when I was still considered a guest of the town. And I had Katie to think of—not to mention bringing humiliation to the Mathis home. I mortified Mrs. Mathis enough after my conduct at Governor Smith's Christmas party.

"We should try to get some rest. Here." Brett handed the blanket to me, wrapping it around my shoulders. He was embarrassed and disappointed, yet he was still willing to bare himself just to provide me comfort. My stomach growled with hunger, leaving me to clutch my middle. Thunder and lightning rolled in the distance as the storm moved away. Rain filled the pie pans.

Brett put an arm around my shoulders, bringing me to him. I laid my head on his shoulder and closed my eyes, listening to his steady breathing as the fire dimmed to embers. And I felt safe.

26

DAMAGES

I did not know how long I slept, but when I awoke, the world was quiet, except for drips plinking in pie pans and birdcalls welcoming the dawn. I had been semiconscious of Brett through the night, his body's warmth around me, the weight of his arm embracing me beneath the quilt. It was the absence of his warmth that woke me.

Brett was donning his damp clothing when I sat up.

"We best be on our way." He did not look at me.

I shrugged off the quilt. My body ached from lying on the hard floor. I did what I could to adjust the stays beneath my dress, the bones of the corset digging into my sides. My feet screamed at me in protest, unaccustomed to sleeping in riding boots. Brett left to prepare the horses, while I hastily picked up hair pins from the floor, doing my best to pin them into place. I grabbed my hat and gloves before following Brett outside.

Brett saddled the horses and helped me mount. He swung

himself up into the saddle with ease, but he still did not look at me.

The cool air wafted through the branches, allowing water to drop from the bows. Brett's back was stiff as he led us back to the road. Was he regretting last night? Was it my refusal?

We trotted down the road, and still, Brett said nothing. I bit my lip and attempted to break the silence. "The storm has cleared."

Brett looked up into the heavens, where blue sky was peeking through a thin layer of clouds, the orange sunrise breaking over the ridge of hills. "Yes," was his simple reply.

I allowed the silence to settle again as we trudged down the road where we had left Clara and Downs the day before. Mud kicked up with the horses' hooves, and I cantered up to ride beside him.

"Are you not going to speak to me, Corporal?" I chastised, irritated at myself and him for allowing our physical needs to leave this intolerable silence between us. The man did not have any shame in flirting, yet he couldn't confront his own feelings.

Brett's head snapped back, his eyes narrowed on me. "It's nothing, *Miss Coburg*," formality putting space between us.

"Brett, please," I softened.

He swung his horse around, positioning our mounts nose-to-nose. His anger and frustration evident across his reddened face.

"I want you to know, Ella, that I adore you, and I think I'm deeply infatuated with you, if nothing else. You trust me enough to share secrets with me. We shared a moment I thought we both needed. When you told me about John, I was jealous … *am* jealous. When you stopped us, it made me feel like the smallest man in the world. I don't know why I have these feelings for you, but I need time. Time to think." His brows furrowed.

He turned his horse away. I had no words.

"I'm sorry, Brett," I called after him, following behind.

He left distance between us as we traveled.

When we reached the road to town, I asked him if we would be all right. He merely nodded as we parted ways, saying, "Best we don't arrive together." We exchanged farewells, and Brett lowered his hat over his eyes as the morning sun cut over the hills.

—

"We've been dreadfully worried!" Mrs. Mathis exclaimed at the breakfast table. Arriving in the predawn allowed me to sleep a couple more hours and wash up. I was thankful no one saw me muddy and disheveled, knowing there would already be questions. "Sergeant Downs braved the storm to see if you'd arrived. We're very thankful you made it home safely."

"Did you stay *all* night with Brett Chisholm?" Nora leaned close so no one would hear her question, her eyes dancing mischievously.

I gave Nora a weak smile. The whole family came to breakfast after they'd heard I did not return last night. Renny and Mrs. Mathis both showed genuine concern, but Margaret seemed downright embarrassed. Seth was too busy shoveling food into his mouth to look up from his plate, uncomfortable by his female family members. If I had known I would be bombarded, I would have stayed in my room. I was thankful Katie was having breakfast in the kitchen to keep her kitten from the dining table.

"I'm certain she doesn't want to talk about it," Renny excused, trying to save me from the scrutiny.

"No need to ask. We all know she was with him!" Margaret exclaimed. "I'm mortified!"

"Margaret," Mrs. Mathis chided. "She had no other option at the time. However, the optics do not look favorable."

I flushed. "Nothing happened." But I could feel the lie sour in my belly.

"You can trust I will not utter a word," Margaret promised. I knew it was not for my benefit but for her own.

"Can't expect *Clara* to keep quiet, though," Nora huffed.

Margaret grimaced, confirming my own worries. "I'll pay her a visit on my way home. After she realizes what that will mean for Brett, she won't say a word."

What would that mean for Brett? A pat on the back or a simple slap on the wrist? The fallout of this would mean far more for me, and I knew it as soon as Brett kissed me.

27
HOMESICK
1864 SEPTEMBER

B rett did not speak to me for some time. I did not seek him out or visit the Chisholms. If there were whispers of my overnight stay with Brett during the storm, no one told me. Clara, and even Margaret, avoided me, claiming one obligation or another.

It made me homesick. I missed Pa and Elizabeth. I missed my mother. Pa wrote when Elizabeth left with Grandmother Montgomery to her Paris residence. He did not say it in so many words, but I knew his coffers were empty. He vowed he would send me money for Katie and me as soon as he could. Counting my meager purse of money, I was washed over with remorse in burdening the Mathis family. How much longer before I wore out my welcome?

The wedding for Clara and Downs was a small affair, with only Clara's family and friends. Downs did not have anyone attend for him, and it made me pity him. It was the first moment I had seen Brett. He was Clara's opposite in every way that day. She was bright and cheery, while he was dark and brooding. I did not know if it was due to his disapproval of their union or due to my presence. Sergeant Downs would return soon to his regiment, and Clara held on to him for dear life during the ceremony and reception.

We were also waiting in tense apprehension while Rebel General Early—who had retreated into Virginia in July—was pressuring Sheridan's Army, whose back was protecting Washington. A seesaw effect occurred between the two armies as they retreated and advanced. Victory led our troops to Petersburg, the key to the Rebel capitol, Richmond.

Optimism resurged, and once again, people were saying the war would be over in a month. While everyone waited for the siege to give way and unlock the gates to Richmond, we kept an eye on the Shenandoah Valley where Early and Sheridan marched and countermarched. We waited for news as General Sherman marched into Georgia and campaigned toward Atlanta before heading toward the sea.

Overcome with guilt and hopelessness, I found myself drinking whiskey before supper to douse my guilt. Seth knew, for he was the one to offer it to me, but no one else was the wiser. At night, I wouldn't be able to sleep, drowning my thoughts and dreams of John and Brett with another glass of whiskey. I would wake up early, downing a cup of black coffee and toast, my head pounding while I followed Seth out to our makeshift shooting range. Nora seemed to know I was unhappy because she would give me sad, concerned looks that left me feeling reproachful. I was failing Robert each time Katie begged for me.

28
THE RAID

1864 OCTOBER 19, WEDNESDAY

Clara asked for me to call on her under the pretense she wanted to show me her wedding gifts, but in truth, she wished for me to speak to her brother.

"He has not been himself since the summer," she explained. "Not since ... you know ... the storm." No one spoke to me about that night, and I was grateful for it. I already relived it every time I closed my eyes, wondering how I could heal this abyss between Brett and me. "I'm tired of seeing him moping about. He has been too eager to return, especially after seeing Matthew depart, and Ma and I are not ready to let him go. Can you please speak to him?"

"Does he know I'm here?" I asked.

She looked sheepish. "Please, Ella. I know you once had affection for him, and you treated him so well, so tenderly. You made him happy. I daresay your care is what saved him."

"I'm not sure of that, but I'll try to speak to him if he'll allow me."

Clara showed me to the porch balcony outside his upstairs "sick" room. He did not turn to see who approached, his messed-brown head bowed over a book, his shoulders covered by a beaver-pelt coat to ward off the autumn chill.

"Brett," Clara spoke.

He turned to look over his shoulder, our eyes meeting for an instant before he returned to his book.

"I'm in no mood for company today."

"Brett, this has gone on long enough." Clara put her hands on her hips. "Ella's here now, and you *will* speak with her."

"Clara, I don't know—" I began.

"Ella! He's acting childish and stubborn. I'm closing these doors, and you both are staying out here until some reconciliation has been made."

Before Brett or I could say a word in protest, she closed the double doors, locking them behind her.

"I'm sorry. She doesn't know when to not meddle," he said.

I stood there in silence until Brett gestured to the chair beside him.

"We don't have to speak if you'd rather not. We can just tell Clara we have agreed to remain civil."

Brett shook his head. My heart clenched with disappointment. I missed our friendship.

"I'll be returning to my regiment soon. I need to be with the other men through this last stretch." He closed his book. "So much is happening right now, and I'm missing it all. Sherman's marching toward the sea through Georgia. Petersburg remains under siege and soon it will break, then we'll march into Richmond. Early still poses a threat. He's a stubborn Southerner, that Jubal Early. He doesn't know when to give up, does he?"

"No, I guess not."

"The Rebs will be surrendering soon. We're reclaiming land and freeing their slaves, and they will soon be able to do nothing *but* surrender. Everyone is saying this war might be over by the New Year. All I have to say is, I better be involved before it's over. The blockade is getting tighter by the week, and the Mississippi is practically ours ..."

I stared out toward town, trying to find the words I wished to speak. Brett was a good man, kind and passionate. I cared for him—and there was an attraction there—but he knew I could never love him. Not the way he wanted me to.

The view of the town from here was obscured by trees, but church steeples and rooftops separated the landscape from the gray sky. The trees were turning now ... yellows, oranges, and reds. My eyes strained, attempting to see beyond the horizon, beyond the hillsides. Everything seemed so far away, like I was nestled back in the wooded hills of another earth, forever distant from the conflict. It neither seemed real nor right that I sat here in comfort when men were fighting to the death, murdering one another for freedom, injustice, preservation, or rights they believed in.

"Who's that?" Brett broke the silence. "Seth Mathis?"

Seth ran toward the house, Moses barking at his heels.

"Seth!" I stood to wave at him.

He stopped below the balcony, his chest heaving as he tried to catch his breath between words. "Rebels ... cavalrymen ... in town!"

Brett barreled out of his chair and leaned against the railing. "What?"

My heart pounded against my ribcage.

Seth raised his voice over Moses's barking, straining through his labored breathing. "Rebel cavalrymen are in town! They're robbing the banks and burning houses and killing people! Their officer is claiming he will shoot the first man to offer resistance. They're in possession of the town now!"

Brett and I both looked toward town and saw, to our horror, a Confederate flag now waving on the Village Green above the treetops. Smoke trailed skyward.

I gasped. "They'll burn down the town."

Brett gripped my hand. The tough muscles of his hand squeezing mine. "When did this happen, Seth?"

"Just a minute ago! They herded a bunch of people onto the Village Green, and they're going to shoot them all! I'm off to warn Ma and my sisters."

"What should we do?" I asked Brett.

"You need to hide somewhere, Brett!" Seth called up to us. "They're going to kill every soldier in the hospital!"

"What's going on?" Mr. Chisholm asked, coming out onto the front porch below us.

"There are Rebel cavalrymen in town, sir," Seth replied. "You need to hide Brett. I don't know if they'll stop with the hospital. They may be raiding, searching for any young men."

My chest tightened as I stared back at Brett. "Where should we hide you? The cellar? The barn?"

Brett shook his head. "I can't endanger my family. I need to leave the property and hide in the woods. I can't have the Rebels finding me if they search the area for Union soldiers."

"You can't just hide out in the woods, especially if the Rebels are here to stay, Brett." Fear gripped me, but my mind went into action.

"Seth and I will take horses and go hide in the old Williams' cabin. Go tell the Mathis women, Seth, then meet us by the road west. Come on." Brett pulled me with him.

Reaching the door, Brett rattled the handle. "Clara!" He hit the door with his open hand. "Goddammit! Let us in!"

The lock turned, the door flinging open. Clara met us with wide eyes.

"You'll hide in the barn," Mrs. Chisholm demanded, rushing into the room.

"I won't let you be accountable for hiding Federals on your property, Mama. I will leave and hide in the Williams' cabin. I know the way, and we can take horses. If I need to, I can continue toward the Notch."

"You'll hide in a cave? I think not! You're my son, Brett, and you will do as I say. You are staying on the property where it is safe, and we know you're nearby."

Brett crossed the floor and gripped his mother's arms. "Listen! I will not have this family in danger. I can't stay here. Do you want to have the enemy raging in here and searching every corner and turning every bedsheet to only find me? Do you know what they would do if they found me? This is war, Ma. They would drag me out to the driveway and have me shot in front of you. I won't have that happen, you hear?"

"Fine, Brett. Go to the cabin. But if you don't come home, I don't want to live the rest of my life wondering if you're alive or not." Mrs. Chisholm surrendered, withdrawing her arms from her son's hands. "But we can't have you keep a horse up in the woods. They're needed, and if the Rebels spot it, they will know someone is hiding there."

"Then someone will have to go with me to bring it back."

"Have your father take you."

Brett fastened his holster with dueling pistols. Clara handed him his hat to shove onto his messy hair, and we all followed him on his swift feet outside. Mr. Chisholm met us at the door, a hunting rifle in his hands and his lips pursed with anger.

"What's the plan?" Mr. Chisholm asked.

"I'm going to hide out in the old Williams' cabin." Brett turned to his father.

"Ah, good idea." Mr. Chisholm set to loading his rifle.

"Pa, we're going to need horses, but you'll have to bring the horses back."

Mr. Chisholm's head jerked up from the rifle, his face aghast. "I can't go with you, Brett. I have to be here to protect the women. There is no one else to do it."

"I'll do it. I know the way to the cabin and back," I volunteered.

"No, it's out of the question," Brett said. "I won't put you in danger."

"Brett." I pushed past the Chisholms, ready for battle. "I won't have you going up there by yourself. You need someone to bring the horses back, or they will discover you. I'm a fast rider, and I know the way. I can do this."

"It's not a matter of whether you can do this or not because I have no doubt that you can, but I won't put you in danger. You must stay here until it's safe to return to the Mathises' home."

I lost my patience. "I don't care about the danger. I'm coming along whether you like it or not, and we're only wasting time arguing. Now, come on, or you'll have no time to hide."

I pulled Brett's arm and led him off. Brett brushed off my hand, angry with me again, but acquiescing.

We ran across the lawn to the barn. Jersey was watering the horses, unaware of the invasion. Brett called for two horses to be saddled, and without delay we mounted. Brett glimpsed back at me, checking I was securely in place, before we took off through the back property and toward the worn road, toward the hills.

We galloped at full speed, the horses lunging forward. We leaned close to our horses' manes, hoping to conceal ourselves from the enemy. Seth joined us at the bend of the road on his nut-brown horse, a hunting rifle across the saddle. We slowed only for a moment so he could ride alongside us.

"Here," Seth said, handing me the handle of my Colt revolver.

"Thanks." I could feel Brett's eyes on me.

The wind blew, causing the trees to sway and orange leaves to scatter. With our speed, we reached the cabin in under an hour. The little house no longer looked eerie but lonely among the trees.

"Now return posthaste," Brett told me as he and Seth dismounted. "And if you fear any danger, hide. Can you shoot?" His eyes went to my lap where I hid the revolver.

"You bet she can!" chimed Seth.

Brett gave me a lopsided grin.

"I'll take the tree line," Seth offered, double-checking his rounds.

Brett came to my side and gripped my hand. "Take care of yourself, angel."

Warmth flooded my chest at the use of his endearment for me. I didn't realize I missed it. "You, too, Brett."

Brett tethered the horses to my saddle, and the two men disappeared to their posts without another word. Fear and anxiety pounded against my temples, pushing me back down the hill. I rode as swiftly as I could with two other horses in tow. The wind whipped my hair, causing strands to escape the pins. Everything seemed like a blur, for there was only one focus, and one focus only—to reach the Chisholms' house and hide from the inevitable danger.

I turned off the trail and headed down the dirt road, winding back through the trees. My heart thumped in my chest. I would have vomited if I had stopped our canter. The other two horses trailing behind prevented me from breaking out into a gallop.

Without warning, three men in civilian clothes on horseback came up the road. We saw each other at the same moment, and I found myself pulling up on the reins. They stopped in the road, smirks on their lips. My mind rushed, trying to find a way around them.

"Why, look who we have here?" the man in front said, his horse inching closer, causing my own horse to back up a pace. "Where do ya think yer goin'?"

"Home." My voice cracked.

"And in quite a hurry."

"What's yer name, li'l darlin'?" another man asked, his beard smeared with dried tobacco juice.

"Move aside, sirs!" If I was to feign courage, I would do it to my death.

"Oh, the poor thing is scared, Sam. What do you say we help her relax?" They exchanged lascivious grins. "Should we call in Harris?"

"No need to call me in, gentlemen."

That voice. So familiar.

My blood ran cold.

How did he find me?

"*Ethan*," I bristled. I hope he felt the visceral anger seething from my voice.

"Seems she knows *you!*" the bearded one, Sam, teased.

He perched on his black stallion, his Confederate-issued, wide-brimmed hat shading his eyes. His newly grown beard made him look fierce.

"Hello, Ella. My luck is better than I thought," he sneered. "No matter how far you run from me, fate brings us back together, now doesn't it? I do believe, my dear, that you have underestimated my abilities and my determined desires."

The cavaliers seemed to be closing in on me.

"How did you find me?"

"It wasn't difficult. He just fell right into my grip. Don't worry, it took a lot of effort to break him."

"Who? What are you talking about?"

A sneer crept across his mouth, and a guttural laugh escaped.

"He's been reported missing for some time now, hasn't he? I suppose it's been since last spring when my plan went into motion." He looked at his men, who nodded in confirmation.

My hand flew to my mouth in realization. "John!"

"Yes, I suppose that was his name. Well, let me put your mind at ease as to his fate. There is no way he would have survived my ministrations."

Shock scoured my insides. My breath caught. And my muscles clenched. John ...

Before I could regain composure, Ethan was off his horse and grabbing me around the waist.

"It's time we end this!" Anger raged through his voice as he yanked me off the horse. Blood pulsed through the blue veins that accentuated his neck.

"No!" My senses returned.

Several shots echoed from town, and my mind reeled with images of assassinated men, women, and children in the Village Green. Ethan and the Rebel cavaliers barely flinched from the distant explosions. This was all part of their plan. I wondered if this was how my life would end. This was not how I pictured my death.

I writhed in his vicelike arms. "Don't, Ethan! Please, don't do this!"

Ethan turned to the men. "You three! Keep watch! Listen for Young's signal, and shoot anyone who approaches."

"Leave some for me," one cavalier hollered. And the others laughed and made lewd comments. Ethan ignored them as he pulled me away from the road, toward the cover of the trees.

"Ethan, please. Please. You don't want to do this."

"Shut up!"

"I'm untainted, Ethan. You know this. Please."

"You saved yourself for me, did you? My bride-to-be? I hope you are telling the truth, for your own sake. Or are you a lying, deceitful bitch after all? You and your family have only sought to ruin me!"

"If you're ruined, it is your own doing!"

I wiggled my hands free, attempting to scratch his face, but he retaliated with a quick slap across my cheek, causing a searing, burning pain to shoot across it.

"You'll think twice before you speak back to me!" Ethan's grip tightened; he trapped my arms against my sides to keep them restricted. I tried to kick as he pulled me into the brush, but his palm came across my cheekbone again. "You're going to make this worse for yourself if you keep fighting."

Without warning, he pushed me down to the ground, his entire body weight against me. His hat fell off in the struggle, and his blond hair flopped into his piercing, gray eyes, gleaming with lust and rage. His hand darted under my skirt and crawled up my leg.

"Help! Help!"

I prayed Seth or Brett might hear me. Hoped my voice would echo through the trees.

"Shut up!" Again, another sound slap crossed my cheek. This time, a bitter, metallic taste bloomed in my mouth and my ears rang.

"This will only go one way. It's time I end this curse once and for all."

He rent my stockings. The tear of fabric brassy in my ears. He paused, and I prayed he was rethinking his plan. Instead, he pushed the Colt revolver into my face.

"Still have my brother's Colt? It was of little use to him and will be of little use to you too."

Ethan flung it away from us, crashing through the bushes.

His weight crushed the whalebones in my corset into my ribs.

"Please, oh, please, Ethan. Please, don't do this," I panted.

His hand gripped my throat. "Not another word, darling. Not another fucking word. Or you're as good as dead. You owe me for the trouble you've put me through." More fabric ripped as my bodice was torn to my waist.

"Oh, dear, why have we waited so long?"

I sobbed as his hands searched under my skirt once more, pushing fabric aside until his fingers touched my most private place.

Oh, Lord, this can't be happening. Save me from this. Please, save me.

Gunfire went off nearby, and men began to yell.

"Help." My voice came out a strained whisper. I lifted my hips to try and push him off. "Help!"

Ethan backhanded my face. Gripping my neck, he banged my head against the ground. I struggled to breathe. His hand on my throat. Blood in my mouth.

More shots and shouting. The cavaliers called after Harris for reinforcement.

He growled in exasperation. "Stay here!" he commanded as he rose. "Move from this spot and you're dead."

Drawing twin revolvers from his holster, he pushed through the brush back to the road.

I sucked in air. Rolling onto my side to cough and spit blood. The shock of the encounter left me raw and numb. The revolver glinted in the weak, gray light, beneath the bushes. I fumbled to my knees and pushed myself through the brush. Pushing back the branches, I reached in and grabbed the revolver. Cold and heavy in my hand, it was like a spurt of energy in my veins, propelling me to my feet and out to the road.

"Ella! Don't move! Get down!" Brett yelled as bullets whizzed past me.

My knees buckled at the sound of Brett's voice, and I flattened to the ground. What was he doing? He was supposed to stay hidden. He was going to get himself and Seth killed.

The three Rebels climbed on to their mounts, still shooting.

"No!" Ethan bellowed. "Don't retreat!"

A signal sounded in the distance, and the three men turned, galloping toward town. Ethan, still exchanging fire with Seth and Brett, hesitated, his eyes locking with mine before mounting his horse.

"They're getting away!" Seth shouted.

Brett rushed to my side as Seth reloaded his pistol, firing after them.

"Ella." Brett helped me to my feet.

I refused to live in fear if Ethan survived this. Blood rushed in my ears. The whole earth tilted, but I managed to cock the hammer. Aiming it at Ethan's back, I squeezed the trigger.

Ethan jolted forward against the horse. The bullet hit. The horse galloped on. I prayed it was a fatal shot as he disappeared down the road.

Brett draped his coat around my shoulders, bringing me close. My head spun, and my whole body burned with nausea. My vision dimmed around the edges, but strong arms were there to catch me.

29

BLAME

The room was dark. Blinking and rubbing my eyes, I cleared my vision to see I was in a spare room at the Chisholms' house. I winced at the bruise on my cheekbone. Chills racked my body. I pulled the blankets to my chin. I did not dare close my eyes again in fear of seeing Ethan's face. I could still feel his hands on me. And hear his harsh voice ringing in my ears. Tears rolled down my cheeks, gathering in my hair. The shivering would not stop. I hugged my legs to my chest. Nausea rolled over me in waves and I leaned over the bedside, thankful for a washbasin left with rags and murky, red water to catch my vomit. I collapsed back against the pillows. Why can't I stop shivering?

A knock sounded on the door, and I pulled the blankets up to my face, attempting to muffle my sobs.

"Ella?" asked Mrs. Chisholm. "May I come in?"

"We need to take her home, Mama," Clara said.

"Shush, dear. Let me have some time alone with her." Mrs. Chisholm knocked once more. "Ella, may I come in?"

Despite my lack of response, Mrs. Chisholm opened the door, shutting it behind her.

"Ella?" She approached the bed. "I'm sorry this happened."

I was sorry too. This was all my fault. Ethan did this to their town because of me.

"Did he …" She fiddled with a pleat on her dress. "The Rebel. Did he force himself on you?"

I closed my eyes and put my hands to my face, sobs escaping.

"He did not succeed. This is all my fault," I cried. "I'm so very sorry. I should know by now, wherever I go, I put other people in danger. He found me. He brought them here. I'm so sorry."

"What do you mean, he found you?" Bewilderment cut through her concern.

"I'm sorry, it's my fault. I need to go home. I have to go back to the Mathis house."

"I don't think that can be done right now. You need to stay here."

"Please, Mrs. Chisholm, please. I shouldn't be here! I have to leave."

"Rebels are still in the streets. We must wait till it's safe."

A hard knock pounded on the door. "Mama!" Brett called. "Open the door, Ma!"

Mrs. Chisholm hurried to the door, opening it a few inches. "This needs to wait."

"The Rebels were chased out of town, but they got away with money they robbed from the bank."

"The bank! Oh, dear! What about the smoke we saw?"

Brett gave a short chuckle. "Mostly from Greek fire that failed to ignite the town."

"Praise the Lord."

"That Southern sympathizer no one really liked, Morrison, was shot, and one other gentleman. And one Rebel was killed. His body was found floating in Sheldon Creek. The rest of the Rebels burned a hay wagon on the bridge. The whole thing is aflame to keep us from following them across the Canadian border. Captain Conger's on furlough and is in pursuit with several townsmen. He's capable. He'll arrest them before they escape with Federal dollars."

"Who would have thought? Here in our own town."

"The town is safe now. How is she?"

In the dark, I could see Mrs. Chisholm shake her head.

"Brett," I cried out to him. "I need to leave!"

Mrs. Chisholm turned from the door. "No, Ella, you shouldn't leave yet. I don't think you are well enough—"

"I need to leave. Please, Brett, please take me home," I pleaded, sitting up in bed.

Brett pushed past his mother and came to my side, grasping my hands.

"Are you all right, Ella?" His eyes went hard when he saw my cut and bruised face. "I should have never allowed you to accompany us to the cabin to bring back the horses."

"Please, Brett. Don't blame yourself. It's my fault this even happened to St. Albans."

"Of course not."

"He came because he heard from John Mathis I was here."

Brett's eyes went round. "What? Why? John would've never exposed that information to a Rebel."

"He was forced … tortured. And that man wasn't just any Rebel. It was Ethan Harris."

"Ethan Harris? The man you were betrothed to?" Even in the

dark, I could see Brett's jaw muscles flicker.

He had a right to feel angry.

"John? He's still alive?"

"Ethan …" My tongue was thick in my mouth. "Ethan, he said …"

The cut on my lip burned with the taste of salt. I deserved the pain. I wanted to feel it all. The Mathis family would never forgive me.

"What is it? What did he tell you?"

Somehow, I managed to break the words from my tongue. "He said John didn't survive. Ethan broke him … to get to me." The truth settled over me like a wool blanket, scratchy and suffocating. I squeezed my eyes shut, fresh tears cascading down my cheeks. Brett brushed them away.

"Shh, my angel." He brought me into his arms. "Everything will be well."

It was a lie. To soothe me, to dismiss the truth. I shook my head. "What do I *do*, Brett?" I asked him, helpless.

"Let's take you home."

I leaned out of Brett's embrace. "Oh God! What am I going to tell Mrs. Mathis? I don't think I can tell her that her son is dead." My hand flew to my mouth. "And Ethan? Is he still alive?"

"You shot him, Ella."

Was Ethan the body that was found in the creek? That had to be a fatal blow. I'm glad I did it.

"Come, let's take you home."

Brett lifted me from the bed. My arms wrapped around his neck.

—

Mrs. Mathis said nothing. Her face was bleached of color. Her dark eyes stared, stupefied, as she listened to what I managed to tell her. Nora joined in my sobs while we huddled in Mrs. Mathis's bedchamber late into the night.

"I knew John would never live a long life," she said woodenly, more to herself than to us.

My dress and stockings were still torn, and my knees scraped the floor as I knelt beside her, begging her pardon. "I'm so sorry, Mrs. Mathis. I'm so sorry. None of this would have happened if I hadn't come here. I brought this here."

"Don't you dare blame yourself for the wrongs of men. I will not hear another word. It's late, and we all need our sleep."

She brushed my cheeks, offering a compassionate smile, and I stood up and released her hand. Sleep was the last thing I wanted.

I knew what I would see as soon as I closed my eyes.

30

HIS DECLARATION

1864 OCTOBER 20, THURSDAY

S leep eventually came. A brief, restless sleep, filled with dreams. When morning arrived, all I could do was stare at the torn dress I pushed into the corner. Late in the night, when whiskey had made me feel brave enough, I shed the garment to examine my body in the candlelight. My lip was swollen, my cheek bruised. Marks along my neck and legs were left behind by his hands, and I hated myself for it. I brought this upon us.

My stomach soured when Kay brought me breakfast and I pushed it away, refusing to be bothered. My head pulsed with an agonizing headache.

I did not know how long I remained in bed until Nora pushed herself into the room. Her voice soft and tearful, she told me Brett Chisholm arrived to convey his condolences to the family and wished to see me. She understood if I denied him, her eyes full of sympathy when she looked upon my face.

I shrugged on a dressing robe. "No, bring him up."

Both my body and heart ached. Nora went to fetch him. Needing to numb the pain, I gulped a sip of the whiskey flask from under my pillow, then did my best to calm the hair around my shoulders.

"May I come in?" Brett sounded at the door.

"Come in, Brett," I rasped.

"I won't stay long, but I wanted to bring you this." He handed me my revolver. "Seth said it belongs to you. JPH?" he asked, gesturing to the engraving on the handle.

"Something I took from him a long time ago. I'm glad it found its mark."

Brett nodded in acceptance. He understood why I needed to do it. For myself. For John.

"I couldn't sleep last night. My mind was uneasy, thinking of you," Brett admitted.

His Adam's apple bobbed with his swallow, his cheek flinching. We hadn't spoken in weeks. I did not know if he would forgive me for hurting him, for hurting this town, for hurting this family.

"I don't know what I would've done if something worse had happened to you. I would've never forgiven myself."

"Forgiven yourself?" I asked. "I should be the one asking forgiveness."

"No. I had no right to put my own expectations on you. You have been nothing but kind and compassionate toward me. A true friend. But knowing something could've happened to you yesterday. I ... I ..." He stammered, reaching for my hands. I could feel his fear of losing me in his grip. "I don't know what I would've done without you. There's something I realized last night, though. I feel I owe it to you to tell you ..."

I reluctantly nodded, unsure if I wanted to hear what he had to say.

"I realized I'm in love with you. I have been for months now." His eyes drooped.

In my heart, I always knew this was how he felt. My care for our friendship had pushed the thought away. I was too absorbed by my feelings for John.

"Oh, Brett, I—"

"Please," he interrupted. "I know. You love John. I don't expect you to reciprocate."

Tears sprang to my eyes. I was so tired. So tired of crying. And I would only hurt him.

"Everyone I have ever loved is in the earth. You don't want me loving you."

"No, angel. I would die a happy man knowing I have your love … if you could ever learn to love me." Brett coughed. "I will be returning to my regiment soon. I would like to protect you the only way I know how. I know this is not the most appropriate time, but war steals our time, doesn't it?" His eyes glistened. "My name can give you protection. My pension can take care of you. If anything were to happen to me, you and Katie would be provided for. I will make sure of it."

"Brett, I couldn't ask that of you—"

"You didn't ask, Ella. I'm offering it to you because I love you. You would honor me to become my wife. I can provide for you and Katie. I know you're grieving and hurt, but I only have a couple of weeks before I must make roll call. Will you marry me, Ella?"

My muddled brain struggled to keep up, to push the well of sadness away. John was gone. I did not have a home to return to. I only brought pain and burden to the Mathis family. There was my promise to Robert to care for his sister. And I failed in every way.

Katie deserved better. She deserved a family. I needed redemption. I needed to redeem myself after the countless failures I made, and Brett was offering it all ... and more. I could learn to love him. He was the kind of man most could easily love—charming, strong, and generous. Yes, I could do it. If not for him or myself, for Katie.

"I'll marry you before you leave then," I found myself saying.

"You'll marry me?" he asked, his brows springing to his forehead. I nodded. "I'll do anything you ask." His eyes sparkled with joy, but he remained serious.

"Protect us. I need help adopting Katie to ensure her protection. I made a promise I have struggled to keep, and if something were to happen to either one of us, I need her cared for. Adoption would ensure she does not become a ward of the state but would have the protection of your family."

"Adopt Katie as our own?" He attempted to cover up his surprise and confusion.

"I already have the papers."

"Well, you certainly plan ahead." He brushed his fingers through his hair.

"I need to fulfill my promise to Robert in some way. This is the best way I know how, but an unwed woman cannot adopt. You said you are offering protection."

I could tell I was hurting him. He rubbed his temple. I cringed, feeling guilty asking so much of him, already taking advantage of his declaration of love.

Brett set his jaw. His eyes stern with determination. "You have my protection, and I'll help you with the adoption papers."

I breathed a sigh of relief, but a pit in my stomach growled my heart's betrayal.

31

PROMISES

I did not sleep well anymore, too scared to close my eyes to see Ethan hovering over me or John left in a shallow grave. I kept myself busy with wedding preparations, but my heart was not in it. Brett came every day to visit me and make plans.

The first snowfall arrived the first of the month, forcing us all indoors. I could tell Brett was worried about me, and he offered to help me with wedding plans, but I told him that he had more important matters. Brett and Mr. Chisholm were confirming the adoption papers and going through the process without me. Along with this business, Brett was on the search for a home for us.

He found a small, two-story home on the outskirts of town. The property was off the road that led to the lake. It was a quaint, cottage-like house with four bedrooms upstairs and a parlor downstairs connecting to a dining area and a cement kitchen. Beside the house was a compact vegetable garden that would do well in the spring. A small apple orchard with two dozen trees descended down the hill from the back property, and an old, weathered barn stood at the southeast corner. Mr. Chisholm gave Brett two horses and a cow to put in the barn. Brett said there was enough room to eventually add on to the house as our family grew, his face lighting up with the potential.

And he promised by then he would have more to provide. He was making a lot of promises to me. Brett made plans to join his father's law firm when he returned so he could have a stable income to provide for Katie and me. He was doing everything to prove I made the right choice in accepting him.

—

Seven days. Then he would be gone. The day was a blur to me. I spoke to no one. I was more alone than ever before. Sitting alone in a dream amidst a blur of people buzzing, invisible to them all, even though they were celebrating my wedding.

The day before, a package arrived from York, Pennsylvania. Pa sent the wedding dress Mother had been working on for my wedding with Ethan. She never finished it, but inside was a note pinned to the front of the dress.

> My darling daughter,
>
> It pains me not to be there for you, but circumstances keep me here. The least I can do is send you this. I know your mother never managed to finish this dress before she left us, but Mrs. LeDoux agreed you must have the dress she intended for you. Mrs. LeDoux completed the stitching, and I send it to you now with all my love.
>
> Pa

I cried when Mrs. Mathis helped me dress in the white gown. The delicate, handstitched lace Mother added to the décolletage and sleeves made me feel as if she were embracing me. Oh, how I wished Mother and Pa could be here to assure me that I was doing the right thing. Mrs. Mathis wrapped me in her arms, and she let me cry on her shoulder until I had no more tears to shed.

My feet carried me down the aisle of the church, alone, to exchange halfhearted vows with Brett Chisholm. He reassuringly pumped my hand, knowing my difficulty. I couldn't help but wish my life had turned out differently, but I convinced myself that this was best for Katie and me. We had no hope of John returning. He was gone, and my heart had gone with him. I did not know if I had anything left for Brett. Numb, I barely noticed when the reverend pronounced us husband and wife, and Brett pressed his lips to mine.

After the ceremony, Brett and I were alone in the carriage, on our way to the Chisholm home for the reception. I was quiet and gazed out the window at the cold wind blowing through the bare tree branches. The carriage wheels whipped up slush and mud. He didn't ask me questions or even mention John, but he knew I was still grieving. Brett embraced me and whispered words of love and compassion, promising he would be back soon, and then we could really start a life together. He repeated his promise to provide and protect us.

"Let's live in the moment, angel. We don't know what tomorrow will bring, but I'll do everything in my power to make you happy."

He was right. He would be leaving. We did not know when or if he would return, but he did this for us. I was grateful he signed the adoption papers, and I was fulfilling my promise to Robert.

—

Katie's head lay in my lap, and Brett sat across from me in the dimly lit carriage as we left the reception. My belly was warm, and my head was fuzzy from the champagne. I wish I had eaten more, but I had little appetite. Brett couldn't stop looking at me and beaming. I tried to smile for him, but my lips only trembled.

When we arrived at our new home, Brett hoisted Katie from my lap. My heart lurched seeing Katie in his arms. She now had a father and I a husband. Brett laid her down in her little bed and waited, while I took off her shoes and coat before tucking her into the covers.

I turned to Brett, and he brought his hand to my cheek.

"I promise we'll have a good life," he whispered, sadness in his eyes.

"Please, Brett, no more promises tonight," I pleaded.

"No more promises." He took my hand and led us to our own bedchamber.

The room was furnished with cherry wood furniture. The bed was magnificent, with bedposts grazing the ceiling and gold, brocade curtains hanging from the canopy. Mrs. Chisholm had outdone herself when she insisted on furnishing the little house. Brett dimmed the lamps around the room, then excused himself, allowing me privacy to change into my nightgown.

While I changed, I studied the stitching of the dress Mother made for me. I was a different person when she started it. So much had changed. I wondered if Mother felt as nervous on her wedding night as I did. Her circumstances were different, of course. She was in love with her husband. I cared for Brett and I trusted him, but still, my hands shook with nervousness. I took a couple swigs from a hidden whiskey bottle, and then hid it beneath my undergarments in the chest of drawers.

Brett knocked moments later, and I sat on the side of the bed, ready in my nightgown.

"Come in," I beckoned, hoping he would not hear the anxious catch in my voice.

Brett tiptoed in and closed the door. I kept my back to him and listened as he took off his clothes and moved into the bed. His hand went out to me, drawing me toward him, and I crawled under the covers beside him. Brett's arms went around me and pulled me against him, his bare skin warm. I trembled, and he brought me closer to him as if I was cold.

"Nervous?" he whispered in my ear.

"A little," I replied.

"You're safe with me." True to his word, he did not promise.

I said nothing, my throat still burning from the whiskey.

"You know I'll never hurt you, don't you?"

I didn't want to tell him that I was scared, that I still thought of Ethan's hands on me. Yet, I was also curious as to what it would be like to be with Brett, too embarrassed to share that with him. I nodded.

He tipped my chin up. "Look at me, angel."

Gazing into his passionate, blue eyes made tears slip from mine. He was so gentle with me. I did not deserve his love.

"Oh, my darling, please don't cry." He brushed his fingers across my cheeks. "It will be all right. You trust me?"

"Yes, I trust you." I did trust him.

"I'll love you enough for the both of us." He held my face in his hands, and his thumbs stroked the hair at my temples. "The last thing I want is to see you in pain. If it hurts, we'll stop right away, all right?"

I nodded. His face leaned toward mine, and I closed my eyes as his lips brushed mine. I wondered if he could taste the liquor on my mouth. His lips were tender and consoling. Brett's arms embraced me, and his hands rubbed my back to comfort me.

"I love you, angel. I'll never hurt you," he repeated over and over, like a balm to my soul, as his kisses became more and more persistent.

I returned his kisses, remembering how comforting his kisses made me feel in the cabin months ago. Unbidden desire started to burn in my belly. I surrendered to his kisses.

His skin burned against me, and his hands caressed my sides. He rucked up my nightgown, and I cringed at his hands running up my thighs. I pulled away from his lips and searched his eyes. They only returned my look with concern.

"Are you all right?" he asked.

"Yes," I lied.

I closed my eyes and tried to push the thought of Ethan away from my mind, but it kept invading my head. My eyes sprang open. Brett's mouth meandered down my neck to my collarbone. He unbuttoned my nightgown while his lips traveled down my chest, between my breasts. A hand cupped my breast, and I gasped when his other hand touched between my legs, my hips lifting in response. He looked up at me as if to ask permission, and I nodded in consent.

He settled himself between my legs, parting them with his hips, and my breath caught when he pressed against me. I winced as he prodded. He moved slowly, inching into me.

"Breathe," he reminded me as he pushed into me, allowing my body to adjust to him. I kept my eyes open and bit my lip the whole time, refraining from the sounds that threatened to break free. Water gathered in my eyes with the burning pain and blood, but the pleading love and passion in Brett's eyes kept it from spilling over. He moved above me, thrusting his hips. Soon, he sighed in relief, and his eyes closed as he fell back on his pillow.

I pulled my nightgown back down to cover myself.

"Did I hurt you?" he asked, needing assurance.

"No, Brett," I managed to say, the pain gone as soon as he left me.

We lay there side by side, listening to each other's breathing. I did not know how I could sleep, my heart still pounding in my ears. Brett's breathing deepened into a gentle snore, and I knew he was asleep. I curled up in a ball and wrapped my arms around my middle, the liquor rolling around in my belly.

I rushed from the bed and went to the washbowl to vomit. Sweat beaded on my neck. With another wave of nausea, I vomited again. Cold and shivering, I made my way back to bed and pulled the blankets up to my chin. Brett turned in his sleep and his arms went around me, bringing me against him. When I did finally find sleep, it was the first time in a long time I did not dream.

32

SWEET FAREWELL

He would leave today. The house sat quietly in wait. The dawn yet to break.

Still in bed, I pulled the down comforter up to my chin. I rubbed my cold, exposed nose to warm it. Brett was like a heater against me, his arm lay across my belly. His shallow breathing stirred the hair at my neck. He looked peaceful and content, almost like a boy if it wasn't for a shadow of a beard along his square jaw. The scar on his cheek was fading. It had been nearly a week since we exchanged vows, and I was already preparing for his departure. I could love this man, I decided. My heart still ached for John, but life proved unfair a long time ago. I had to be strong, and I had to build a home for little Katie. Brett would make a good father once he had time to be one.

We were out of time, though. He was leaving this morning.

I nuzzled against him, burying my face in the crook of

his neck. He pulled me against him. I was growing accustomed to belonging to someone. He loved me and showed me in every way he knew how. He would live up to his promises. But I would not depend on him. I couldn't depend on anyone anymore. He was leaving, and I only had my Montgomery strength to lean on now. I did not know if Mother would be proud, but I could learn to be proud of myself.

The bed curtains parted at the foot of the bed, and I looked at the floor-to-ceiling window where drapes hid the view outside. The early morning was still and silent. There was a peace to it that came with something.

I inched out of bed. Making sure I didn't disturb my new husband, I pulled the blankets up over him to keep him warm as I removed my body from his embrace. I shuffled my stocking feet into slippers and made my way over to the window. Cold air penetrated my nightgown, and I wrapped my arms around myself. I pushed the drapes aside to see it was snowing. The dark sky had a gray-brown blanket of clouds. I leaned against the windowsill and watched the white flakes float down to earth. The world around us was silent. The snow buffered the earth from noise.

The falling snow reminded me of last winter. I couldn't help but think back to the morning John left. I didn't want to think about that right now. John never returned after that morning. Brett would leave to finish the war, but I was supposed to believe him when he said he was going to come back.

"Can you not sleep?" Brett's voice was husky with sleep.

I turned to see Brett push himself up to peer at me.

"It's snowing."

"Is it?" He gave me a lopsided grin, still half asleep. His tousled hair falling across his forehead lent him a boyish look.

"It's really beautiful. I never have gotten tired of it. Vermont snow is different from Pennsylvania snow."

"Because there's more of it?" Brett chuckled.

"Well, there is that, but no. It's the feeling it gives me. It makes me feel like this is the only place on earth. That this is the only world there is, and all the other things we hear about—death and war—do not even exist. As if those terrible things are all a figment of our imagination."

"We must have horrible imaginations then," Brett teased, his smile growing wider.

I rolled my eyes. "I'm serious."

He sobered. "Vermont does feel secluded at times. War even reaches here, though."

I turned and glared at him, wishing he was not there or he was still asleep. "Do you think I don't know that? I saw them. I knew him. It was all because of me."

"No, I'm sorry." We hadn't spoken of that day since it happened. He spared me that much. "That's not what I meant. I mean war reaches here in people. Each and every one of us are proof of this war. We're fighting this war even at home. There is not a family here that is not affected. You're proof of that and I'm proof of that." He touched his cheek, and his fingers ran across the scar. I wondered if it still itched him. "It's surrounding us and falling all around us like the snow outside."

I said nothing, even though he waited for me to speak. I had nothing to say. He was right. We were our very own reflection of the war outside our home, states away from us.

"Why don't you come back to bed, angel. It has to be cold by that window, and it's still dark outside. We have a while before we have to get up. I want to take my time in leaving you."

I went back to bed, and he wrapped me in his arms, snuggling against me beneath the blankets.

"See. You're cold."

"I'm all right," I whispered.

He rubbed his hands against my arms to warm me. "I spoke to Mrs. Zimmerman and Miss MacKenna. I told them to watch out for you and to make sure you are always happy." He spoke of the two hired help he employed two days ago.

"I don't need looking after."

"Sure you do. I want my wife to be content and protected while you're waiting for me to return. I shouldn't be gone long. Maybe only a couple months. The war is almost over. I'll be back by next year, I'm sure, and then we can finally start our life together. The whole country will be starting new lives. There will be a union again, just like our union. Our children are going to build the next Roman Empire. I can feel it."

I couldn't help but smile.

He kissed my forehead, his lips trailing down my jaw to my collarbone. His hands roamed the slopes and swells of my body, and I brought his mouth to mine, opening his lips and finding his tongue. Our daily practice in lovemaking was coming easier for both of us, and I needed him to remember this moment, to be able to carry it into battle. I ran my fingers through his chest hair and along his arms. I took his hand, kissing his palm, and then laid his hand on my hip. His hand pulled up the hem of my nightgown, and I parted my legs for him as he touched and stroked me. I pulsated with pleasure—it was unlike anything I ever felt before. I wanted him more than was most likely appropriate for a modest wife.

"I want you," I whispered, breathless.

He moved on top of me, and I wrapped my legs around him as he pulled my nightgown over my head. My hips arched toward him, and he entered me as his hands cupped my breasts. I moved with him in a synced rhythm until both of us were spent, my hips arching toward him as if taking him all in. He collapsed beside me and drew me into his arms, kissing my head before we both fell back to sleep.

—

The pale light filtered through the window when we awoke. Brett lay his head on my belly, his right hand caressing my side as he muttered. I wondered if he spoke to a hopeful child in my womb. His words chanted in a singsong fashion, and I knew he was reciting poetry.

"... *and straight her arms, of snowy hue,*
About her unresolving husband threw.
Her soft embraces soon infuse desire;
His bones and marrow sudden warmth inspire;
And all the godhead feels the wonted fire."

He was speaking the words of Virgil, quoting the story of Aeneas and Lavinia.

"Trembling he spoke; and, eager of her charms,
He snatch'd the willing goddess to his arms;
Till in her lap infus'd, he lay possess'd
Of full desire, and sunk to pleasing rest ..."

I feigned sleep as I listened to him, yet I knew he was aware of my consciousness. He did not let on, nor did he raise his head to make it known that he was aware. I hoped he would fall back to sleep until the time came to rise. We remained in this position for an hour more until the house began to move with the dawning day.

—

We had taken our time at breakfast, as if stalling for more moments together. But now he was actually leaving. I folded the last of Brett's clothes into his canvas bag, which sat on the bed. Brett picked up his ragged book, *Pharsalia*, and my tintype from his bedside table, and settled it on top of his meager belongings. Two articles evidently the most important to him. I beamed at my uniform-adorned husband. He would carry us to battle—to victory. I closed the bag.

"All set," he said, picking me up in an embrace, my feet lifting from the floorboards.

"Put me down. You're going to wrinkle your uniform, and it was just pressed too!"

"I don't care one bit. I'm going to hold my wife like I want," he teased, and I could see the excitement in his eyes. But then his mood turned somber. "I'm going to miss you terribly."

"I know. You'll keep busy fighting off the Rebs, though."

"I'll be worried about you here by yourself."

"Please, don't worry. There's nothing for you to worry about. I'm capable of handling things on my own. Just stay focused on bringing yourself home. That's all I ask."

He pressed his lips to mine. I could feel his passion building, the electricity radiating through my mouth, yet restraining himself from taking me back to the bed.

A knock sounded at the door, and Brett set me down, hesitating to pull away from our kiss. He pecked me on the lips once more and went to open the door.

Maureen MacKenna, the maid he hired, stood in the doorway. "Your family's here in the cutter, Corporal."

"Thank you, Miss MacKenna. Tell them I'll be down in a moment."

"Yes, sir." She left us to our moment.

"Well," Brett said. He wrapped his arms around me, bringing my head to lie against his chest. I could hear his heart drumming in my ear. "I can't believe I'm leaving you already. I'll pray these months go by quickly."

I pulled my head away from his chest to look into his clear-blue eyes. "You'll be home before you know it. You'll take care of yourself, though, won't you?"

He cupped my face in his hands. "Of course. After all, I have more than one reason to live for now." He kissed both sides of my cheeks and then swooped me into his arms, as if he had to or he would lose me. "I love you, Ella. I really do."

"I know you do."

He pressed me harder against him, as if to keep me there from an outside force pulling me away from him. "Can you please tell me you love me, too, even if it's not true? I know love will come with time. I just want to hear you say it right now, so I can hear it in my memory while I'm marching in the cold."

Despite his tight embrace, I tilted my head to rest my chin on his chest. I searched his eyes to see what was there. He knew my love wasn't for him, but he pleaded for me to say it just the same. He was hungry to be loved back by me, even if I had to pretend.

"I love you, Brett Chisholm," I murmured, forcing my eyes to stay locked on his, even while I lied. "I *do* care a lot about you," I emphasized so he could also hear the truth. "I would be devastated if you never came back to me."

His lips curled into a soft, boyish grin. "I'll come home to you, angel. A herd of wild horses couldn't keep me from you."

I patted his chest, and he loosened his grip. "Well, we better get you to the station." My husband of a week was leaving me so soon. Anxiety creeped in as he hefted his bag across his shoulder and took my hand to walk downstairs together.

Katie sat on the bottom of the stairs, and the Chisholms and Clara stood at the door, ready to leave.

"May I go see the train too?" Katie pulled at my sleeve.

"No, darling. You have a little cold, and it's snowing outside. Say goodbye to Brett here."

Katie pouted and looked through fringed eyes, watching to see what he would do. Brett stroked her cheek. "Be a good girl while I'm gone, and maybe I'll bring something back for you." She smiled but didn't say a word.

I leaned over and kissed her on the head. "I'll be home soon." She bent her head and wiped her runny nose on her sleeve, while Maureen took her by the hand.

"All right, let's be on our way," Mr. Chisholm said, taking Brett's bag.

I shrugged on my winter jacket, scarf, mittens, and knitted bonnet as we headed out the door. Flurries still fell from the sky, and the ground was coated white. It would have been a beautiful winter morning if it hadn't been for our approaching farewell. Clara and Mrs. Chisholm sat slumped in the cutter. We did not speak a word as we rode to the station, Mrs. Chisholm and I on either side of Brett. She clutching her son's arm for dear life, and Brett holding my hand for his own comfort. Across from him, Clara sniffled behind her hand muff.

Mr. Chisholm sat straight, his face emotionless except for the slight annoyance whenever he glanced at his wife and daughter. I kept taking deep breaths, causing little puffs of vapor to float from my mouth into the air. Most of my concentration was in keeping myself sane and trying to keep morbid thoughts away from my mind—I'll be saying goodbye to him, maybe forever. I couldn't think that way. It was as though I were trying to push an unwanted gofer back into its hole, but its head kept popping back up and ruining my garden with its little mounds.

The station was busy when we approached. Other cutters and horses lined up along the street beside the station. The train hissed with hot steam in the cold snowfall. The platform was loud with the commotion of a loading train. Brett pulled out his ticket as we pushed our way through the masses. Others were returning to war, recovered from wounds and illness, itching for action and the approaching victory. They all wanted to be a part of it. To me, they were one and the same, all soldiers heading back off to perform their duty. They were all faces to me, and I paid little attention.

The railroad reminded me of past goodbyes. Goodbye to Robert, goodbye to my family, goodbye to Landon Greene, goodbye to John—which I would always regret not doing—and now goodbye to Brett.

"You'll take good care of yourself, won't you, son?" Mrs. Chisholm asked, hanging on to Brett and dabbing her eyes.

"You have nothing to worry about, Mama."

Brett leaned down to kiss her on the cheek. Clara sniveled into a handkerchief, yet to say anything to her twin. Brett and Mr. Chisholm exchanged hearty embraces, patting each other on the back.

"I'm proud of you, son," Mr. Chisholm said in his ear. I averted my eyes to give them privacy. More words were whispered in each other's ears, and then Mr. Chisholm handed Brett his bag. Brett nodded at him. They both understood each other.

Brett turned to me, his face sad and his eyes hard with longing. "I'm missing you already," he said, embracing me, lifting me off my feet.

"I'm going to miss you so much."

That was the truth. I buried my face into his scarf. My chest tightened. I was scared for him and for myself, but I never would have told him as much. I needed to show him I was strong so he wouldn't worry over me. He needed to keep his mind set for the fighting. He could get himself killed if his thoughts were elsewhere.

He nestled his nose in my hair above my ear and whispered to me, "I'll think about you every night. That will keep me warm." I giggled at his intimate whispers. "The memory of you will keep me alive, angel. I'll be home by the New Year."

"Please, just be safe, all right?"

"I will. Those Johnny Rebs will be sorry that I'm back." He chuckled, then kissed my cheek and set me on my feet. "I almost don't want to leave you."

"You have to go, my dear."

"I know. I need to finish my enlistment." He paused to stare into my eyes. He held my face, brushing his thumbs along my cheeks. He looked so handsome standing so close to me, his face full of love and admiration. He leaned down and locked his lips to mine, wrapping his arms around me. The train whistle blew, and the conductor yelled for everyone to board. We pulled away from each other.

"I love you, Ella."

I smiled at him and lied again just so he could live on my words. "I love you too."

He smiled back, a sad, farewell smile. "I'll write to you when I get the chance."

I nodded and adjusted his jacket collar.

"I'll see you when I come home."

I stood on my tiptoes and reached up to kiss his cheek, my upper lip brushing against his scar. "Goodbye. Take care of yourself."

"'Bye, angel."

We embraced once more, and he walked up to board the train.

Clara and the Chisholms stood behind me, both ladies sobbing and Mr. Chisholm saying, "There, there" over and over again. I didn't look at them but watched the train, watching him leave. Brett kept looking back at me, a waning smile on his lips. When he reached the car door, he glanced back at me for the last time and waved goodbye.

33

EXTRADITION

The winter was cold all alone in that house. Everyone was tired of the war. We were ready for it to end. Lincoln was running against General McClellan. Lincoln's reelection seemed doubtful, especially after his veto of the Wade–Davis Bill, which required the majority of the electorate in each Confederate state to swear past and future loyalty to the Union before the state could officially be restored.

But as newspapers blared news about Sherman advancing day after day toward Atlanta, the old excitement of the war flared. This time with relief. The war was almost over, and we saw our victory looming over the horizon. The New Year would bring the restoration of the Union. Then, as we had all hoped, Sherman marched into Atlanta, burning it, blazing a trail. The president must have been mighty grateful for this victory. He must have been praying for it fervently day in and day out more than any of us, for his prayers were answered. He was reelected by a wide margin.

Each day, I combed through the editorials and columns, searching for news on the St. Albans' raiders. Searching for his name. I had to be sure he was dead. I had to be sure he was the one left dead in the creek. But the papers were quiet on it, too filled with election news and the whispers of victory.

Letters arrived from Brett expressing how tired he was from marching in the rain. He desired to fight. And he missed me more than he had ever missed a single human being in his life. I would reply to him with short letters, telling him what was going on in St. Albans and informing him about the weather and the colds that passed between Katie and me. In each letter, he asked about my health, and I wondered if he hoped we had made a child. But when my menses arrived at the start of December, I knew it was not to be. I was relieved and made no mention of it to Brett. Let him continue hoping to carry him through to the end.

Katie and I went to the Mathis house every Sunday evening for supper, and they invited us over for Christmas. Christmas felt melancholy to me for the first time in my life. Just any other day. I tried to be lighthearted and joyous for Katie's sake, but I just wanted tomorrow to come. Katie was spoiled with gifts from the Mathis and Chisholm families. The money Brett had put in the bank for my use was already dwindling fast on the servants' wages, repairs on the house, and groceries. I had only enough free money to spend on a new porcelain doll for Katie and a new Christmas dress for each of us.

I wore my new, dark-blue, taffeta dress to the Smiths' annual Christmas party. Just like the year before, I sat beside Mrs. Mathis and the other St. Albans' matrons. No one spoke a word to me while I sat there listening to the women's idle gossip and watching the dancers.

My mind wandered, imagining myself last Christmas, dancing in John's arms. I would have given anything to go back and have that Christmas again. I would have done many things differently if I had known I'd never see John again. I would have done anything to have that moment again. Now, I would have accepted John in a heartbeat. But I forced myself out of my reverie. I was bound to another man. I was moving on with my life, and I wanted Christmas to pass so I could move on. Christmas brought too many painful memories. I was relieved to wake up the morning after to sunshine beaming through the frost-covered windows.

A blizzard arrived in mid-January, leaving Katie and I snowed in. I was unable to dig out the barn to reach the horses until Seth came to give me a hand. Mrs. Mathis made a visit to bring us groceries and treats for Katie. I told her it was unnecessary, but she insisted, saying she would have a responsibility to me until her death. Her eyes were full of sorrow when she told me this, and I knew she called on me for John. I thought back to the letter I gave to her when I first arrived, and I still wondered what he had written to her. There was more spoken between those two than I realized. I acquiesced and accepted her help. It was the first time I had seen her smile in a long time. She left, and for the rest of the winter, she religiously visited me when I could not go to her.

One day, Mrs. Mathis arrived with a turkey Seth had shot, potatoes, and news that the last port of the Confederacy had been sealed off. The blockade runners could no longer reach the South, and the Rebels were beginning to crumble under the complete siege. They would have a shortage of food and supplies and would soon surrender. Brett would most likely be coming home soon.

Rumors came in February of a peace conference between Lincoln and Jefferson Davis. We found out a week later that Davis had agreed to send delegates to the conference but insisted on Lincoln's recognition of the South's independence. Lincoln then refused, and the conference never commenced. So, the war raged on.

By April, the snow had melted. Seth came to help clear the apple orchard and vegetable gardens, and he brought a newspaper. Throughout the winter, news reports trickled in from Canada where the St. Albans' raiders were now in custody. I scanned for Ethan's name among the defendants, but he had yet to be mentioned.

"They made mention of a 'Yankee' who assisted their escape from Camp Douglas in Illinois, but that is all," Seth explained, handing the paper to me. The Montreal court transcripts revealed the arrested men were mostly escaped prisoners of war.

The trial had concluded, the eighty-eight thousand dollars they robbed was returned to the banks, and they were to be released by special train to the Confederacy.

"They refused the extradition," Seth explained, "insisting Canada remain neutral in our conflict. And that is not all the money ... just what Montreal law enforcement was able to recover."

"You think Ethan is the Yankee they mentioned?"

"Must be. Why they haven't mentioned his name or any others' involvement, other than their Canadian contacts, I don't know. Their commander, Bennett Young, is claiming they were given official command to rob the banks and burn and surround the town in retaliation for atrocities committed in the Shenandoah Valley by our troops."

I shook my head at this news. Seth grumbled, frustrated they were not being charged for robbery and arson, that all of the money was not returned, and they would not be extradited to face judgment in a federal court. I did not have peace in the outcome, either, but for obviously different reasons.

34
SAD TIDINGS
1865 APRIL 10, MONDAY

The day the world righted itself was the day my world tilted on its axis. It happened when Mrs. Zimmerman found me in the vegetable garden clearing winter debris. The rain had let up, and although still cold, the sky was clear.

"Better come inside," she ordered in her thick, German accent. "No good, no good."

She always looked at me with disapproval. Nothing I did seemed to please her, and getting my hands dirty made her frown.

"I'll be in for the noonday meal," I told her, turning back to the discarded detritus in the garden bed.

"Better come inside, Mrs. Chisholm," she demanded again.

"Why?" I finally asked.

"Post is here."

I stopped, confused, searching her face for an answer. Obviously, her English was lacking. Otherwise, she would have been able to explain herself better.

"News and a letter," she repeated. "From the army."

My heart lurched. Mrs. Zimmerman followed behind me, waddling on her thick legs. She didn't say a word as we entered the house. I went to the table in the entryway and saw the newspaper folded, with two letters on top. The paper was dated today, and headlines blared with news of the Confederate surrender.

The war was over.

I exchanged a look with Mrs. Zimmerman.

"It's over," I told her, shocked. I never thought it was going to end. And just like that, it was done.

For the first time, Mrs. Zimmerman's face broke into a brilliant, wide smile. She said something in German I did not understand, clasping her hands and looking to the heavens. Although I did not know what she said, I knew she was praising God.

I picked up the two letters. One from Pa, and the other had been posted from North Carolina, but I did not recognize the address. It bore the mark of the Fifth Vermont Infantry, Brett's regiment. Blood rushed in my ears, and I knew what I was about to read. Mrs. Zimmerman did as well, as she worried her lip. I opened the letter, and it was dated March 23rd. Three weeks ago.

Dear Mrs. Corporal Brett Chisholm,

I regret being the bearer of sad tidings. Your husband fought honorably during our most recent engagement at Fort Fisher. He even saved one of our officers, shortly before he took a bullet in his side. Corporal Chisholm was the most loyal man I had ever had the privilege to know. He was a warrior, if ever I saw one.

Today, I visited him in the hospital, and he wished for me to write to you to tell you he was sorry he could not keep his promises. He said this was for the best, though, because now he would be with his Lord, and he hoped you would find peace in knowing. Shortly thereafter, I received word he had passed away in his sleep. He felt no pain as he slipped into the afterlife. He will be buried along with his comrades, who sacrificed for the preservation of the Union and the freedom of all. I will send his effects to you after I post this note.

Again, I regret to be the one telling you the sad news. He will be gravely missed among his regiment and his comrades. I hope this letter finds you well. Many condolences to you and his family.

Sincerely,

Lieutenant Charles T. Allchinn

I read it again to make sure I understood correctly. My mind fogged. The war was over, yet he was gone.

"Vhat?" Mrs. Zimmerman asked, but I ignored her.

Brett was dead. Shot by a Rebel bullet. Shot in the side. Bled to death. He would not march home. The war was over, but he would not march home.

"Lieutenant Charles T. Allchinn," I whispered to myself as I finished reading it over for the second time.

"Who?" She appeared nervous, rubbing her hands together in apprehension.

"He's dead," I told her, handing her the letter, not knowing if she could read it.

She looked at me in shock and then glanced down at the letter. I turned away from her, opening Pa's letter. I barely digested his words as he revealed he will surrender the ironworks and himself to the authorities. He was going to confess everything he knew about Ethan and his involvement with the Confederacy. I was angry. I was furious. I would never be able to return home.

I was angry at Brett for leaving me, for dying and breaking his promises. I was angry at Pa for betraying me, for his involvement with Ethan, for putting me in this position, and for his damn honor that demanded his confession.

An unbidden sob wrenched from my chest. I clapped my hand over my mouth. I left the letters with Mrs. Zimmerman and ran to the bedroom, shutting myself in. I had to remind myself to breathe.

Trembling with searing fury, I shuffled through my drawers until I found my hidden whiskey bottle. The sip seared my throat.

I screamed, not caring who heard me. I wanted to rage, to flail my limbs until I was spent. The bottle, cold in my grip, left my hand with my throw, shattering against the wall.

Glass scattered on the floor like the remains of my heart.

—

Mrs. Chisholm sat in shock, her chin trembling and her eyes glistening. "My last, and youngest, son is dead?" she asked for confirmation.

I nodded and she parroted my nod.

"Well," she whispered, her voice cracking with emotion, "you should probably go tell Clara. I don't think I can."

I squeezed her hand, but she withdrew it away from me and clutched her handkerchief to dab at her eyes. She was trying her best to hold her composure. I stood up from the settee and left the parlor.

As soon as I stepped onto the stairs, I could hear her gut-wrenching sobs muffled in the settee cushions. I bowed my head, sad for them more than for myself. Of anyone, I dreaded telling Clara.

When I went to Clara's room, she said, "I'm not well today, I'm afraid. My company will be poor."

She didn't look sick, but her hair was down in a long braid, and she was dressed in a green-and-gold-threaded, silk-embroidered dressing gown. A wedding present.

"I need to speak with you. May I please come in?" I asked.

"I suppose so," she said, opening the door all the way so I could enter. She walked back to her bed and got back under her quilt, propping herself against the pillows. I followed her in, closing the door behind me, and took a seat by her bedside.

I fidgeted with the ends of my shawl. Silence passed between us, and then I finally took a deep breath and gathered all the courage I could muster.

"I got a letter today—"

"From Brett?" Her face lit up.

"No, it wasn't from Brett …" I began. This was hard. I just needed to come out with it. The shock and adrenaline were starting to wear off. My shoulders drooped. "The letter I received this afternoon was from a lieutenant in Brett's regiment. He was shot at the Battle of Fort Fisher. He didn't survive his wound, Clara."

Clara stared at me. She appeared paralyzed, her eyes unblinking and her lips parted. She didn't breathe, but just sat still, her face like stone, like an alabaster bust. Her eyes grew wide, as if she were seeing a fire gaining before her and she was unable to escape, but watched helplessly while it engulfed her and burned her mercilessly to death.

"Brett's dead," I said again, as if she hadn't understood, but the truth was, I was beginning to fear the look on her face and the sudden, stale silence. Thick like the musty air in a cellar.

Her eyes watered, her lips quivered. "He can't be. I would have known. We're like one, he and I. We're twins. We came into this world together, we should leave this world together. No …" She tried to repeat herself, but instead, her words were repeated in silent sobs. She shook her head and then buried her face in her hands. I placed a comforting hand on her trembling, arched shoulder. She brushed my hand away. Blotches of crimson stained her wet cheeks, her eyes a fiery glare.

"How dare you!" she yelled. "How dare you!"

I recoiled back into my chair. "W-w-what?" I stammered.

"You took him away from me! You deceived him! Made him think that you loved him, but you never did! I bet you haven't even shed a tear for him yet! I'm ashamed to ever have called you sister!"

"Clara, I'm so sorry." I did not know what else to say, I was so taken aback by her outburst. But part of me understood. I was angry too.

"You are the most selfish person I've ever met! You led them on. You let them hope, and then you killed them!"

"Pardon?"

"Don't act like you don't understand me! You know rightly well what I'm talking about! I'm not daft! I *know*! You took them away from me—both John and Brett! I loved them both with all my heart, and you took them away from me! They are the only ones I've ever loved, and both of them loved you. Now they are dead because of you! Oh, and I must not forget *Matthew*!"

She knew! How much did she know?

"Don't you dare!" She held up a finger, stopping me when I opened my mouth to speak. "I know he fell in love with you, too, and he proposed, but he wasn't good enough for you! I'm not blind! I saw how Matthew looked at you! All the men look at you like that! I won't be surprised if my own husband dies and never returns! And you know what? I'll have you to blame! You're like poison! You come on quickly without warning and kill them while they gradually become paralyzed and blind with obsession, and then you consume them, and they are lost forever! They all fell in love with you, and they are dead! Think about it, Ella. Think about the destruction you've caused! If you genuinely loved them, as I did, they would both be alive!"

Her tirade burned like a hot poker. I swallowed the sting, not wanting her to see the effect of her words.

"Get out of my room! I never wish to lay eyes on you again! You are nothing but a conniving, manipulative whore! Get out!"

I sat there in shock. She threw off her blankets in a flurry and stood, glaring at me, her eyes burning. When I didn't move, she raised her hand and slapped me. I didn't notice the force of her long, thin fingers, but as soon as her hand left my face, my cheek burned. I put a hand to my jaw and moved my mouth to release the numb, tingling feeling in my lips.

"You don't know what you're talking about," I told her. "I loved your brother, and I loved John with every fiber in my being. Maybe it is my fault that I let them both love me, but don't ever think or even tell me that I was the cause of their deaths!"

"Oh, shut up! Shut up!" She covered her ears with her hands, like a child who didn't want to hear she was wrong.

"It's because of this war, Clara, not because of me! It's taken everything we love. Yes, it is my fault that I let them both leave without telling them how I truly felt, but I wasn't the one at the other end of that barrel! I wasn't the one with my finger on the trigger!" I didn't even know why I was trying to defend myself. I was beginning to feel the shame of guilt, just like the burning in my cheek.

"Get out!" she screamed again, walking to the door to show me out. She stomped her foot.

I swallowed my pride and anger. I wanted to hurt her with words worse than she used to hurt me. When I reached the door, her hand flew over her mouth, and she rushed to the washbasin by her vanity to retch. If she hadn't angered me, I would have been by her side to rub her back as she vomited, but now I didn't care. I left the room and the sounds of her gagging and sobbing.

I leaned against the wall in the hallway and slowly melted to the floor, gathering my knees against my chest and finally succumbing to tears. I couldn't help but wonder if Ethan was right about a curse, whatever that was. Whenever I realized I actually loved someone, it was always too late. I lost them all—Robert, Mother, John, now Brett and Pa. I could have loved Brett. My affection for him could have turned to love. He was easy for everyone to love. Now I would never be able to tell him that. He knew when I said I loved him that it wasn't sincere. It was only for his sake. Oh, Brett, I'm so sorry.

What had I done? I sat there, my face buried in the folds of my dress, and muffled my whimpers, these thoughts haunting me and circling me like vultures. I couldn't live like this. I just couldn't! Everything was lost to me now.

I must have sat in the upstairs hallway for quite a while as I regained composure because when I got downstairs, I was surprised to find Mr. Chisholm in the parlor. Mrs. Chisholm still cried in her handkerchief while her husband comforted her. They both looked up when they heard my footsteps.

"How did she take it?" Mrs. Chisholm dabbed at her face.

I shook my head and looked down at my clasped hands. "Not well."

Mr. Chisholm nodded. "I'll be over to see you tomorrow."

A dismissal. I pulled my boots back on and walked out of the house—numb and fatigued—to leave them to their grief.

35
WHILE FROM THE SHORE AROSE SUCH LAMENTATION

B rett's belongings arrived the next day, wrapped in brown paper. On top was a square, polished, oak box. When I opened the box, my hand flew to my mouth. There, lying in the velvet-lined box, was an honorary medal. Round and golden with a blue-and-gray ribbon. On the medal was the head of Lincoln, and surrounding him, along the edge, was inscribed: "With malice toward none. With charity for all." On the other side were the dates of our long-fought Civil War. I marveled at the medal and touched its cold surface and the silk ribbon.

Below the box was the worn and rugged edition of Lucan's *Pharsalia*. I picked up the book carefully, the binding loose, and opened to a place marked by a piece of paper. I noticed the handwriting as my own, and I recalled what I had written in my last letter. I did not need to reread it to refresh my memory, which was filled with brief descriptions of house chores and gossip. Instead, I went directly to the text:

'Twas through her that Fortune gained

The right to strike thee. Wherefore did I wed

To bring thee misery? Mine, mine the guilt.

I had not heard truer words. I was a wife unworthy, only to bring him misery. Surely, I broke Brett's heart. I skimmed the page, noticing that Brett had underlined a passage in charcoal.

In the boat

He placed his spouse: while from the shore arose

Such lamentation, and such hands were raised

In ire against the gods, that thou had'st deemed

All left their kin for exile, and their homes.

I knew after reading the marked text, as if peering into his soul, that he was sending me the most heartfelt and intimate goodbye he could possibly send. He understood me more than anyone ever had, and yet he loved me with unfaltering conviction.

"Thank you, Brett," I murmured.

Setting the book aside, I picked up the folded clothing. A single, cream-colored shirt, spare pants, undergarments, and his uniform jacket. I held them on my lap, caressing my hands on the fabric as if I were touching Brett. I pressed the clothes to my face and inhaled his scent. It still smelled like him—like soap and cedar—but I could smell the strong, pungent stench of battle and war still clinging to its fibers. Brett's sweat and the acrid scent of gunpowder intertwined with wood smoke.

I started to unfold the shirt but stopped when I realized the shirt had a tear on its side. I stuck my finger in the tear and noticed, at once, a large, white spot surrounding the tear. It appeared as though it were a stain of milk, but I knew by putting my finger through the torn material that it was the hole of the bullet that killed Brett. Somebody bleached away the bloodstain, trying to help his widowed wife not be subjected to the stain of her own husband's death, but unfortunately, they did not know me. If I had been there, I would have told them to leave it, not conceal the truth. He was dead. It was not necessary to spare us the sight of his own blood. Oh, how I wish they had let the stain be!

I peeled open his jacket. There, nestled inside, to keep from breaking, was my pocket-size, framed photograph he had carried with him through battle. The glass was unbroken, and there were a few finger smudges blemishing its surface. I puzzled at the woman within the gilded frame. I could not hold a smile, I knew, but there was a tiny blur of movement around my lips, as if I was trying not to laugh at something. The rest of my face was pale and serene, my eyes small and looking away from the photographer at something in the corner, at a distance. My hair appeared lighter than in person because of the light used in the photography studio. It looked like a halo around my head, the curls hanging down my neck like coiled, gold shavings. The dress, one of my best taffetas, was plaid-patterned, decorated with silk fringe on the bodice and sleeves. I appeared amused by something, but it was as though I was trying hard to look innocent and angelic. I was none of those traits. I tried many times to follow my mother's example, but I continually failed. Too stubborn and strong-willed.

A knock sounded at the door just before noon, and Miss MacKenna ushered Mr. Chisholm in. I offered him a seat beside me in the small parlor.

Mr. Chisholm cleared his throat, eyeing the contents of Brett's belongings before me. "I see you received Brett's things."

"Yes, they arrived today." I could feel the discomfort and grief radiating off him.

"I'm certain my wife will be wanting to see those at home."

He was right. I had no right to Brett's belongings, but I wanted to keep some part of him. His father was going to make this harder for me than I thought. "All due respect, Mr. Chisholm, but these were sent to me, his wife. I would like to keep them as a remembrance of him."

"Your marriage was short." So was his speech. "We'd appreciate his possessions with his family."

"If you must, may I at least keep his book and my picture?" I asked, touching those things beside me as if to protect them.

He thought for a moment and let the silence settle around us.

He nodded in acquiescence. "You may keep his book and your picture. We have no need for them."

"Thank you," I said, gripping the book and picture frame to my side.

"Now, about the property. Brett bought it on a loan from me, but unfortunately, we are going to have to sell it. We do not have the financial means to maintain two properties."

I was taken aback. "Perhaps we can profit from the orchard and the garden?" I wanted to find some solution to keep the house for Katie and me. We had no other place to go. "Between Seth Mathis and me, we spent many days cleaning it up and preparing it for new growth. There should be an abundance of apples by September."

"I know how you've been tending the grounds, but even if you were able to sell your produce, you would still not have enough to pay back the loan. This is a time for us to be reasonable. Not only can you not afford it, but there is no possible way you can maintain this house without the help of servants. I'll pay off their services today, but I cannot continue paying their wages. Since you have cleaned up the property a great deal, I'm certain I'll be able to sell it for a profit, and that will be sufficient for the amount I will lose in servants' wages. There is no way around this. I'm sorry, Ella. It may be best for you and Katie to return home to your father."

"I won't be able to return to York," I told him. I did not want to share Pa's arrest.

He did not ask why. "I'm sorry to hear that." He neither said more nor offered a place in his home for his son's widowed bride. I wondered if Clara had something to do with this.

I bowed my head, convincing myself they were grieving and doing what they thought was best.

"This is a difficult time for all of us, I know, but there is nothing that can be done. You're going to have to dismiss the servants, and I will send them their wages for the time they have been with you."

"When do we have to move out?" I asked, resigned.

"Well, I don't want to rush you, but as soon as you have packed and found a place to live. I won't let my son's wife be homeless."

"And yet you're kicking us out of our home."

"I didn't expect this to be easy for you. It is not easy for us either. He was my son."

"And he was my husband."

"Yes, you are right. Still, there is nothing to be done."

"Sir?"

"Yes?"

"I did not deserve Brett," I confided in him.

"Perhaps not." The truth stung.

"But he chose us."

"You're right. He loved you, and you made him happy. I'm thankful he left this earth with you choosing him." His voice caught on his words, emotion pinching his face.

Mr. Chisholm dismissed himself before he could let me see his tears. Leaving me clutching what remained of him and me.

36

REMEMBER TO BREATHE

1865 SPRING

I packed our home alone. Brett's belongings would return to the Chisholms for their own disposal or revered use. Mine, along with Katie's, were packed haphazardly, for I no longer cared about my material objects. Besides, all my dresses were to be dyed black now. Dull and heavy, Katie and I were moved back into the Mathis house, while the Chisholms prepared the cottage for sale.

The day I arrived at the Mathis home, Nora met us at the door, followed by Renny, Seth, and Mrs. Mathis. They all wore sad smiles when they greeted me. I wondered, for a moment, if my return reminded them John would never return, but then they told me the news President Lincoln had been shot. And it felt necessary we were together to process the tragedy. We gathered around the table for supper.

"I hope they catch everyone involved and they all get what's coming to them!" Seth said, pounding his fist in his hand.

"Oh, Seth," Nora said, grasping her brother's arm. "Do you think this means the war will resume?"

Katie grabbed my hand, hoping to find comfort by my side.

"I don't know, Nora. I hope so, just so I can find those bastards and slit their throats!"

"Seth!" Mrs. Mathis exclaimed, looking at him in shock. "There are innocent ears!"

"Please, Seth, Katie—"

"I'm sure it's nothing she hasn't heard before. Right, Katie, my sweet?" He nudged her chin.

Katie giggled at the attention he paid her.

"For goodness' sake, Seth." I pulled Katie closer to my side.

"What?" he said, appearing baffled. He shrugged his shoulders at my accusing glare.

"Seth," Mrs. Mathis scolded, "let's keep that kind of talk to a minimum at the dinner table."

"Yes, Ma."

"Thank you." Mrs. Mathis poured us all some wine. "Now, I know it is going to be hard to go through the rest of the day knowing that President Lincoln has departed, but we must do it. We are welcoming Ella and Katie home."

Home. I wanted to breathe in that word and fill my limbs with it.

"If John were here with us right now," she continued, "he would tell us to go on fighting the brave fight, no matter what comes knocking. I think he would also tell us that we have nothing to worry about because our government has everything under control, and they'll take care of us so no further harm will come to the Union. Everyone is too tired of fighting. We're at peace now, and I'm certain everyone wishes to keep it that way. It is only a slim minority, such as this Booth character, who think the war is still going on, so we have nothing to worry about. Mr. Johnson will see us through this tragedy. Before we eat, let us pray for Mrs. Lincoln and for our country."

She bowed her head, and her prayer was full of gratitude. I couldn't help but hide my emotion behind a secret smile when she thanked God Katie and I had returned to where we were meant to be.

—

Festivities were arranged ... parades for returning troops, soirees, church picnics, and a grand ball at Governor Smith's home. There was so much joy and relief, but a shadow still hung over everyone. The president was gone, and so were so many. Disbelief the war was over made the celebrations feel insincere. People reveled in the victory but did it hesitantly, as if it could all be taken away from us again.

Renny, Nora, and I followed Mrs. Mathis into the ballroom where tables were laden with dishes of homemade food upon linen tablecloths and surrounded by flower vases. It almost reminded me of an elegant, indoor church picnic. Already, the military band was setting up on the makeshift stage to play for entertainment. After we girls had finished helping Mrs. Mathis set out our prepared dishes, we all retired to a corner where Margaret sat with baby John on her knees. Cole already disappeared to speak to a client about business.

"Nora," Margaret jested as soon as we sat down, "why don't you go stand with all the other young, unmarried girls?"

Across the room, a group of young girls giggled and flirted with the uniformed soldiers. Nora was five to ten years older than most of them. She scoffed.

"I'm certain one of those handsome men would dance with you."

Nora glared at her older sister. "Why not ask yourself the same question?"

"Nora!" Mrs. Mathis said, astonished by her sarcasm.

"I'm a married woman—with a baby! I have no need for dancing." Nora rolled her eyes.

"What's the matter, darling?" Mrs. Mathis asked, her eyes softening with compassion as she grasped her daughter's hand.

"I'm sorry, Ma. I think I'm just going to find something to drink." Nora excused herself. She walked off before I even had a chance to ask her if she needed company.

"What has gotten into her?" Margaret asked as soon as she was out of earshot.

"I don't know, dear. She has been acting depressed ever since last week. Do you know anything amiss, Renny?"

Renny shook her head. "She hasn't confided in me recently. It's hard to read her sometimes."

"Ella, has she said anything to you?"

I did not know if I was allowed to tell them of her concerns about Bradley House or if I should keep it confidential. She was worried he would not be returning home. It was not my place to share. "No, she hasn't."

Seth was bringing Katie over, her hands grasping two doughnuts.

"Excuse me," I said, before they approached. I wanted to get away before they inquired more about Nora and to intercept Seth, who was surely spoiling Katie's supper.

"Mama! Look what I got!" It warmed my heart at hearing her refer to me as such, and I could not get over the fact she was mine. *Look at her now, Robert.*

"*Have*, darling," I corrected her.

"Look what I have," she said, showing me the two greasy doughnuts.

"I see. You're going to have to wait and eat them after you have your meal."

"May I at least have one?"

"I told her she could have them," Seth explained, his charming smirk reminding me so much of John.

"Seth, you're of no help." I sighed. "Very well, you may have one doughnut before dinner, but you must promise to save the other one until afterward."

"Thank you, Mama!" And she immediately stuck half a doughnut in her mouth.

Seth and I both laughed at her eagerness, and her cheeks filled like a chipmunk.

"Chew well before swallowing or you might choke," I warned her. "There are seats waiting for you." I gestured to where Mrs. Mathis and his sisters sat, and I went to find Nora.

As the crowd of flirting girls and young soldiers dispersed onto the dance floor at the first strike of the band, I found Nora in a lonely alcove with a champagne flute in her hand. She did not notice my approach, or if she did, she did not let on. Her eyes stared into the alcove's dark shadows.

"Nora?"

She took another sip of champagne. "Margaret's always known how to get a rise out of me. I wish she'd bite her tongue, especially when she knows I'm practically engaged."

"Have you heard any word from him?"

"No, but I'm sure I will soon, now that they're all starting to return. It should be any day now, I would assume. It would be hard to believe he would not come home alive after so many have died." She took another sip. "God wouldn't take Bradley too. That would mean I'm destined to be an old maid like Ma and Margaret believe me to be."

"I'm sure you won't be an old maid, Nora. If not the wife of

Bradley House, then surely the wife of someone just as worthy."

"I'd rather be a widow like yourself. You are the only wise woman I have known my whole twenty-six years. You did what you needed to do to survive in this world."

"I haven't been all that wise, Nora." I had so many regrets.

She gripped my hand, and we sat there in the shadows of the alcove until neither one of us felt so alone, and we both remembered to breathe.

37
THE CONSEQUENCES OF WAR
1865 MAY 28, SUNDAY

We all stood in church, fanning ourselves while we sang the usual hymns. So many wore mourning. Many more wore patriotic pins or black ribbons on their breasts. The grief over the loss of so many of our brave boys in blue was palpable in the congregation. Others beamed in celebration of their returned soldier. Renny was one of them, gripping Landon Greene's arm as if she never wanted to part again. I even noticed Matthew Downs had returned. Clara gave me a haughty look when Matthew dared to raise his hand in greeting to me. She pulled him away despite his protests.

Nora tugged my sleeve, disrupting my singing. I turned to her and saw her staring at the back of Mrs. House a few rows in front of us. Nora's eyes were wide and her jaw set firm.

She turned to look at me, her face pale. "Mrs. House is here," she whispered. "That can only mean one of two things."

No one had seen Bradley House's mother enter a church since the last time her entire family was home. Her husband was never the churchgoing type. When she did come to church, it was either a holiday or one of her daughters or sons were home, all of whom were married and had families of their own. For a long time, Bradley, the youngest, was the only one who came with her on Sundays. As soon as Bradley had enlisted, she stopped attending.

After service, Nora nudged me as we watched the reverend's wife approach her. Her mouth moved as she spoke a few words to Bradley's mother, grasping her hand. Mrs. House raised her head to acknowledge her, revealing her profile. Her pale face was blotchy and grim with lines. She gave a weak smile and nodded her head, closing her eyes briefly. She spoke a few words in response, followed by the reverend's wife's own words, and then she departed, leaving Mrs. House to turn her head straight ahead once again.

"He's not here, Ella." Her eyes scanned the room. "He must not be returning, or he did not survive."

"You can't know that."

Nora looked at me, her eyes moist. "Why else would she be here? And alone too?"

"I don't know, but there has to be another explanation. Maybe she has come to pray for his safe return. Not all the soldiers are back yet."

"Owen Childe is back." She pointed him out beside his folks. "He doesn't even look worse for wear. He just appears a little older. He was in Bradley's regiment."

His brown hair was greased, his jaw shaved, and his uniform freshly pressed. He stood between his mother and an unfamiliar, blonde woman. We had all heard of the Southern wife he returned home with; it was a source of teatime gossip wherever we called.

"Maybe you should speak to Owen. He might have some answers

for you."

She bobbed her head, determined.

"I noticed Mrs. House in the front row." Renny sidled up beside us, her brows furrowed with concern. She gave Nora's arm a squeeze.

"I'm fine." Nora brushed off her sister, avoiding her worried, dark eyes.

The service concluded, Nora linked her arm with mine and pulled me toward Owen.

He stood, speaking with another soldier who shook his hand, and left as we approached. His dull, gray eyes lit up like moonlight when he saw us.

"Why Nora Mathis!" he exclaimed, taking her hand to pull her close. He gave her a quick peck on the cheek.

"It's good to see you alive and well, Owen," she greeted. "We're all very proud of you."

The light in his eyes dimmed a little. "Thank you."

She glanced at me, gesturing. "You remember Ella Coburg, don't you? I think you may have met her on your furlough a couple summers ago. She had just arrived to stay with my family at the time."

"Ah, yes. It's a pleasure, Miss—"

"She's Mrs. Chisholm now," Nora interjected.

It registered with him then. "Mrs. Chisholm, it's a pleasure once again. I'm very sorry for your loss. If it's any consolation, ma'am, Brett spoke very highly of you during his last days. I had never seen him so happy. He was a great soldier, a superb military man who loved his country."

A sacrifice for our country, just like all the other men who will not return, who are cold and decomposing in the earth. I smiled despite my dark thoughts and said, "Thank you, Mr. Childe. Your words are a comfort."

Owen Childe gave a wry smile and then turned to the petite woman hidden behind him who was speaking to his mother. "Mother, may I steal Josie from you for a moment?"

"Certainly, dear. Good morning, ladies. Nora Mathis, Mrs. Chisholm," she said, nodding at each of us.

"Good morning, Mrs. Childe," Nora and I both greeted, nearly in unison.

"Excuse me, I must see what Mr. Childe is saying to the reverend."

"Very well, Mother. Don't want Pa to rile him up," he joked.

Mrs. Childe rolled her eyes and left us.

"This is Josephine, my wife." Owen Childe beamed down at her. "We met in Virginia when her family found refuge over our line. The chaplain married us the day after the Confederate surrender."

"Well, how do you do?" she said in a thick, Southern accent, leaning in to shake our hands.

I was so surprised by her voice and the strength of her grasp because of her appearance. She was younger than Nora and I, probably seventeen or eighteen. Her golden hair was curled and piled on top of her head with emerald-studded combs. Her brass-colored hat with ostrich plumes, and the taffeta ribbon beneath her chin, were a little too extravagant for Sunday church service, but it was obvious she didn't seem to care and even took great store in her new hat. Her face was beautiful with a small, pointed nose, blue eyes fringed with long, light-brown lashes, and a bow-shaped mouth that curved to reveal her straight, cream-colored teeth. Her figure was perfect but for the small bump she tried to hide beneath the flounces of her green dress. After noticing she was pregnant, I surmised that must have been the cause of their hasty marriage.

"Welcome to St. Albans," I said. "How do you like it thus far?"

"Oh, my, it's quite a change from the family farm in North Carolina.

But the farm ain't there anymore. My pa was the only man in Surry County who wasn't a secesh. 'Cause we were Union sympathizers, the militia burned down our home. We ran into Owen's regiment, and we took such a liking to all those soldier boys, my family decided to stay awhile, and we did. Pa and Johnny signed up to fight, and Ma and I helped cook and nurse sick boys. My three little brothers helped cut firewood and did odd jobs around camp for pennies. And I helped nurse Owen when he came down with malaria fever, and that's how we met—me nursing the poor boy back to health. He was a sorry sight, but I nursed him up, and even after the fever, I helped him regain his strength. Then, before long, we were in love and decided to marry."

Owen cleared his throat, embarrassed by his wife's rambling. "Anyway, Josie and I just bought a new house out toward the country with a pretty, little orchard. In fact, we bought it from Mr. Chisholm." He bit his cheek when his eyes landed with mine.

I smiled to assure him I did not mind he was to live in the house Brett and I were newlyweds in. I did not care who had the house. I never considered it my home.

"I'm very happy for you and Josephine," Nora said, but I knew she was cringing inside, desperate for news about Bradley. "It's good to have you back, Owen. Everyone has been filled with anxieties while waiting to see who comes home. It's especially hard since John is gone."

Owen gave Nora a wry smile. "Your brother was a good man. A true hero."

It was rare to hear people speak well of John, but since we'd found out he was dead, everything changed. They seemed to have forgotten his hand in Robby Chisholm's death. He was just another local soldier who sacrificed for the Cause.

"Thank you, Owen. He is greatly missed. Have you heard news of anyone else? Any of the other men?"

Owen's mouth drooped. "I suppose you noticed Mrs. House here today, and I suppose that was the reason you came over to see me to begin with."

Nora's cheeks flamed crimson. "You've always been one to jump to the quick. You know that wasn't the *only* reason, though. I wanted to speak with you. I'm so glad you're home, I really am."

Owen guffawed. "At least you admit it. Mrs. House most likely came to pray for Brad."

"Is he … is he …" she struggled to speak the words. She fumbled with the fringe of her shawl as she waited for him to save her.

Owen heaved a great sigh. "Near Fredericksburg, a shell exploded by a line of tents. What tents were not blown apart combusted into flame. Bradley House was in one of those tents, Nora."

"But is he … is he … I mean, he's alive, isn't he?"

Owen nodded. "I think he wishes he hadn't survived, though. He's not in a good way."

"Then he's home?" Her eyes welled.

"Yes, but I must warn you. He's not himself anymore. His face and body are marred—from the burns. He's not the man you remember, Nora. It's a miracle he's even alive."

She brushed silent tears away. "I have to see him."

"I don't know if that's a good idea. He doesn't talk the same way either. The flames scorched his vocal cords. He won't ever be able to live a normal life. It left him crippled."

"That doesn't matter. I have to see him."

My heart broke for her, listening to her desperation in receiving the news.

"I don't think Mrs. House is allowing visitors. I haven't even seen him since he's been home. The last I saw him was in the Washington Hospital before taking the train home."

"Did he speak of me?" Nora asked, desperate for something.

Owen shook his head and then said, hoping to give her some reason for it, "He doesn't speak much anymore."

Nora bowed her head, dabbing at her eyes with her handkerchief. Young Mrs. Childe bit her bottom lip and rocked on her feet, embarrassed she was privy to this moment. I searched around for Mrs. House, but she was already gone.

Nora grasped Owen's hand. "It's so good to see you, and congratulations on the wedding. Ma will have to invite you and Josephine over for dinner one evening."

"We'd be delighted." The corner of Owen's lips tipped. "I'm sorry to be the bearer of bad news."

"I'm glad I found out instead of worrying myself to death." Nora pulled me away and hurried us through the departing church crowd.

We passed Mrs. Mathis, Seth, and Renny, who all looked at us with concern. I gave them all a half smile and followed Nora out to the carriage. She did not speak a word once we were inside but looked out the window at the street, where people still mingled, reciprocating pleasantries.

Mrs. Mathis and I exchanged sad looks. She knew, and she was heartbroken for her daughter.

38

LOVE AND LOSS

1865 SUMMER

s soon as Nora was brave enough, she sent a letter to Bradley, hoping he would see her. Weeks had passed, but no answer arrived. Nora moped around, sending a new letter at the end of each week. Finally, at the end of the month, a letter arrived for Nora, but it was from Mrs. House, stating her son was not accepting visitors. It said nothing about whether Bradley wanted to see Nora or not, and Nora was convinced Mrs. House did not speak for her son, but for herself. Ignoring her refusal, Nora waited until it was market day, then went to their home to deliver the message herself, giving it to a recently hired manservant for Bradley.

A week later, Nora received another letter, this time from the manservant. The letter was transcribed from Bradley. Nora was happy after that day because there was hope. Bradley promised to speak to his mother about allowing

Nora to visit. A couple of days after Bradley's letter, another letter arrived. This time, it was from Mrs. House, consenting for Nora to visit her son.

When she returned two hours after her visit, Nora did not speak a word but closed herself in her bedroom for the remainder of the day, refusing food and company.

The next morning, when Kay was taking Nora's breakfast platter up, I stopped her in the hallway and took the tray from her. When I knocked on Nora's door, there was no answer. I turned the knob and was surprised to find it unlocked. The room was dark, all drapes were drawn over the windows, and Nora's bed remained made. I found Nora asleep on the floor, the quilt from John's room wrapped around her. I kneeled beside her, touching her shoulder. Nora's red-rimmed eyes fluttered open.

"I brought you breakfast. Pancakes, sausage, and fried eggs. The maple syrup is fresh too. Kay just got it this morning."

"Thank you," she said, hoarse with sleep. She sat up, yawned, and stretched. "It was too hot to sleep in the bed."

"You must be famished," I commented, sitting down beside her with the tray.

She nodded, and we sat in silence while she filled her belly. I would stay until she asked me to leave.

When she was nearly done, I told her, "You can talk to me about it. I won't say anything. I'll just sit here and listen."

Nora's eyes were tired—not just the tired of poor sleep, but the tired of being emotionally spent. She brushed hair out of her face with her hands, the curls from yesterday gone.

"I'm so confused, Ella. For the first time in my life, I don't know what to do. You should have seen him. He's so thin and weak. He said all he can do is sit in his chair all day and read the paper. The entire left side of his face and his left hand are completely deformed from the burns." She blinked and took in a deep breath. "He has a patch over his left eye, and the only good eye he has left is so sad and lifeless. It was painful to watch him and hear him try to speak. I had to bite my tongue the whole time to keep from crying."

She wiped her wet cheeks. "He used to be so tall and strong and manly. He was so handsome before the war, and I could hardly believe he chose me to be his sweetheart. Then when he enlisted, he said that he would come back in a month and we would be married. None of us knew that the war would go on for four years. Too many of us are victims of it. You and I both, Ella. We have both loved and lost, and look where it has brought us!"

I clasped her hand but she pulled it away, leaving my hand to lie on the quilt. I rubbed the fabric between my thumb and forefinger, letting the silence settle us.

"This is John's quilt," I eventually said. "It used to be in his room. I think about him every day, and I still can't stop missing him. It hurts sometimes to think what could have been. I regret it so much. But it hasn't made me worse for it. It's made me adjust my priorities. I told myself I had to move on—and I did—and at least getting married allowed me to make Katie my own. It may not seem like we can find joy in this right now, but Bradley is *alive*, Nora."

"I know I should be happy about that, but if only you saw him. It's obvious he wished he had died that day when the shell exploded. He's miserable and in pain every second of every day. Even when I was speaking with him, Mrs. House came in to give him his laudanum pills. Ma told me I should move on. She might be right. You did."

"John's dead. What else could I have done?"

"Well, Bradley might as well be. He'll never marry me now. He can barely walk."

"Give him time, Nora."

"You know, I asked him why he didn't write to me. He said if I had known, I would want nothing to do with him. He said we can't get married because he would never be a good husband. He wouldn't be able to give me children. He said he's useless, and I deserve better. But then I told him I would rather be an old maid if I wasn't to marry him." She wiped at her wet cheeks with the edge of the quilt. "He said, 'Fine then.'" She laughed a little. "He's always been obstinate."

"Are you going to visit him again?"

"I told him I would. Well, until he goes to Philadelphia. He leaves in a month to see a specialist. Bradley says he's the best, and he will help him regain more mobility."

—

For the remainder of June, Nora went to visit Bradley as often as possible. No one saw her shed another tear. She went on with her days as if she had a purpose. And then when Bradley and Mr. and Mrs. House left for Philadelphia, she began visiting the local hospital to help nurse the boys who had come home and were waiting for surgery. There were even burn victims in the hospital, and she learned how to apply the dressings and appease their pain.

More and more veterans came through St. Albans on their way home to other parts of Vermont, New Hampshire, and Maine. Some would even knock on our door, asking for a warm meal or a drink of water. We did our patriotic duty and gave them nourishment to hold them over until they reached home. Sometimes we would even get men who fought at the Wilderness alongside the 118th, and we'd ask if they knew Lieutenant John Mathis. More often than not, they would say, "Ah, yes, that ol' boy was a fierce soldier. A truly brave man and a great leader." Then they would tell us what we already knew—he'd been captured and they heard he was dead.

Mrs. Mathis and I helped Kay and Louise cook the food, so there was always enough for any wandering soldier. Sometimes, if a man arrived at suppertime, we would give him his meal and allow him to sleep on the porch with Moses. Nora and I both complained about this and told Mrs. Mathis she should at least let them sleep on the parlor floor where it was warm and comfortable, but she refused, saying she wouldn't have any of them stealing things or bringing in pests.

"Besides," she said, "they've been living outdoors so long, I'm sure a porch awning is like a roof anyway."

Nora and I just rolled our eyes and let her suggest the porch for the next soldier who arrived at suppertime. None of them ever complained. They were simply happy to be going home to their families and eating a home-cooked meal.

39
A GHOST

The church held a picnic in honor of the surviving veterans and in celebration of the harvest. Stubborn Nora even broke Mrs. House down into allowing Bradley to participate, setting him up beneath a shady tree. Nora's steps bounced when we left to return home.

We all descended from the carriage, laughing and chatting, with even Mrs. Mathis chuckling at her son's teasing. Moses came bounding around the back when he heard our laughter, barking and wagging his tail in greeting.

Stopping on the porch steps, I realized I had lost a glove. "I think I dropped my glove in the carriage."

Mrs. Mathis gestured to Thad to remain.

I turned back to the carriage and halted at the top step, peering out past the gate.

A man walked a slow, defeated gait up the road toward the Mathis property. From where I stood, he appeared a slim silhouette, bent over from the weight of his baggage, and his head bowed beneath a worn cow hat. There was a limp familiar to sore feet and fatigue.

"Another one?" Mrs. Mathis asked. "I thought we had seen the last of these vagabonds. I was sure they had all reached home by now. I'll go tell Louise to make a plate for him. Nora, can you help Ella find her glove?" Kay took Mrs. Mathis's shawl, and Seth scraped off his boots before they went inside.

"Are you sure you dropped it in the carriage and not at the picnic?" Nora asked.

"I think so ..." I still watched the man approach the gate and stop to look in our direction. He stood there, his gaze shadowed beneath his hat. Moses remained at the foot of the steps, sniffing the air, and let out a low woof.

"Ella?" I could feel Nora's eyes boring into me. Moses panted, and his tail thumped the ground. "What is it, boy?" Nora asked. He released a subtle woof and started jogging toward the stranger at the gate.

"A moment," I told her, my eyes watching him. So many times I glimpsed John in a returning veteran. My mind convinced me that he wasn't dead and that he would mysteriously appear one day. Longing played tricks on your mind.

But ...

It couldn't be him.

I hadn't realized I was holding my breath until I released it with his name, "John?"

My mind raced, trying to comprehend what I was seeing, trying to make out whether it was truly him.

Impossible. I only wished it was him. He was gone.

"What?" Nora and I exchanged looks. Her face had drained of

color, her brown eyes wide. She turned back to look toward the road. "It can't be."

I was afraid to learn my eyes had deceived me, if he was truly a figment of my imagination, or if he were a ghost.

My legs seemed to carry me forward. I stopped to look back at Nora, who stood still on the stairs, staring at the man at the gate. I glanced back at the man. He had not moved, contemplating whether to approach or wait for me to advance toward him.

Moses reached the stranger first, sniffing his feet, and accepted a pat from the man. My steps were measured, unsure to what or whom I was nearing. I was ten feet away from him when he looked up and turned back to the road, revealing his profile to me. I knew at once, despite the gnarled beard and dark, tired complexion.

"John?" I called. "How—" How was this possible, I wanted to ask.

"I didn't think you'd still be here," he rasped, his back turned to me. I didn't realize I missed the sound of his voice until I heard it and my breath caught in my throat.

I swallowed the lump. "You're alive?"

"I'm here, aren't I." His words were sharp. He turned around. His eyes were dark and withdrawn.

I took a step, but he held up a hand to stop me.

"Don't come any closer. I'm infested with pests and reek of dysentery."

He took off his hat then, and I could see a tan line where the brim rested. Dark circles shadowed his crow's-feet, his lips were cracked and blistered, his dirty, matted hair brushed his shoulders, and his beard was left tangled. He did not wear his uniform, but brown, homespun pants that skimmed the tops of his deteriorating, brown, leather boots, a cotton shirt, and a gray, wool jacket—holey either from moths or bullets.

His gaze took me in from head to foot. I searched him for some sort of emotion, some sort of sign. I did not know exactly what I wanted to hear from him or see in his eyes, but I could feel my heart sink.

"Still wearing black, I see." Then his eyes paused, looking at my left hand by my side, seeing the gold band I still wore for Brett. "Oh," he said, as if he understood everything now.

I wanted to explain it all. I wanted to tell him that everyone thought he was dead, but I couldn't bring myself to do it. I clenched my hand, attempting to hide it.

Nora rushed to my side then and stopped when John extended his hand. "No, Nora," he warned.

Her cheeks were wet, and I could see the evident pain etched in her expression, but she managed to restrain herself beside me. "John. But it can't ... oh, John. Is it really, truly you?"

"How come you're looking at me as though I were a ghost?" he asked, a dry, sardonic tone to his voice.

Nora beamed. "Oh, my dear brother! It is really you, isn't it? I'm not imagining it." She stepped toward him till she was within arm's reach.

"You better not move an inch closer, Nora Lee, or you'll get every insect I've inherited," he asserted. "I'm going to stay out here. Tell Ma she's needed in the backyard."

We both bobbed our heads and watched as he lumbered around us, Moses following on his master's heels. As John disappeared behind the house, Nora wrapped her arms around me.

"This is by far ... the happiest day ... of my life," she blubbered.

I patted her arm. Disappointment and confusion burned my throat. It all seemed so surreal. I had dreamed of John's return—even when I knew he was dead. We would always greet each other with desperate kisses. Kisses I still remembered. That turned my blood molten and left tingles where his beard scraped my skin. We would apologize profusely, only stopping our caresses to whisper words of love. This scene was nothing I had dreamed of.

"Let's go tell your mother," I said, taking Nora's hand.

"Oh, Ma. She's going to be beside herself when she sees him alive and well."

"Alive, yes, but well ... maybe not."

Nora sighed. "Ma will doctor him back to new, though. He just needs a bath, some home cooking, and a warm bed to sleep in."

She let go of my hand, hiking up her skirts and running as fast as she could toward the house.

"Ma! Ma!" she yelled. "Ma! Come quick! Ma!" Once she entered the house, I could still hear her yelling.

My feet felt numb as I walked back to where Thad stood with the carriage.

"Is that really ...?" Thad probably feared he, too, was seeing things.

"It appears John Mathis has returned from the grave." My voice sounded like someone else's in my ears.

"Apparently so. I wonder where he's been all this time?"

"Obviously, not in the ground." I shuddered as soon as I realized I said it aloud.

Thad ahemed and rocked on his feet. "Here." He handed me my glove. "Found it wedged in between the seats."

The small, white glove was so crisp and clean in my hand. Balling it up, I pushed it deep inside the pocket where its companion hid, waiting.

"Thank you," I managed to say as Thad turned away from me, climbing back into the driver's seat. He clicked his tongue and flicked the straps against the horses' backs, lurching forward and clattering off toward the stables.

—

Mrs. Mathis and Nora embraced, laughing through their tears. Even Katie mewled at seeing Mrs. Mathis and Nora cry. But I did not know how to feel. My heart ached, my soul soared, but my eyes were dry.

Seth stood awkward among the women, not knowing what to say for comfort. Instead, he fetched the large bucket Louise filled with scalding-hot water, and a bar of lye soap, to take out to John. Thad was setting out his scissors and razor, ready to give him a cut and shave.

"Send for the doctor, and stop at Margaret's and Renny's on your way back," Mrs. Mathis instructed Kay, shoving her bonnet in her hands and guiding her out the door.

I felt like I was floating, my soul slowly peeling away from my body. Mrs. Mathis tasked me with preparing John's bed, and I could not help watching him from his bedroom window, his slim frame shivering in the backyard while Louise ordered him to strip. My chest tightened, humiliated for him as he tried to cover himself with his brown hands. My face heated at his frail nudity. His tan lines were sharp at the base of his neck and at his wrists. Red, jagged scars crisscrossed his white back. Other scars, obvious bullet or shrapnel wounds, puckered on his chest, neck, and upper arm. Anger flared in my gut, knowing at least one man who had put those there. I wanted to shoot Ethan again for what he did to John.

I was too afraid to move from the window, afraid this was all a dream. I wanted my eyes to stay on John forever, to make sure he was real, to make sure he wouldn't disappear as soon as I turned away.

Voices in greeting echoed from downstairs when the Smith family and then Renny and Landon arrived. Instead of going downstairs to welcome them, I shut the bedroom door and stayed at my post to watch John.

—

The lights were extinguished throughout the house, except for the upper hall near John's room. The doctor had come and gone a mere hour ago. I walked past the door, and through the open crack I could see Mrs. Mathis rocking in the chair beside his bed, knitting while he slept.

"Ella?" she whispered.

I peeked my head in through the door. "Everyone has left, and Seth and Nora are talking in the parlor."

Mrs. Mathis beckoned. "You've stayed away from us all evening."

"I'm sorry. I just didn't want to intrude on your reunion."

Mrs. Mathis set down the needles and yarn. "You know you're as much family as my own sons and daughters." She patted her side, as if to say, "Come." I did, kneeling beside her, resting my head on her lap. She laid down her knitting and stroked my head, taking out pins and removing the locks of coiled hair at the nape of my neck. "It scares you that it might be different between you, doesn't it?"

Her maternal touch unraveled me like my hair. "I suppose … well, I really don't know … what I'm thinking."

With a clean-shaven jaw and combed hair, he looked more like the John I remembered, just older, more distant, and haggard. His breathing came in jagged gulps as though even in sleep, his trials continued.

"I understand. I have many questions I want to ask him, but right now, I must be content with the relief he's alive. I had come to accept his death. We all had. So, I think confusion is normal. I keep asking myself, if he were dead, how is he now alive? Where was he all this time?"

I nodded my head against her lap.

"Are you tired?" she asked me.

"No. I don't know how I'm going to sleep with all this mulling in my head."

Mrs. Mathis ran her fingers through my hair, releasing tangles from my long, wavy hair. "Well, my dear, I think I'm going to try and get some rest. Do you mind sitting here for a while with him?"

I lifted my head and looked at her kind face. "Of course not."

Her wrinkled hand cupped my chin. "If he wakes, feed him the broth. No water yet. If you need anything else, don't be afraid to wake me. And, dear, please don't be dismayed. He'll eventually realize you've loved him all this time. If he's anything like his old self, he's as stubborn as his father was."

I smiled, grateful for her comforting words. She leaned down and kissed my forehead. I helped her to her feet and handed her the knitting. She patted my cheek as she left the room and closed the door, leaving me completely alone with her son.

John slept restlessly, waking through the night with shuttering gasps and coughs. His eyelids fluttered open and then relaxed back into sleep as he realized he was back in the comfort and safety of his own home. My heart warmed with the thought my presence brought him peace, but he never once acknowledged I was the one who remained at his bedside.

40
DIRTY LAUNDRY

The dawn birds chirped outside John's window, rousing me from my dozing sleep. Darkness still loomed, but already, John was waking and trying to kick off the sheet and quilt.

"I'm not used to these damn things," he muttered, untangling himself and rolling onto his stomach. His eyes landed on me and stopped to stare.

"You're not feverish, are you?" I reached out to touch his forehead.

He brushed my hand aside, his face turning beet red. "No, I'm fine. Dammit!" he yelled into the pillow when he noticed his wet sheets were soaked with brown fluid and fecal matter.

"I'll go find Kay to have your sheets changed and get you clean clothes."

He pulled the blankets back up to cover himself.

"You better not," I warned, peeling the blankets off. "You'll get it all over."

"I've turned into a fuckin' baby!"

I was taken aback by his outburst and embarrassed for him. "I'll just go fetch Kay," I said and rushed out.

John punched his pillow in frustration and anger.

Down in the kitchen, I found Kay helping Louise with breakfast.

"Is everything all right?" Kay asked, taking in my appearance.

I knew I looked tired and disheveled, my dress wrinkled from sitting all night, my hair tangled around my shoulders.

"He needs his bedding and undergarments changed."

"Very well." Kay wiped flour from her hands. "Lead me to the child."

John still had his face buried into the pillow.

"Now, Mr. John, what's all this pouting for, sir? You've been in the army long enough to know that dysentery's common and not something to be embarrassed about." Kay spoke to him like she spoke to Katie.

"Is she still here?" His voice was muffled by the pillow.

"Who, sir? Mrs. Chisholm?"

John looked at me by the door. His eyes burned with fury, and I knew Kay said the wrong thing.

"Whatever her name is," he gritted through his teeth. "Tell her to leave."

It stung.

"Aye, sir," Kay replied, herding me out the door. "I'm sorry," she mouthed, but it was already too late. John knew I had married Brett Chisholm.

—

Nora and I sat on the back porch, folding John's laundry. I remembered

Nurse Fisher insisting I roll bandages on the rainy day in Gettysburg. She had known I needed the chore, to stay busy, to stay the grief—if only for a moment. It was a brief respite, even now, but it did not keep me from dwelling on what John now knew.

Nora's eyes bore into me. "You know it's not your fault. He's just as stubborn and as arrogant as he's always been. He was never keen on feeling helpless. And right now, his condition has him vulnerable. I think he's embarrassed you're seeing him this way."

I shook my head. "That may be so, but it's not that." I paused and placed the folded pillowcase on top of the pile. Looking at her, I could feel myself shriveling up inside. "He *knows*."

She looked at me, confused, trying to figure out what John knew that would cause me to feel so bereaved. I wiggled my ring finger. Recognition dawned on her face, and her mouth formed an O.

"Kay called me that, not realizing."

"He would have found out eventually."

"I know, but I was hoping to God he would find out by me, and that I would still be Ella Coburg to him."

"I understand." She sighed. "If only we could all start where we left off."

"Oh, Nora."

"I'm sorry, Ella. I'm just so confused, and I don't know what to do about Bradley. His mother would rather I wasn't there, and she hovers whenever I am, so he probably doesn't even know how much I still care for him." Tears cascaded down her cheeks.

I wrapped my arm around her. "It's so hard. I feel so guilty for marrying Brett."

"But we all thought John was dead. You were doing what you thought you needed to do. For you and for Katie."

"But I don't think he's going to understand that logic when he's been alive all this time. He probably feels betrayed."

She lifted her head to look at me. "You should speak with him. Tell him how it was while he was gone."

"You said so yourself, that he is stubborn and arrogant. He's not going to listen to a word I say. He won't understand."

"You should at least try."

"You should too."

"That's impossible with his mother always supervising."

"Maybe, if she would allow, I can come over with you and she can show me her garden. I hear she prides herself over her roses."

Nora gave me a watery smile. "That she does. Oh, Ella, that would be such a great help! Then, maybe—finally—I can speak with Bradley … privately."

41
HYSSOP AND LICORICE ROOT
1865 SEPTEMBER 9, SATURDAY

Dark clouds covered the afternoon sky, causing nightfall to arrive prematurely. Rain had been falling for nearly a week now, and the roads were muddy and sodden. Seth entered the back door into the kitchen, letting in a wind gust before he shut the door. The fire in the hearth flickered with the bluster. Kay and I glanced up from shucking corn cobs, and Katie's face bloomed at Seth.

"Well?" Louise asked, turning away from the boiling pot of chicken and vegetables to look at the soaked, young man.

He stomped the mud from his boots.

"What in heaven's name are you doin'?" she scolded. "Not in my kitchen! You know better than that!"

"Ugh! I forget my manners when I'm stressed."

"The hell you do! That's a lousy excuse, Seth Mathis, and you know it. Now clean that up before you take another step in here."

Louise threw a rag in his face, and he hustled to clean up the tracked-in mud.

"So? Were you able to get the herbs?" Louise planted her hands on her hips, impatient.

"Here." He pulled out two little, glass jars from his coat pockets labeled hyssop and licorice root. "Doc is standing by, too, just in case he's needed."

Louise didn't say another word and went right to making the tea.

"Thank you," Kay said.

Seth bowed his head, finished cleaning up, and went back out to help Thad untack the horses.

"This should do the trick." Louise put on the kettle, adding the herbs with some thyme into a tea strainer.

Once the kettle hissed steam, she placed the strainer in a clay mug and poured the steaming water over the strainer. "Ella, let this steep for a while and then carry it up to John."

"You should probably have Kay do it," I told her.

Louise shook her head. "I need her down here to help me with supper. You take it up."

Nora and Mrs. Mathis entered the kitchen with a basin of wet rags.

"Have Seth and Thad returned yet?" Mrs. Mathis was flushed, but she did not look concerned. I suppose John's fever was the least of her worries now that she realized she could survive his death.

"Yes, ma'am," Louise replied, stirring the broth and then going over to check the roast on the stove. "Supper will be ready in about half an hour. I still have to boil the corn, but we need to wait for the broth to be done."

Mrs. Mathis eased herself into the chair beside me, and Nora followed suit.

Louise fetched a tray to dish out a bowl of broth. I took out the tea strainer from the mug and placed it beside the bowl. When the tray was set, she gestured for me to take it. I hesitated, but Mrs. Mathis gave me an encouraging smirk. Straightening my shoulders, I left the kitchen.

John's room was dim and warm, lit only by the fire in the hearth and the lamp beside his bed. He opened his eyes when I came in. His eyes were heavy on me as I set the tray next to the lamp. His wavy hair was damp around his face. The blankets piled on top of him were pulled up to his chest, his bare shoulders rising with each breath. He scooted up onto the propped pillow and pulled the blanket up around his collarbone.

I took up the mug, blowing on the hot tea. I watched him over the rim, his eyes resting on my pursed lips. A glint of heat I had yet to see from him flickered in his gaze, sending a little thrill down my spine. A hint his feelings for me were not entirely absent.

"Here, drink this." I brought the tea to his scabbed lips.

"I can do it." Affronted, he took the mug from my hands, causing the tea to slosh over his hand. His eyes blazed for another reason. "Were you going to scald my throat with this?" he asked, wiping his hand on the sheet.

"Sorry," I murmured. A red scar puckered above his right nipple, still pink with new skin. A near-fatal bullet wound? Silver lines, like hatch marks, marred his chest. It looked like a knife was taken to him, meant to cut him into ribbons. I averted my eyes, wondering which ones were from Ethan and which ones were from war. He brought the mug to his lips.

His face pinched and he spat. "What vile drink did you give me?" He pushed the mug back into my hands. "Are you trying to poison me?"

"It's an herbal remedy to bring down your fever."

John coughed, hard and rasping, an old-sounding cough I had heard from the hallway. I waited as his lungs spasmed. When the attack subsided, he moaned, pained and spent by the wracking coughs. He reached back for the mug, but I pushed his trembling hand away.

"Let me. Please." He must have seen the pleading in my eyes because he relented, allowing me to bring the tea to his lips. His muffled cough sounded painful as he closed his mouth over the rim, drinking until it abated.

"Enough," he croaked, and I placed the mug back on the tray.

"Broth?" I asked.

He shook his head and plopped back onto the pillow. He closed his eyes, and I waited for a while before I got up to leave.

"May I ask," he said, "why you aren't home in Pennsylvania, back at Woodhue? Is your threat not gone? Aren't you now a widow? You could be back home with your family." He was not being cruel, but his deep-brown eyes showed obvious curiosity. I wondered if he knew about the Raid, and how I left a bullet in Ethan's back. He obviously knew about Brett.

"Yes, he's gone. There was a raid last October—"

He winced. "I'm sorry."

"Why? You couldn't have been here to defend me or St. Albans. I should be the one apologizing. They could have chosen any northern town to raid, but they chose here … because of me."

He didn't say more, but the shame on his face confirmed that what Ethan said was true. John surrendered my whereabouts under torture. Guilt washed over him like a tidal wave. I ached for him. My fingers and limbs itched to touch him. To smooth the pinched wrinkle between his brows, to massage the tightness from his jaw. To feel his warmth again, even just to ensure he was real.

Instead, I changed the subject. "Mother died last year. And Pa … well, Woodhue is nothing like it used to be."

"I'm sorry to hear that."

We sat in silence for a time. Him taking another sip of the tea.

"Some whiskey may improve this."

I shook my head. "The doctor said to avoid spirits and coffee."

"Did you love him … Brett?" he asked, frowning into his mug.

I sighed and cleared my throat. "He was good to me. I cared a great deal for him. I was alone. You were dead. And he offered protection and support for Katie and I. He was a good man, and we could have been happy." I didn't know what else to say. His eyes drooped with sadness, still avoiding my own.

We still did not know everything that happened to John, and we probably never would, but he was not the same man I had met in '63. Ethan, war, and imprisonment broke him. My chest was tight. I ached to hold him, to touch him, to force him to look at me. To see the love I still bore for him. My throat was thick with emotion, and I swallowed.

"I wrote to you. Did you receive it?" It was the question that had haunted me since the moment we learned he was missing.

"I've been imprisoned since the Wilderness." His eyes were on me now. Hard and cold. "Did you expect the damn Rebs to give out federal mail to Yankee prisoners?" The furrow between his brows deepened. "Ah, I see. You expected a very different reunion if I had received this letter? Would I have changed for the better if I had?"

Tears pricked at my nose now, coming dangerously close to seeping out. "Of course not. I just …" I sniffed.

"You just wanted to apologize and hope I would completely forget about Christmas night, and we could go on with our friendship as before? Or"—he smirked—"perhaps you realized your deep, undying love for me and wished we could make a happy home together? Or maybe it was just that you felt guilty for rejecting me, and you were feeling sorry for poor, ol' me? Well, my dear, *Mrs. Chisholm*, I need nothing from you, and I especially do not need your sympathy."

I frowned; his words stung. I hated hearing him call me by my married name. "My letter ... my letter ..." I couldn't get the words out, too taken aback by his own. Would he reject me now if I told him what it said? "You've changed, John," was all I managed to get out.

John snickered as though I had just recited a silly joke, as if he were laughing at my expense. "Of course I've changed. You're so naive. Did you expect Brett to return to you unscathed as well?"

"Of course not. I—"

"No man who has lived through this war of hell or the Rebel prisons can return a whole man! You women are all the same. Romanticizing us soldiers as heroes, while ignoring the husks that return."

"Oh, don't flatter yourself. Romanticizing? Indeed!" I shook my head vehemently. "You might have gone through hell and back, but we were all left to tend to things while our hearts were away fighting this damn war." I pointed a finger at him. "You insult me, John. How dare you belittle what I've been through, what your mother's been through, what Nora's going through with Bradley."

"I simply state the facts. You know nothing of the horror I witnessed."

"Nothing? You tell me I know nothing? When you brought me to Gettysburg to sit beside Robert for hours, watching him die? I nursed so many boys while they'd suffered bullet wounds, infections, and disease. I held their hands as they cried for their mothers and asked for their wives.

"Brett was killed while we were still newlyweds, leaving me a *naive* widow and Katie fatherless, still. I had to be strong for everyone who was mourning around me, dying around me, and despite the compassion and sympathy I showed others, I was ridiculed for being a mother to Katie and allowing Brett to marry me. Clara thinks it's *all* my fault … that if it weren't for me, you and her brother would still be alive. They blamed me for it all. And yet, I stood strong, comforting your mother and sisters when they'd heard you were missing, trying to give them hope. And then when we were told you were dead, it was as though the rug was pulled out from under us. I was alone, unable to stand on my own two feet. Then, when the Rebels invaded, I did what I could to protect those they wished to harm."

Tears stung my eyes now as I thought of that day. Remembering Ethan's face, hard with anger and revenge, his breath sour with ire. I shivered, recalling his hands on my breasts and my legs.

"Ethan Harris helped lead the raid," I told him, his face growing white despite the flush from his fever. "He found me and nearly raped me, if it hadn't been for Brett and your brother." I blinked my eyes, hoping to ward off the tears that threatened to spill. I hated telling this to John. He had been punished enough just by knowing he was the one to leak my location. I could only imagine him lying in a cold, lonely cell, possibly bleeding to death, knowing Ethan was on his way to St. Albans and he could do nothing to stop him. "You're right. How can anyone live through war and not change?"

The lines of his mouth were firm, and his jaw was clenched. I wanted to say more, to soothe his anger, but I was angry too.

I would not cry in front of John.

"You know nothing of war," he reiterated. His eyes were dark and glaring. His hands balled up into fists in his quilt. "Did you march, day in and day out, rain, sleet, heat, or bone-chilling cold and then fight to the death? I think not! You have no notion of lying in trenches, waiting for enemy fire to rain down on you. You don't know what it's like to march out onto the battlefield, your life hanging in the balance, your life in the hands of God, and you are helpless to save yourself, and you have to admit to yourself that you may die in the next second, in the next hour, tomorrow, or next week.

"I watched as men fell around me, as cannons blasted through our lines, killing dozens at once, and all the time, Rebel bullets were whizzing past my head, capable of striking at any moment, yet my life was spared each time. *You* saw a mere effect of war, but you did not see the surprised, paralyzed faces the very instant they were hit and then hear their bloodcurdling screams when they realized they were missing a limb or their guts were hanging outside their bodies."

I shivered at his words.

"No, you neither witnessed war nor do you know what I went through. You have no idea what it was like to be imprisoned in so many cells I cannot remember them all. They seemed to all melt into one never-ending nightmare, where hunger is eternal and fear of whether you would be the next to die in your own filth and others' grime is continually present.

"I won't go into any further detail. Neither do I wish to recall the images, nor do I wish to make you sick with every scene and sight and thing I heard in prison. We became greedy, skeletal animals. I have changed tremendously from the person I once was, and I fear you shall never know me, nor do I wish for you to know who I've become. There is no going back to the way things were."

I stood up and backed away from the bed. "I suppose you're right," I snapped, straightening out the creases my sweaty hands caused on my black dress. "I'll leave you to rest."

John did not say a word to stop me as I left.

I angrily brushed my wet cheeks as I marched to my room, slamming the door behind me.

—

That evening, John grew steadily worse. The rain returned, and Thad went on horseback to fetch the doctor. Nobody slept that night except for Katie. Mrs. Mathis and Nora stood beside the doctor while he assessed John's condition. Seth and I placed chairs in the hallway, attempting to read while eavesdropping.

"I'm surprised he lived through his imprisonment. If he completely succumbs to pneumonia, I fear he will not survive. He's too weak and undernourished. I'm not sure his body will withstand it," the doctor told Mrs. Mathis and Nora behind the closed door.

Did John only come home to die? He survived all odds, and now he was going to die from congested lungs? I did not pretend to understand it.

"Have him gargle with saltwater and take hot baths to loosen the mucus. Hot and cold compresses are necessary, but for short periods of time. Keep his chest and neck fully covered. It is also very important that he moves, so make sure he rolls on either side and sits up in bed. Continue with the broth, and he can drink any fruit juices. If his condition worsens, let me know. I'll be by to check on him in the morning."

The door opened and I peered inside. The doctor had put on his coat and gathered up his bag and hat.

"Thank you, Doctor." Mrs. Mathis followed him out the door. He acknowledged both Seth and I, and then they walked down the hall to the foyer.

Nora sat on the edge of the bed with John's hand in hers. Seth and I went to his bedside.

"He's going to be all right, isn't he?" Seth asked.

Nora shrugged. "I'm not sure. We just have to wait and see. At least he's sleeping now."

His face was pale and glistened with perspiration. His breathing was shallow and rattled when it went through his chest.

"Those damn Rebels!" Seth cursed.

Neither Nora nor I said anything but watched John's every breath. We both wanted to curse the enemy too.

Mrs. Mathis returned to the room, a tattered, leather-bound Bible in her hand. "I found it in his belongings."

It was the Bible I gave him back in Pennsylvania. Robert's Bible. He kept it with him all this time. Even through imprisonment. My heart warmed at the thought.

"It was Robert Moore's," I croaked. My throat constricted and my nose stung.

Mrs. Mathis beamed and handed the Bible to me. I opened it and saw new markings, obvious bookmarks and penciled underlines that John added—markings that weren't there when I gave it to him. There, tucked between the pages of Matthew 11, was a letter I sent to him.

"Thank you for encouraging me to stay the course. I don't know if I could stay here if it were not for you. I'll forever be grateful for the safe haven you've provided me. John, I look forward to the day I can show you how much your protection means to me," I wrote. There was so much hope in my words.

"Please read a passage," Mrs. Mathis requested, taking a seat.

I found another letter marking Romans 3. My eyes landed on my scrolled script, *"there is not a day, a moment, when I don't think of you. I shudder in imagining where I would be now if you didn't come to find me after Gettysburg."* In reading back my words—how could I ever not realize I was in love with him? John had been sure of his feelings then, confident I would share his love when he confessed that Christmas night.

I swallowed the lump in my throat, turning the letter over to read the scripture. Through blurred eyes I recited, *"For all have sinned, and come short of the glory of God; being justified by His grace through the redemption that is in Christ Jesus: whom God hath set forth to be a propitiation through faith in His blood, to declare His righteousness for the remission of sins that are past, through the forbearance of God; to declare, I say, at this time His righteousness: that He might be just, and the justifier of him which believeth in Jesus."*

"Oh, I hope he has found peace." Mrs. Mathis sighed. "It was never his fault."

I wondered if she knew he had told Ethan where I was, and that I was the cause of last year's raid. But I did not think so, so I assumed she was speaking of Robby Chisholm's death.

"He's a good man." Nora grasped her mother's hand. "I wish Pa could've seen that."

"I think he saw it, dear. I just don't think he fully understood your brother." Mrs. Mathis rubbed her forehead and closed her eyes for a moment.

"Tired, Ma?" Nora asked.

"It's been a long day."

"Why don't you go to bed? Ella and I can stay up for a while and keep an eye on him."

"Certainly," I agreed.

"Thank you, dears." Mrs. Mathis hoisted herself out of the chair and rubbed her weary eyes.

"Here, Ma," Seth said, holding out his arm for his mother to take. Mrs. Mathis put a tender hand to his cheek. "Thank you, Seth."

"Do you think he has found peace?" Nora asked once Seth and Mrs. Mathis left the room.

"I hope so." I turned to drape a cool cloth across his forehead while I wiped the silent tears that escaped. His brow pinched even as he slept. "Oh, how I wish things were different," I whispered, more to myself than to Nora.

"Me too."

"I just imagined things would be different if he ever returned." I breathed deeply, sucking back the tears. "He hates me for not reciprocating his love when he gave it to me. That I went on to marry Brett. Nevermind that I only ever loved him."

"But you still do!"

I shushed her. "You'll wake him. I don't think he really knows how I feel. He never got my last letter. So as far as he knows, I've never loved him. I've loved Robert and Brett, but I've never loved him."

"You have to tell him, Ella. You have to tell him that you've loved only him all these years. You should give him a reason to fight."

"But I don't know if he still loves me." My chest ached voicing my fear aloud.

"Of course he does. He wouldn't be so angry if he didn't still love you."

I scoffed.

"Well, it's true," Nora insisted.

"That sounds absurd."

"He talks about you—when it's just him and me. He always asks after you and Katie. He hasn't said it outright that he still loves you, but I know my brother."

"Well, if I tell him that I love him, will you tell Bradley House?"

Nora bit her lip in thought. "That's a little different."

"Not completely."

"I plan on talking to him anyway, as soon as I get the chance."

"Well, as soon as I get the chance—when he stops hating me—I'll tell him."

"You're as stubborn as he is." Nora's lips tipped up, her eyes glinting with silent laughter. "I'm going to get some more hot water." She took up the basin and damp rags and left the room, giving me a very unladylike wink as she closed the door.

—

Nora had been gone for nearly an hour, and I had to fight the pull of sleep in the quiet room. To keep from dozing, I hummed "Oh Shenandoah."

John's eyes fluttered open and peered at me beneath sleepy lids.

"Ella?"

"Oh, I'm sorry. I didn't mean to wake you."

"Why are you still here?"

"Er—Nora and I are supposed to stay up, but Nora went down to the kitchen a while ago. She should be back soon." Or she purposely left us alone in this room together.

"No, what are you still doing in St. Albans?"

"John ..."

"Why are you still *here*?"

"There is no home to go back to. Pa turned himself over to the authorities weeks ago."

"Oh," he said, his voice raspy with sleep. I didn't blame him for not having the words. I didn't either.

Of course there was more to it. Maybe I still hoped John would show up alive. Maybe fate kept me here to see him return. I didn't know. Was that what he was wanting me to say?

"I'm very glad you're home," I told him. "It broke everyone's heart to learn you were dead."

"Did Ethan tell you he killed me?" he asked.

I nodded.

John grimaced. "He nearly did." He pointed at the gunshot wound on his chest. "I'm so sorry, Ella. After beating me to submission and finding out the necessary information, he shot me and left me for dead. I thought I was going to meet my Maker. I don't know how much longer afterward, but the next thing I knew, I awoke in a damp, dark cell in some Virginian prison. A fellow Union prisoner, a surgeon, took care of my wounds while I was unconscious, and by some miracle, God spared me. He said I should have died immediately after receiving that bullet. He said it was divine intervention the bullet missed my lungs. I really don't know how I survived my wounds in those putrid conditions, but I did."

"I'm glad you did," I told him.

"Are you?"

"Yes."

"I'm sorry for this," he apologized, gesturing to us. "I won't be here much longer."

"Of course you will."

He shook his head.

"Of course you will," I said more firmly.

"As soon as I regain my strength, I'm going west. They need Lieutenant Mathis out there."

"John … what about us? What about your mother?"

"She will be saddened, but she'll understand I need to do what I feel is necessary. I can't stay here. You wouldn't want me to stay here. I would be a constant reminder of your hardship."

"That's not so—"

"Is it?"

He began a coughing fit just as Nora entered the room with a large basin of steaming, fresh water, followed by Kay, who brought in towels and a mug of the tea concoction.

"Just in time, I wager?" Kay said.

The timing couldn't have been worse.

42

A CHOICE

1865 OCTOBER

The month passed as John recouped his strength; however, the doctor suggested John needed a warmer and drier climate if he was to improve his health. If he stayed in Vermont, he would have chronic lung ailments, which was on the verge of consumption. Knowing that's what took his father, I knew he would fight to avoid it. His health would be compromised for the rest of his life, which would be considerably short if he were to remain at home. The consequences of surviving prison were grave.

John, once again, mentioned going west, but this time, he told the whole family. Mrs. Mathis understood the gravity of the situation, but she demanded that she go with him. John, of course, refused, giving a list of reasons—the trip was far too risky for his aging mother, Seth still needed a mother's stern hand, there would be no suitable living arrangement in camp for mothers, and besides, how would it look for a lieutenant to have his mother coddling him and following him around? It was out of the question. Therefore, Mrs. Mathis pleaded her son go somewhere else without rejoining the Federal Army, someplace closer where he could begin a respectable career and eventually settle down.

"I have already sent a letter to the War Department. I should be hearing from them soon. When they need me, I will go, if not sooner," John said.

"But winter will be coming soon!" Mrs. Mathis exclaimed. "You won't even be able to go until March when the snow melts."

"That's why I should leave as soon as I can, to beat the early snowstorms and settle into quarters before winter."

"But why the army, John? You finished your service. Do you really think it would be wise for your health?" she asked him.

"Ma, it gives me a purpose. Without that, I'm nothing."

"Don't say that. What of your writing?"

"What of it? I will always write in my spare time, but it will never earn me a living. I'm no Dickens or Sir Walter Scott."

"But you always used to write beautiful prose, closely equal to their talents."

"Only to you, Ma. No publisher would be interested in my work. Besides, my writing is lacking spirit these days. A change of scenery may do it some good."

"I do not deny that. But can you not be stationed closer? The military is still needed in Georgia, South Carolina, and other Southern states. The papers are buzzing with President Johnson's Reconstruction Plan."

"I just returned from there. I *will* not go back. The humidity and insects would definitely kill me!"

Tired of arguing, Mrs. Mathis released a great sigh. She raised stubborn children. "Very well, but you must stay till March, at least."

"We'll see, Ma," John said, which he repeated on several future occasions whenever the time of his departure was brought up.

—

"I thought maybe we'd try something new." Seth romped through the tall grass, two repeating rifles slung over his shoulders. I had missed our early mornings at our makeshift shooting range.

"Something new?" I set my Colt back in the haversack.

"Thought it would be fun for your birthday."

"You remembered?" Despite his wild streak, Seth was surprisingly thoughtful.

He shrugged, his cheeks staining pink, while he handed me the rifle. "I'll need a hunting partner once John leaves."

"Oh, I don't know if you want me for a hunting partner."

"Why not? You're a quick learner and a great shot. And you don't mind rising before dawn, unlike most of my comrades."

Seth set to showing me how to load the cartridge.

"That's it. Now push the lever forward as far as it will go, then straight back." I copied his instructions as he modeled for me. "That will cock it. When you're ready, hold the butt against your shoulder like this. Right. Now aim the muzzle and fire at your target."

I pulled the trigger. The rifle jolted, and the shot sailed over the tin cans on the split-rail fence.

"It will take some practice. Watch." Seth demonstrated, the whizz of the bullet and ting of the can echoing in the quiet woods. "Try again."

We both reloaded, and Seth showed me where to place the butt to limit the kickback. "Here. Allow me."

He stepped behind me, helping me bring the muzzle level with the fenceline.

"Shouldn't you be getting ready for school?" A voice cut through my concentration.

Neither one of us heard John approach. Seth sprung away, and I lowered the rifle.

"Seth's been a great teacher," I told him, needing to defend him.

"I can see that." He narrowed his eyes at his little brother.

"It's a birthday present for Ella." Seth jutted out his chin.

"Happy birthday, Ella." His eyes flitted to me before turning back to his brother. "Get going, Seth, before you're late. Ma said you've been late every day this past month. No university is going to want a student with a history of truancy."

"Who said I'm going to university?"

"Seth," he growled. "Git! I'm in no mood to fight you."

Seth grumbled, relinquishing his rifle to John and trudging back where he came from.

"He's been helping me, John."

John turned to me, his eyes ablaze. "He's been teaching you to shoot?"

"So I can protect myself."

John nodded without a word, simply leaning Seth's rifle against the tree and coming beside me. Of anyone, I knew he'd understand my need to protect myself. His cool hands repositioned the butt against my shoulder and took Seth's position behind me. The heat of his body radiated through my back, his arms wrapping around me to steady the rifle. Wounds, words, loss, and love had passed since he last touched me, but it was like no time had lapsed. My body recognized him like a moth to a flame, leaning into him.

"Aim a little lower." His voice was gravely. The moist warmth of his breath caressed my ear, prickling my skin.

"Like this?" It came out a breathy whisper.

"That's right. Now pull the lever back." I pulled the lever back, my hips bumping into his when I did. "Take a deep breath." We inhaled in unison, his hands resting on top of mine. Rough. Strong. "Pull the trigger and release your breath when you fire."

I exhaled, squeezing the trigger, and heard the familiar whistle and ping, the can flying off the rail.

"I did it!" I couldn't help but laugh, proud of myself. It only took two tries to hit a target. I'd be a proficient markswoman in no time!

"Ella?" My name rumbled in his chest. The vibration penetrated me. His hands guided the muzzle down, and I turned in his arms.

My breath caught. His brow was pinched in worry, and his eyes were at half-mast, landing on my mouth.

"Ella," he said again. His gaze explored my face. "I failed you. I was supposed to protect you, and I failed you."

I let John take the rifle from my hands. "You didn't fail me. I'm still here, safe."

"But if not for me …" His throat bobbed. "He hurt you, didn't he?" Pain etched his face, bracketing his mouth. His eyes pleaded for the truth.

My throat stung. "He did."

He flinched. I cupped his cheek, needing to comfort him. His beard had grown. It was coarse and thick beneath my fingers.

"You are not to blame, John. Ethan would have always found a way to reach me. I needed to rely on myself. I needed to know how to protect myself." And I couldn't blame myself anymore either.

John grasped my hand, stilling it against his cheek. "You shouldn't have had to feel like you needed to protect yourself. I could have done better by you. You and Katie deserve to feel safe and loved."

"We do deserve to feel those things." My thumb stroked his

whiskers beneath his hand. "But what if we think you can be best for us?" I asked tentatively.

"You deserve more. I know I can't be good for either of you. You moved on once before. Before, when you thought I was dead. I know you can do it again. You found happiness with Brett. You're capable of finding it again, and I *can't* be here to see it." His eyes glistened with unshed tears.

My heart was impaled by his words.

"It doesn't have to be this way." I pulled my hand away, and he let it drop to my side. "What about what *I* want? I have a choice in the matter too. You can't just push me away because you don't believe you deserve me."

"I wouldn't be able to make you happy. To give you what you want."

"You haven't asked what I want. But I'll tell you anyway. *You're* what I want, John."

"No, I'm not. I'm leaving. I can't provide for you, to care for you like you need to be. I can't be a father for Katie or anyone else. You need someone who is whole, who is capable of giving you all of life's comforts."

"Stop telling me what you think I want! Nora was right. You are pigheaded. But your self-loathing needs to stop. You went through a war. You were a prisoner. You faced death. But it does not mean you are broken. It merely means you were tested and didn't fall apart. You fought your way home. You are a survivor. I'm a survivor. And you are so deserving of love and happiness. Two things I want to give you."

"Ella—" He reached out to touch me.

"Don't." If I let him touch me again I'd either push him to the ground and consume him until he relented or I'd collapse into a watery mess. I was neither going to beg for him nor allow myself to fall apart.

"You know my choice. I'm not going to stop you from making yours."

Before I could lose all strength, I turned on my heels, finding my way home through blurry vision.

43

THE CURSE

1865 OCTOBER 28, SATURDAY

"Apple pie, applesauce, apple dumplins—you name it, I've cooked it and eaten it. I don't think I've much room for more." Josephine Childe giggled, patting her round and heavy belly.

The Childes were insistent about Katie and I visiting, knowing it was once the home Brett and I shared—even if it had only been a short time.

She loaded up a basket for Katie and me to take home to the Mathis household.

"That's the last of them. Thank goodness! They're more ya'lls than mine, anyhow. I'll be glad to not see another apple until next year. Come back in a week, and I'll have jars of apple butter for you."

We promised our return and bid our farewell.

It was a dry, fall day, and puffy, white clouds sailed across the blue expanse. Katie and I took the lake road home, marveling at the last of the autumn foliage. There was a crisp chill in the air promising early snow, but we had yet to air out our winter woolens.

The heavy baskets slowed us, but we didn't mind, and Katie did not complain of the load. Birds chirped and flitted from branch to branch, and for the first time, it felt like this was home. Despite John's obvious avoidance, I was at peace. He knew where I stood. And I patiently waited for him. The heated glances we exchanged told me it was only a matter of time before he realized what was true in his heart.

His strength was returning, and I knew that time was soon. Just that morning, John and Seth left to check their traps and hunt wild turkeys. Over his dawn cup of coffee in the kitchen, I noticed color returning to his cheeks, promising his previous vitality. It warmed me, seeing his health return, watching him and Seth sling their hunting rifles over their shoulders, don their hats, and trudge out to the woods with smiles on their faces.

I was deep in my reverie when a branch snapping caused me to stop and look toward the tree line.

"Katie." I stopped her.

"What is it?"

I shushed her. The birds stopped singing. Black bears were not known to come down to the village, but knowing they were fattening up for the winter, it was not unheard of. For a moment, I wished I had my Colt, even if it was just a cat stalking its winged prey.

Movement caught in the corner of my eye. A man pushed through the brambles, stepping out of the shadows. His hat was pulled low over his face, and his hand was heavy with something. I gripped the handle of my basket as if I could wield it. Alarm bells started ringing in my ears.

He took another step into the road, lifting his face from the shadows.

I sucked in a breath, pushing Katie behind me.

Ethan Harris lifted his hand, pointing his revolver.

"Ethan." My voice sounded level, but my heart pounded like a drum in my ears. "I shot you."

But I knew in my heart he wasn't dead. All those months searching for any sign of him in the newspapers, and there was none. But I knew.

"Hurt like hell too." He rubbed his shoulder as if it still ached.

"What do you want?" I hissed.

Ethan laughed. "You, darling. Don't you know that by now?"

He inched forward, his firearm steady in his hand. A glint in his eyes told me that he was determined, and I could feel the cold grip of fear creep up my spine. I took a step back, edging Katie back with me. I could feel her little body trembling behind me, but I was thankful she did not say a word.

"Is that yours?" he gritted through his teeth, gesturing to Katie. The muscles in his jaw twitched.

"Robert's sister." If omitting the fact she was mine now would save her, I would do it. "Let me send her home. This is between us."

Ethan rubbed the stubble on his chin, remembering something. "She's mute?"

I did not try to correct him. If he thought she would not say a word about his presence here, it would keep her safe.

"Go, Katie." I nudged her. "Run home."

She looked up at me, her eyes large with worry.

"Go," I said again, gripping her hand and trying to silently communicate with her to find help. "Please." I pumped her hand one last time and she gave a quick nod, dropping the basket at her feet, apples tumbling in the dirt. She took off running down the road, her heels kicking up her short skirts.

"You're going to have to come with me, Ella," Ethan ordered.

I turned back to him. "I'm not going anywhere with you."

"I need to get my life back, and this needs to end now."

"I don't know how I can help you with that." I took another step back as he approached, his weapon still aimed at me.

"There are only two ways we can do this—you can either leave quietly with me now, or we can do this the hard way."

I wondered how far John and Seth were on their trapline from here, or if there was anyone nearby who would hear me if I screamed.

"Leave to go where?"

"Woodhue, Ella."

"Woodhue? You can't go back there. You're a traitor, Ethan. Pa confessed everything. They'll arrest you as soon as you step into Pennsylvania."

"That's where we have to go. It was stolen from me, and it has to end there."

I needed to get away. He was two yards away from me now, and I had to do something.

Desperate, I threw my basket of apples at him.

And ran.

I pumped my arms, trying to get away, my feet pounding on the dirt road, the cool autumn air filling my lungs, but it was not enough. He was quicker and stronger.

Ethan's arms went around my waist and crashed us to the ground, knocking the wind out of me. *I can't breathe*, I thought for just a moment before the butt of the revolver cracked the top of my head and everything went dark.

—

My head ached. Cold penetrated my bones. I tried to peel my eyes open, but I was so, so tired. My head was heavy on my neck, my chin resting on my chest. Stretching my neck, willing my head to rise, I grimaced.

He must have heard me moan because he was then in my ear. "You chose the hard way. I'm sorry, Ella. You didn't give me a choice."

I blinked. I didn't know where I was, but I knew Ethan was with me. My vision blurred and was tinged red from the blood dripping in my eye. My limbs were so heavy.

Cold earth. Cold stone. Damp, loamy air. Darkness engulfed us, but for gray light coming from my right.

I tried to move again, to shift my limbs, until I realized I was propped against a stone wall, my feet and hands bound.

"Where … where are we?" I managed to say. My tongue was thick in my mouth.

"A cave."

We were still in Vermont! Smuggler's Notch. The trapline was not too far from here. If I screamed, would they hear me?

"We'll stay here just until I find a horse." The dark was heavy. I could not make out his face, except for a vague outline.

My head swam, and I gulped down bile rising in my throat.

"A horse?" I managed to say with a steadying breath.

"We'll need a mount to travel. But here's how this is going to go. I need you to listen to me if you don't want any harm to come to you or that little sister of Robert's."

I steadied my head, my neck straining to look at him. My head felt so heavy.

Ethan crouched before me, hovering.

His stench enveloped us, taking over the earthy scent of the cave. My eyes adjusted to the grayness, and I saw his jaw clench beneath his scraggly beard. He had shed his coat, wearing a linen shirt stained yellow from sweat, and brown, wool pants. His boots were muddy, and he had set aside his hat, revealing greasy, dark-blond hair. I had never seen him so unkempt. His eyes were wide and wild.

"You're coming back to York with me, and you're going with me willingly. If you go with me, I'll tell the authorities everything. I'll tell them exactly what I did—profiteering, selling arms to the Union and Confederate Armies, helping Southern troops advance and prisoners escape. I'll even tell them how I orchestrated the raid on St. Albans."

My eyes narrowed. "Why would you do that, Ethan? They'll hang you."

"No, they won't, because then the curse would be broken."

The curse! Just like the other times he had cornered me. "What curse?"

"Do you believe in curses?" It was a serious question.

"I don't know what to believe."

He nodded, understanding my hesitancy. "I didn't either, not until Father died without cause, the money was gone, and so was Woodhue. Woodhue was meant to be mine, my own, separate from Father, separate from the Harris estate. That and Emilyn Murphy. They were both stolen from me. Your father stole Woodhue, and my brother stole Emilyn, and my father did nothing, even though he knew they were mine. And Emilyn used her Irish tongue to curse us."

My mind scrambled to comprehend what he was telling me, searching for all that I remembered about Emilyn.

"Your brother killed her?" I asked, although I knew the truth.

"Jeffrey was in love with her, but Emilyn chose me. He shot her so neither one of us could have her. Shot her right in front of me, so I killed him."

I sucked in a sharp breath. I knew the story, but I knew it as

Jeffrey taking his own life after he took Emilyn's.

"Before he killed her, she cursed us.

"*'May you only feel death and loss. May all you claim fall into ruin and be torn apart. May all men of your blood feel yearning, never to be quenched. And may the curse only be broken when a bride spills blood onto stolen ground.'*"

His eyes were distant as he remembered, speaking the words he had heard her say years ago. A bride? Did he mean *me*?

"When Father died, I discovered that over the years, he had given thousands of dollars to Christopher Coburg. His friend. Your father stupidly reinvested it back into the ironworks, thinking it would turn a profit. But Father was too entrenched in debt, leaving me with nothing but his house and his failing company.

"When the war came, I knew munitions were the only way out, so I convinced your father to turn it into a weapon manufacturer. I never did have much allegiance to the Cause or a desire to fight—only a loyalty to money and a need to end this curse. That's when I met Mr. Pocket, a Southern sympathizer who helped me contract with the Confederate Army and the Union, sending guns to both sides. By the time your father discovered his signature on the orders, it was already too late because I had his permission to marry you. And you are my way out of this curse."

I latched on to his words about Pa. Ethan used him, and he admitted it. He could save Pa. He could tell the truth, just as he said he would.

"You would tell the authorities everything then? That my father is innocent?"

"As I said, if you go back with me willingly, I'll confess, but your father is anything but innocent. He already surrendered. His signature is on all the orders. He knew, but he said nothing."

"Because you threatened him!"

"Yes, because he wanted to keep you and your family safe. I did everything I could to protect your family, even protecting you from ruin by sending that boy away."

"You might as well have killed Robert yourself!"

"He agreed to go. You see, money and fear are powerful things. So powerful, in fact, you would leave the woman and sister you love."

"You know nothing! You are so blinded by your greed and hate, you would hurt anyone and everyone in your path. You sent Robert to his death! You beat John nearly to death! You've forced yourself on me—twice—and you think I'll willingly go with you in hopes you will turn yourself over to the authorities and my father will be let free? Do you think I'm daft? That I would go because I believe you?"

"Nearly to death, huh?" His eyebrows rose. And I knew I had slipped up. "He's alive ... and ... here?" He saw the realization dawn in my eyes and straightened, checking the rounds in the revolver.

"No, Ethan! Don't!" I twisted on the ground, hoping to release my hands, to grip him, to stop him. I struggled against the bindings.

Ethan was pacing now, his mind working through this new piece of information I let slip.

"Ethan, please! You can't!"

"Shut up! I can't hear myself think!"

"Please! Leave him alone! He doesn't need to know I'm here with you! Please!"

"I said, shut up!"

He gripped me by my throat, pulling me back, only to let my head bounce off the wall of the cave.

44

BURNING

1865 OCTOBER 29, SUNDAY

I sucked in a shuddering breath, as if breaking through a watery surface. Gulping down stale, musty air. Swallowing felt like a million tiny shards of glass going down my gullet. My ears rang, and my body and head screamed. Blinking open grainy eyes, I steeled myself, expecting to see Ethan hovering over me again, but instead, I was alone.

Moonlight shone through a glass window, partially covered by a scrap of fabric. A cradle before a cold hearth. Dusty shelves of discarded preserves. The Williams' cabin!

I was bound to a chair, and he had left me here. I didn't remember moving to the cabin or how long I had been unconscious. Taking stock of my limbs and body, I ached all over and my neck and head felt particularly painful, but it didn't seem like he had harmed me in any other way. How long had he left me here?

Then I remembered.

John!

He was going out to find John.

The only other one who knew his plan to raid St. Albans. The only other one, besides Katie, I was protecting. The only other one whom he could possibly use as leverage to make me go with him. I had to do something. I had to get out of here. I had to stop Ethan before it was too late. Katie must have reached the Mathis house by now. She would have told them. John would be out looking for me.

I struggled against the strips of cloth Ethan had fashioned into bindings for my wrists and ankles, trying to loosen them against the chair rungs. They would not budge. I searched the floor for something to use, anything to help me get out of here.

A nail! A nailhead stuck out from one of the floorboards. I would have to tip the chair, scoot it across the floor. But it could help rip through the cloth.

Using my body to hoist myself, inch by inch, I shuffled the chair along the floor. Taking another painful, deep breath, I closed my eyes, throwing my body to one side. I tipped. The chair carried me over, impacting with the floor. A bruising pain shot up my arm. Air wheezed out of my lungs. Letting the agony ebb and flow, I lay there, stunned, waiting for it all to subside. But I had no time. Ethan could walk in at any moment.

The loose nail stared at me like my saving grace. Like an inchworm, I wiggled, wincing each time my arm scraped along the rough floorboards and my neck spasmed. I stopped to catch my breath and calm my stomach, threatening to reject its content.

"Please, Lord." I tried to muster whatever strength I had left to reach that nail. It seemed so far away. I took a deep, steady breath and willed myself to keep going, inching closer, scraping against the floor.

I reached the nail and let out a muffled howl as I tried to move my hands over the head of the nail. The chair pinched and pinned my arm, making it nearly impossible to move my bound hands toward the nail. My knuckles scraped against the rough board, stinging as they broke open, but I did not stop. I would break my hands before I stopped. I wiggled until the nail caught the binding.

Sawing against the nail, I continued to pray, "Please, please."

Then I heard something. I stopped to listen, trying to quiet my breath to hear. Bushes rustled and horse hooves clopped. Not waiting a moment more, I resumed pulling and tugging at the bindings, sawing through them. I hissed in pain as the nail sliced my palm, but then my hands were free. I sat up, my muscles screaming in protest, and I reached for my ankles, fumbling with the ties.

The movement outside came closer. A horse snorted and a bridle jangled. I slumped to the ground, scrambling away from the chair, searching for something—anything—I could use as a weapon.

Ethan was back.

He rushed in, closing the door behind him.

"I was followed," he announced, putting his back to the door. He lifted his eyes to see me standing there, and they flashed black with rage. "How in the hell!"

He flew at me, and I nearly stumbled back over the fallen chair before he had his grip on my wrist.

"No you don't!"

His grip was punishing, pinching, squeezing my bones together.

He whipped a knife from his belt.

And I screamed a bloodcurdling scream.

"Shut the hell up!"

His eyes frantically searched the cabin, landing on the shelves of jars.

"Did he follow you here?" I whispered, hoping John—anyone—

had heard me scream.

Ethan pulled me over to the cabinet, pushing preserves aside until he found an empty jar. Without a word, and before I could even flinch, the cold sting of his blade cut across my wrist.

I hissed. "What was that for?"

I tried to draw back, but he only squeezed tighter, the pressure causing my bones to groan, blood bubbling up from the wound.

He yanked my hand over the jar, my blood dripping off my wrist, the cut from the nail pooling in my palm, then running down my fingers into the jar.

"That's a lot of blood," I commented numbly, my head swimming. The world seemed to tilt, and queasiness flooded me.

"Don't you dare faint," Ethan blurted. "You'll give me as much as I need to end this, and right now, you're proving more trouble than you're worth."

My eyes fluttered from my wrist to the contents of the shelves and cabinet. An arm's reach away was a hammer. A hammer I remembered Brett using to cover the windows. That seemed so long ago. A lifetime ago. I rested my hand inches away from the hammer, leaning against the cabinet as if needing the support to stay standing.

"We got the place surrounded!" called a loud voice from outside.

Ethan startled, taking up his revolver from his holster. The cock of the trigger echoed through the cabin.

"Don't you dare move," he ordered.

"Come out and no one gets hurt!" came the voice again. Seth. I'd recognize his voice anywhere, and I was thankful Ethan did not.

Ethan put his finger up to his lips. His eyes pierced through me, willing me to stay still.

"Leave now!" Ethan called back. "I don't want to hurt her—"

"You already did, you ass," I mocked.

He turned to look at the door and I clutched the hammer, hiding it at my back as boots hit the steps outside.

Ethan gave me a withering glare. "But if you come any closer, I will not hesitate!" He squeezed my wrist, a fountain of crimson running into the glass. I bit my lip to keep from crying out.

Silence followed, and I could hear only Ethan's heavy breathing and my ears pulsing. Someone walked through the brush at the front of the house. I tracked the movement and then heard more movement at the back of the house. Were they both out there? Seth and John?

"I said, leave now! I will put a bullet through her head!"

"Liar," I murmured through my teeth.

"I swear to God … Be … Quiet." His whisper came out sharp and stinging.

I stepped into his body, the hammer still at my back, and tipped my head to whisper in his ear. He flinched against me, his grip loosening.

"You won't kill me, Ethan. Not here, anyway. You need me to go to Woodhue with you. The place stolen from you." I purposefully used the words of the curse. His eyes narrowed and his jaw hardened. "Who's to say what's in that jar is enough? You won't chance it. You need to take me—your bride—so you can spill *all* my blood." I was inches away from him now and could feel the heat of his breath with each exhale.

He was right about one thing. Fear is powerful. Maybe even more powerful than love because in one sweeping movement, he wrapped an arm around my waist, pinning my injured hand beneath his grip and pulling my back against his chest. In the whirl of the motion, I brought my other hand around, and with all my strength, regardless of my hand beneath his, I smashed his hand with the hammer. Ethan yelped and I whimpered, but I ignored the pain. His gun tumbled to the floor, misfiring and blasting a hole through the wall.

Everything happened so fast then.

Ethan and I wrestled to the ground as he tried to get the hammer away from me, holding me back and reaching for his pistol. The window shattered in the back of the cabin and the front door banged open, but Ethan and I still struggled.

I pounded him again with the hammer, this time landing on the shoulder I had shot a year ago, and Ethan let out a guttural cry.

"Let go of her!" The barrel of a rifle was pointed in our faces. Ethan stilled and I lifted my head. I sucked in a breath.

The cabin was so dark, and the man standing before us was all shadows.

"Let go of her now!" he repeated, pushing back his hat so Ethan could see his face. John's eyes were like two orbs of burning ore, his face like stone, as he stared down the barrel at Ethan.

Ethan's grip hardened. "You won't kill me, Mathis. Not for *her*." He sneered as he brought us back up to standing. I didn't turn to look behind us, but I knew Seth stood at the open door, his own rifle positioned. "I know your kind. Proud and loyal until faced with pain. Weak."

"It seems you don't know me at all," John snarled.

"Or me," Seth said.

Just as Ethan turned to look behind his shoulder, Seth pulled the trigger. I winced, protecting myself from the blast. Ethan jerked forward, and his grip loosened enough that I could scramble away from him. John placed himself between Ethan and me, as Ethan melted to the floor.

Blood bloomed at Ethan's lips and he coughed. I could not let him get away this time. I needed to make sure he was dead. That he could never come back. So I would never have to look over my shoulder again.

Rage bubbled up my chest, the hammer steady in my hand, and I pushed past John.

Not until the hammer connected with his skull did I know what I was doing, and I did not stop. Anger surged through me.

Over and over again, I hammered Ethan's head to the ground.

Blood splashed up at me every time the hammer landed, but I didn't stop. I did not want to stop. I needed to be sure he would not come back.

"Ella," came a soft voice. "*Ella*," John punctuated, touching my arm.

I flinched at the contact, stopping my hammering. I looked up at John. His eyes were full of concern and fear. Was he scared of me? Ethan was now a bloody pulp on the ground. My hand started trembling and I dropped the hammer, suddenly afraid of myself.

"He's dead. He's dead," I assured myself.

"Yes, he's dead," John confirmed, pulling me to him.

I couldn't stop trembling. John tugged me tighter against him.

"I killed him," I said.

Seth and John exchanged worried looks.

"I need to get her out of here," John told him.

"What about this?" Seth asked.

John looked around us. The tipped chair, the jar of blood leading a dark trail to Ethan's body. The pool of blood growing beneath him. Then he said, "Burn it. Burn it down to the ground."

Seth gave a firm nod.

Glancing down at my shaking, bloody hands, the floodgates opened. "I can't ... go back ... like this. Katie ... will see ..." Blood was everywhere. My hands and dress were covered in it, dripping off me. I could feel the sticky liquid coating my face and hair. I looked back up at John. He was about ready to combust. His jaw clenched and his eyes darkened.

"I know," he agreed.

His arm did not leave my waist as we stepped around Ethan's body and he guided me outside.

We left Seth behind to set the blaze. John did not let go as we walked away from that house. He helped me step through the dark while I shook and stumbled, his grip firm and in control. I was numb and shattered, my limbs heavy and weak.

"You'll be all right," John whispered, but I could tell he did not believe himself.

Tears streamed down my face, blurring my vision.

"Shh … it's over," he comforted, guiding me down the path until we reached the road.

"He's dead," I said again, not knowing what else to say but feeling like I needed to say something—anything—to hold myself together.

"Yes, he's dead. He's gone now. He won't hurt you again. Let's get you cleaned up."

John led me to a brook that ran near the Williams' place. He helped me kneel beside the water. The moon reflected off the stream, the dark shadows of blood flowing through the silver eddies. The water was ice cold, almost scalding, but it had to feel that way to rid me of Ethan's touch. I scrubbed at my hands and hissed with the sting.

"Let me see." He took my hand in his, examining it. His jaw clenched, anger coursing off him as if he was ready to march back to that cabin and kill Ethan all over again. "We need to stop the bleeding."

"Here. Rip a strip off my petticoat," I suggested, easing myself on my rump and hoisting my skirts.

John's eyes flickered to mine briefly before gripping the hem of my petticoat, and with one great wrench, he ripped through it. My petticoat was already stained with blood, and it bloomed darker as he wrapped it around my hand.

"You are so brave," he whispered, cupping my cheek. "So brave."

He took a handkerchief from his pocket, wetting it and wiping my brow.

The fire had burned out of his eyes, and they glimmered with something else in the moonlight. He brushed the wet cloth along my mouth and jaw, wiping the blood and tears.

"I did everything I could to get away."

"I know. May I?" he asked, gesturing to my hair.

I nodded. My hair had come out of its pins and now hung down in a loose plait. John unbraided my hair, brushing his wet fingers through it, washing the blood out with each pass through. I closed my eyes, my nerves settling, while his fingers threaded through my hair. He wet the handkerchief again, stroking along my hairline to remove the caked-on grime.

His fingers stilled when he reached for the top button of my dress. "John?"

"It's all over," he assured.

I nodded, giving him permission. His fingers worked the buttons, each one bringing him closer and closer to my breasts. Uncertainty was in his eyes, but I did not stop him. Nor did he stop himself, as he helped my arms out of the sleeves. I lifted my hips so he could pull the dress down. His knuckles brushed my sides, and then my legs and I shuddered. I did not know if it was from the cold, trauma, or his touch. He shucked off the dress, his hands stilling at my ankles.

"Ella," he pleaded, his face etched with pain. "I'm so sorry."

"Oh, John." I couldn't help myself, leaning toward him to touch his face, my fingers grazing the roughness of his jaw. "Please. You are not at fault. You never were. I'm sorry I allowed fear to control my heart." I needed to feel more of him, to hold him close.

John needed that, too, because he clutched my calves, drawing me to him, my hands gripping his shirt.

"I've been afraid too."

"We can't be afraid anymore," I told him.

"No. No, we can't be afraid anymore."

"I love you, John. I've loved you for so long."

His lips crushed mine then, searing them. Needy and demanding. I matched him in desperation, my hand grasping his shirt, holding him to me. I sighed, closing my eyes, feeling warmth grow in my belly as his lips devoured mine.

I needed more of him. My tongue flicked against his lips, urging him to open for me, and when he did, I tasted the sweetness of bourbon on his tongue. John moaned in my mouth, and I knew he was feeling the same growing passion I was feeling. His hands roamed the curve of my neck, caressing my cheeks and beneath my ears.

I pulled him tighter against me, my legs wrapping around his hips, wanting more of him, wanting the weight of him.

"Ella." He came up for a breath before returning to my lips.

"Please, John," I pleaded.

He left my lips again, caressing my side, and I kissed his jaw, not wanting my lips to leave him.

"I love you," he whispered against my mouth, easing us to the ground. "I never stopped."

His hand wandered, stroking down and then up my leg, pushing my chemise with it, until I was exposed to him. I arched my back, urging him on, pressing my body against him until I felt his fingers skim between my legs. Tingles fired all over my body, echoing in my breasts and my core.

"So soft," John whispered.

"I want you," I said, breathless.

The friction built with each stroke of his fingers, circling and dipping. Igniting. Our lips were bruising, our teeth nipping and pulling. His beard rasped deliciously across my skin. I wanted to devour him, make him mine in every way. My heart felt as though it may burst into flames.

An orange glow washed over us, dancing across John's handsome features.

John lifted his lips from mine to look up, while I peppered kisses down his neck.

"The fire started," John said, while I kissed him. "We need to go."

I stilled then, looking over my shoulder to see flames flickering above the treetops.

"We can't be here when it consumes the house," he said, taking off his jacket and wrapping it around me.

As soon as he stood, the heat and weight of him left me, and I drew the jacket closer. The cold ground penetrated through the layers. John dunked the dress in the water, wringing out the blood and dirt.

"We may need to burn this too."

I only nodded. The zing in my blood still pulsed through me.

"Come." He helped me to my feet. Flinging the rifle over his shoulder with the dripping dress, he held me close. "Let's get you home."

He kissed the side of my head, and the press of his lips made me wish we could stay here forever. His arm tightened around my waist, leading me away from the brook.

My adrenaline plummeted with each swaying step before John hoisted me into his arms. Wrapping my arms around his neck, I buried my face in his shoulder, closing my eyes, reveling in his strength. I was safe. And he chose us.

45

A CHANCE AT LOVE

1865 OCTOBER 30, MONDAY

I do not know how long John sat there, but when I opened my eyes at dawn, there he was, his head resting on his propped hand, asleep on the chair beside my bed. He had not left my side since bringing me home.

When we reached the house in the early morning hours, the house was alight with gas lamps. Waiting for us. As if it knew we would return. That I would be found safe.

Mrs. Mathis and Nora whispered around me, but they did not speak to me, only speaking to John. Thankfully, Katie was asleep in her bed and would not see me shivering and bleeding.

John brought me to bed, Nora helping me out of my boots and stockings, Mrs. Mathis attempting to shoo John out the door, but he insisted on staying, and I did not deny him. He stayed while they helped undress me. Exhausted, I was barely aware of John's heated gaze when he saw my nakedness before a nightgown was pulled over my head.

I winced when Mrs. Mathis cleaned my palm and head wounds, the cut on my hairline especially tender. John poured me a large glass of whiskey, handing it to me to calm my nerves.

I killed a man today.

The shock was setting in and my trembling resumed, punctuated with nausea.

Mrs. Mathis did not ask where Seth was, and John did not volunteer the information as she wrapped my hand. John poured me another glass of whiskey and she chastised him, but I needed it to sleep. I did not know how I'd rest otherwise, knowing that as soon as I closed my eyes, I would see Ethan's battered and bloody head.

John pulled a chair beside the bed. Mrs. Mathis and Nora did not say a word, leaving us alone. Taking my hand in his, he pressed a kiss to my fingers and promised to hold it until I fell asleep.

Seeing him now when I awoke, my love for him swelled. He sat vigil all night, and somehow, I was able to find a dreamless sleep. My head was tender to the touch, but it no longer throbbed.

Sensing my eyes on him, John's eyes fluttered open. Neither one of us moved, just stared at each other. I could sense the love and worry radiating off him, and I reached a hand out to him.

"Did you sleep?"

"Yes. Thank you for staying with me."

"I'm so sorry, Ella. I'm so sorry this happened. I should have protected you. I should have made sure he never found you—"

"John, don't. Please, don't. You protected me. I'm here."

"I could have done more—"

"Stop it. He did this. He is the one to blame." I would not say his name. Never again. He was dead. "I'm safe now."

"But he hurt you."

"But I'm safe now. I'll survive this."

John brought my hand to his lips, tenderly brushing my scraped knuckles against them. "I could have lost you. I don't know what I would have done if—"

"I know. I know." I had lost him. It nearly broke me. And now that I had him back, I would do anything to protect him. I knew then what I had to do. "John, I love you so much. You have to know you are so deserving of love and happiness. I want us to have our chance. For nothing to stand in our way. For us to have a chance to choose each other each and every day. And I'm so scared I may lose you again … you have to go."

"Go?" He stared at me, confused.

"You have to go west. Take that military commission. Do what you need to do, for yourself, your health, and if anyone—*anyone*—starts asking questions about the Williams' place, and you know they will. There will be an investigation once my pa goes to trial. You need to be gone … long gone. Seth too. Take him with you. Neither one of you should be here when that happens."

"What about you, Ella? I don't know if I can leave you now, not like this."

I gave a soft nod against the pillow. "I'll be here. Katie and I will stay here. And we'll write to each other. We'll survive this." My throat stung. "Once you're settled and ready for me, send for me. I'll do everything in my power to come to you. I promise, I'll come to you."

John reached for me, scooping me up from the bed, and cradled me in his lap. He did not say a word. He did not have to. He pressed me against him, his lips in my hair, my nose nuzzling his neck. I took him in. All of him. The scent of him—soap and grass, and an underlining smokiness of cigar. I took in the feel of him. His chest was filling back out, hard against me, his legs were firm beneath me, and his warmth penetrated my nightgown.

"I love you, Ella," he whispered against my lips.

"I love you, John." It was a goodbye, but I knew, in time, that I would follow him.

EPILOGUE

The note read "Springfield Hotel, Dakota," and I looked up at the unassuming, two-story, wood building. There was no signage, but it was the only large building along the main street. Only a post office, saloon, and a few merchant shops made up the town. Hammering echoed down the road where new building frames were being erected. Civilians and military on horseback and on foot traveled to and fro, kicking up dust. Curious eyes watched me.

I traveled for days, and I was filthy and weary, but my heart soared at the sight of this whitewashed building. It had been too long, and my heart was beating out of my chest, realizing the waiting was finally over.

"Ella Coburg!"

I turned at my name and nearly dropped my bags.

Seth Mathis dismounted his horse at the hitching post. He had grown an inch or two and filled out with riding muscles. He was dirty and dusty, scruff shadowed his jaw, and his hat sat back on his sweating forehead, but he beamed with the largest, whitest grin I had ever seen.

"Why Seth Mathis!"

"Here, allow me," he said, hitching his horse and hustling to my side to take the bags. "We must hurry, though. John's waiting for you."

My stomach flipped at the mention of John. As promised, we wrote to each other. Three years of writing to each other, detailing our lives, sharing our hopes and dreams, making plans we prayed would come to fruition, and now, here I was. We planned for me to come first, marry, help set up a home, and then send for Katie.

"Where is he?" I asked, following Seth into the hotel.

"You'll see." Seth winked, handing the bags over to the concierge. "The room should be under Captain J. Mathis." The lady in charge nodded and sent the bags up to the room. "Come with me."

Seth offered his arm and led me down the road to a large tent beside the construction. We ducked beneath the flap and stepped into a church. Empty pews lined an aisle, and an altar was visible ahead. At the altar, beside the chaplain, waited John.

My heart skipped a beat. John stood straight, his uniform and regalia pressed and shining, his beard cut close to his jaw, and his wavy, dark hair brushed back with pomade. His smiling lips trembled and his eyes gleamed, and I knew he struggled with the same emotions.

A fiddle started playing. I startled, then giggled through tears seeing a soldier, a fiddle in hand, playing a version of the wedding march. Still on Seth's arm, he ushered me down the aisle to John. Our eyes locked, love beaming.

"I'm sorry, I didn't have time to change," I said, embarrassed by my dirty and tired gingham dress. I patted my hair, brushing stray wisps from my face.

John shook his head, the smile not leaving his face. "You're perfect.

Besides, I don't think I could have waited another moment for this."

I knew what he meant. Because neither could I.

"Who gives this woman?" the chaplain interrupted.

"I do," Seth announced. He and I exchanged smiles as he handed me to John.

"Thank you," I whispered to Seth.

He nodded and took a seat on the front pew.

It had been too long since I felt John's hands and I gripped them, wanting to feel every scar and callus. To feel the warmth of them. So many days I imagined the feel of his hands, and it was nothing in comparison to this reality.

I do not know what the chaplain said to us. I barely registered our vows as we repeated them to each other. All I saw was John. His eyes shining, warm and so full of love, and his smile never leaving his lips until we both leaned forward to share a kiss. A chaste kiss, a tentative kiss in front of Seth, the fiddler, and the chaplain, but there was an urgency beneath we knew would consume us.

—

We were finally alone. After a meal Seth insisted on treating us to using his cattle drive money, and my own soak in the bath, John and I lay in the peacefulness of the hotel room.

"Did we rush it?" John asked, worry creasing his brow as he tucked a strand of damp hair behind my ear. His eyes were so full of love and adoration.

I laughed. "Rush it? It's been three years, John!"

The dimples I had missed so much flickered at the edge of his beard. "I mean the wedding. I barely let you step off the stagecoach before I had Seth bring you to the church."

"I would have come anyway. I wouldn't have stopped to clean up if it meant becoming your wife."

"Wife," he repeated, tracing my lips at the sound of it.

His finger left a trail of heat as it continued its perusal of my face, then my neck. My breath hitched when he reached the tie of my chemise. He looked at me then, his eyes searching mine. The softness of affection, turning into smoldering desire. I gave him permission.

Needing to touch him, I reached out to him, my hand caressing his cheek, his beard coarse beneath my fingers. It had been so long since I felt him beneath my palm, and my heart swelled.

"Oh, Ella," he breathed, not wanting to wait any longer.

He brought me to him, pressing his lips to mine. His hands roamed my curves and swells, gripping my back end and pressing me against him. I felt the length of him, all hardened muscle and heated skin, along my body.

Our kisses became hungry, our tongues exploring and tasting, our teeth scraping, and I could feel the heat quicken in my belly. It felt as if no time had separated us.

"I love you so much, John," I promised between kisses.

My words encouraged him, and his fingers found their way under my chemise, lifting it up and over my head. We paused in our exploration. My skin burned as his eyes racked my body, taking in my breasts, stomach, hips, and apex of my thighs. I did not feel shame or embarrassment at his gaze, only love and admiration.

"You are so beautiful," he whispered, then his eyes returned to mine. "I've loved you from the moment I saw you. But I never knew I could love you even more now."

I grasped his neck, bringing his mouth back down on mine. My heart felt as if it would explode from my chest.

We didn't waste time. I helped him remove his clothes while his hands stroked and explored my body. And when my knees parted, his hand finding the curls between my legs, I gasped at the touch of his fingers.

He swallowed my moans, letting me rock against him, holding me tight while I chased the pleasure.

Before I unraveled, I pleaded with him. "I need you."

John did not hesitate, kissing me tenderly as he lowered himself between my legs. He pressed against me and I held him close, urging him not to stop. And when he entered me, we both stilled, settling with the feeling of my body wrapped around his and our connection pulsing. He rested his hands on either side of my head, and we locked eyes.

Our fate was crashing against the rocks and soaring to the highest peak. The world seemed to right itself at that moment. There was no fear or grief. There was only love and safety.

Setting the pace, John thrust against me and I matched him, following his rhythm. We both were tumbling, absorbing each wave of pleasure that hit us. Not wanting it to end. We waited so long for this. And when we both shuddered, we captured each other's moans in our mouths and held each other close until our hearts settled.

Spent and sweaty, we collapsed beside each other. I thought I would cry for joy, but instead, I broke out in giddy laughter.

John's head rolled toward me on the pillow. A lopsided grin on his face. "What's that all about?"

"Love, John. Love. My heart is so full of it, it just bubbled up."

John smiled back, and as night grew late, we held each other close. Between kisses and love, John picked up where he left off from his last letter, weaving an image of the home he would build for us and the family we would grow with Katie. No longer did grief and fear rule our lives. Love and hope would carry us through.

"I love you, Ella Mathis," John whispered in my ear as we fell asleep in each other's arms.

Author's Note

Most of us know the Battle of Gettysburg as the northernmost conflict of the American Civil War. I, too, had known that. It wasn't until my studies during my undergrad classes at the University of Oregon that I learned about the St. Albans Raid. Why haven't we heard about it? Why is there so much literature on the Southern plight that we forget the stories about the Northern men and women fighting against injustice and patriotism? I knew I had to tell their stories.

I had written some version of this story over the years, developing Ella and John's love story in a Victorian world. A world where war tore apart propriety and conservative sensibilities. The women all worked hard to keep their world afloat while the men were off fighting. And I wanted to capture that in the female characters. Their relationships with each other were just as important, if not more important, than the relationships built with their absent men.

When I researched about St. Albans Raid, reading the transcripts of the trial in Montreal, I was surprised to learn most of the men were Union prisoners. A name was never given to the person who helped them escape. It only said a Yankee helped them. I started wondering what kind of Yankee would help Confederate soldiers escape their prison. What would motivate him to do that? Why? That was when I knew I had to create Ethan and his murderous drive to end a curse he believed ruined him, leading him to St. Albans where Ella hid.

For a long time, I put down this story to pursue other interests—building a family, starting a career in teaching Social Studies. It wasn't until the pandemic, when my own mental health battle with post-traumatic stress following the complicated birth of my youngest, that I started writing again. It was like coming home. Rediscovering myself. It was cathartic to write through my own emotions, process mortality and PTSD, all while creating characters who were experiencing their own battles. For a long time, I believed my mental health made me weak. But just as you read, through these characters, they learned that living through their hardships—being tested and not falling apart—made them warriors. In the end, they all chose love over fear.

ACKNOWLEDGMENTS

This story was mine and only mine for a very long time, taking its own twists and turns, sometimes going down a deep spiral, assuming a shape of its own before evolving into the story that it is today. My husband, teammate, and love of my life was not only an inspiration, but he also pushed me to put this book and myself out there. So thank you, babe, for believing in me and motivating me to go for it. Also, a special thanks to my children for putting up with mommy's countless hours of research and writing. I hope one day you both can say I set an example for you on what it takes to go for your dreams.

First and foremost, I'd like to thank the Novel Doctor, Ned Hayes, who met with me at the start of this journey, answering all my questions about writing and publishing. He helped point me in the right direction to get started, which, in turn, led me to my two fabulous editors: Kathy Burge, my content editor, and Joyce Mochrie, my copy editor. Kathy's advice and helpful tips not only assisted me in becoming a stronger writer, but they also helped develop the love story between Ella and John. I am indebted to Joyce for the time and detailed eye she gave to this project. Her words of encouragement and recommendations throughout the process helped build my confidence, making me even more motivated to share my writing with the world.

I wouldn't have gotten this far without my team of book lovers, family, and friends. Thank you to my best friend, Meagan Golden, for always supporting my writing and cheering me on. Thank you for reading the final manuscript and sharing your feedback. I think we can both agree, the dedication of this book means more today than it did yesterday.

I greatly appreciate the proofreading my mom, Dina Balogh, contributed, even if there was a question of how much spice is too much spice. Thank you for always encouraging me, Mom, even as a child when I'd stay up past bedtime writing by the nightlight.

I also appreciate the feedback and suggestions Mari Terhune gave. She has a great editor's eye and was able to catch a few errors I missed. Avid reader and cousin, Crystal Gascon's enthusiasm and suggestions also helped improve the story. I believe our family love of reading may have come from my granny, Tonya Wall, who always has a book or e-reader nearby. She may have been biased, but she has always believed in my talent and has given me great feedback and encouragement since the beginning. Haley Balogh, my sister-in-law, is also a great support, photographing my headshots and offering to be one of my first readers.

My dad, Byron Balogh, set this fire inside of me from the time I could read. Countless nights growing up, he read Laura Ingalls Wilder's *Little House* books. For as long as I can remember, I wanted to grow up to be just like Wilder. Dad was the one who also instilled my love for history, taking my brother and I on road trips and "photo expeditions" to see pieces of the past by driving down historic highways, walking along wagon ruts, and taking photos of old, abandoned barns and pioneer homesteads. One day, I'll write that *Oregon Trail* book, Dad. Thank you for your support and encouragement and helping me set up my website.

I would also like to thank a couple authors who may or may not know they helped me on this journey. Amy Harmon, who has inspired me—as a mom and former educator—to follow my dreams and keep pushing. In a fan email I sent, she replied with the advice to see it all through: *Don't abandon it, but keep shaping it and shoving it forward until you're done, and then do it all again.* Catherine C. Heywood has also been very open and willing to answer questions I have on writing and publishing. Her continued help and support has been invaluable.

Lastly, I'd like to share my gratitude to my two therapists after my daughter's complicated birth and postpartum. I felt like I lost myself for a long time. It was through therapy that I returned to writing, rediscovering my passion and this story in the process. I saw myself in many of the Civil War women I researched—strong and formidable despite the tests thrown their way. I can only hope I did them justice.

ABOUT THE AUTHOR

Jennifer Strand is a middle school social studies teacher, amateur historian, and historical fiction writer.

Raised in Oregon, she studied history at the University of Oregon and Portland State University, and has a bachelor's degree in history and a master's degree in secondary education. She went on to teach thirteen- and fourteen-year-old students about a bunch of dead guys and the importance of why we learn history—so we can better understand the world we live in today and do something to change it.

She lives in Northwest Oregon with her husband, Kenny, her children, K.C. and Skye Lynn, and their Norwegian elkhound, Baldur. When she is not parenting, teaching, or writing, she enjoys cooking, reading romance novels, and obsessing over miniatures.

www.ingramcontent.com/pod-product-compliance
Lightning Source LLC
Chambersburg PA
CBHW020933260626
47169CB00006B/1693

* 9 7 9 8 9 9 0 4 6 5 9 8 5 *